The Sleuth Sisters

A Sleuth Sisters Mystery

By Maggie Pill

GWENDOLYN PRESS, MI

Copyright© 2014 Maggie Pill

Publisher: Gwendolyn Press
Cover Artist: Yocladesigns **(http://yocladesigns.com)**
Editor: Paige Trisko

ISBN: 978-0-9903804-2-9

CHAPTER ONE

Barb

Turning off my headlights, I left the paved road and drove down a bumpy two-track a few hundred feet back from the bar. Once my car was out of sight to passing traffic, I shut the engine off and listened to the stillness around me. A full minute brought no sound except the ticks of the car's various parts cooling down. Reaching under a blanket in the backseat, I picked up a small backpack that held my tools and a large flashlight. Glancing at my reflection in the rearview mirror, I pulled my black knit cap even lower and raised the collar of my black turtleneck. With black jeans and black Easy Spirit lace-ups, I looked like an over-the-hill Ninja.

Through the trees a sign was visible atop a long, low porch. JOES' BAR AND LOUNGE was written in letters three feet high and lit by four large flood lights. Beneath the name, smaller letters read, FINE FOOD AND ALOT OF IT. I'd been here many times during regular business hours. The food was good, but Joe had made mistakes that called for a visit from me.

A single lamp burned at the back of the building, but no figure moved in the square of light I could see. It might have been left on as a deterrent to burglars, but it didn't deter me. With a last look around to be sure there was no traffic on the road, I unscrewed the last of the interior light bulbs and eased out of the car in total darkness.

Shouldering the backpack, I crouched and made my way to the bar, staying near the road but not on it. It's not unheard of to meet a black bear in the woods of northern Michigan, and while I've heard they're not particularly belligerent, even Gentle Ben might be grumpy if surprised in the dark. A car came along at one point, but the night was quiet enough that I heard it a long way off and melted into the trees until it passed.

I'd worried it would be tricky to climb onto the roof of the bar, but there was a convenient step, a discarded video game of the old boxy kind set against the back of the building. Standing gingerly on its top, feet spread to keep my weight on the frame rather than the glass, I laid my upper body on the edge and hauled the rest of myself onto the long, low roof.

The roof was cedar shakes, dry and brittle under my hands. I flattened my body over them, hearing faint cracks as little bits broke off and stuck to my clothing. Again I paused, listening. The night was dark and as silent as only nights in the country can be: no traffic, no sirens, no gunshots. Yet.

Recovering my courage, I rose to a crouch, took the backpack from my shoulder, and moved to the sign. As I placed my feet carefully to avoid noise and a nasty fall, I thought about the owner of this place and what he'd think if he knew of my visit.

As if I'd conjured him, Joe suddenly called from below me, "Who's out there?"

I froze, unsure what to do. If I moved, he might hear me. If I remained still and he happened to look up, he'd easily see me, curled like a fetal child in the harsh lights of his sign. If Joe caught me, if he looked in the backpack, there would be no doubt my intentions were criminal. Following my instincts, I lay still. Joe repeated the question, taking a couple of steps forward. I could see the top of his balding head. He turned a hundred eighty degrees, peering into the darkness. I tried to control my breathing, which sounded like factory machinery in my ears.

A third time he asked his question to the empty night. He took another step forward and I saw he held a shotgun in his hands. It looked big enough to stop a rhinoceros.

Joe made a slow circle of the brick patio that fronted his restaurant. The gun rested easily in his hands, like he knew what to do with it. I watched in dread. His head turned slowly from side to side. His finger hovered on the trigger. When he turned back toward me, I saw the whites of his eyes, larger than normal from fear or possibly anger. I stayed perfectly still, remembering something I once read. People usually look out, not up.

It's true, at least it was in this case. Joe turned around once more, listening to the quiet, and then backed into the doorway beneath me. He must have stood there staring outward for a while longer, but finally I heard the door close with a firm snap and the turn of the deadbolt that followed. I released the breath I'd been holding, but it was a long time before my grip on the knapsack relaxed.

After I'd crouched there a half hour, barely managing to breathe, Joe finally left. During the whole thirty minutes, I argued with myself about whether to stay put or try to escape. When he finally slammed the door, rattled it to test the lock, and headed for the parking lot, I had another panic moment, fearing he'd see my car as he drove away. The taillights never brightened as he passed the two-track, though. Joe was apparently anxious to get home. I was in the clear.

I watched the night for several minutes after the sound of his car could no longer be heard. With hands that still shook a little, I went to work, taking out two small pots of paint, one white, one black, and two one-inch brushes. The actual work was easy, and within ten minutes I was back at my car. As I turned the key in the door, I looked back at my work and smiled. JOE'S BAR, it said, FINE FOOD AND A LOT OF IT. Joe's a fine cook, but his English skills are terrible.

***

It was childish, I know, but the next day I couldn't resist taking my sister Faye to Joe's for lunch. When we pulled up, this time parking in the front lot like normal people, I admired the sign, now grammatically correct due to my late-night visit. No one else appeared to have noticed, but it made me happy. Not only could we get good food at Joe's, but he didn't look like an ignoramus.

Pleased with myself, I almost missed the bombshell. While I ate Joe's excellent coleslaw, Faye laid a proposal before me, watching my face for clues to my reaction. Because I love my sister, I waited until she was done, trying to give the appearance of contemplation.

When she finished and leaned back, apparently composed but exhibiting little signs of nervousness I knew well, I said, "It's not like you think, Faye."

"I know it isn't all night clubs and big payoffs." She dredged her onion ring through some sort of glutinous, artery-clogging sauce.

"It's dangerous."

Her knee jiggled. That was one of the signs. "Who said I wanted to live forever?" She tried for humor. "Remember, I'm sewing a deer costume."

I sighed. Faye claims she's making a brown flannel suit for when she gets too old to take care of herself. She claims she'll wear it into the woods during hunting season and get shot, ending the need for the rest of us to worry about her. I admit it would probably work during any November in Michigan, when hunters crowd the woods. There's one problem, however: neither of us can even hem a pair of pants.

Under the black comedy is a hint of truth. Life has been hard on my sister, and she has no great desire to extend it. That doesn't mean she's suicidal. She's simply averse to a rest-of-her-lifetime lease on a room in a nursing home.

I tried another approach. "We don't know anything about a business like that."

"We've got the basic ingredients, and while I draw unemployment benefits, we can get ready." Faye glanced at the cigarette lying beside her plate, a tacit promise to herself for the moment we were back outside again. "I'm a damn good office manager, despite evidence to the contrary. And you're up to your neck in lawyer stuff you aren't using."

"The law in Tacoma, Washington, not Allport, Michigan." I fished in my pocket for a tissue, an almost constant pastime since I turned fifty.

Concerning Faye's qualifications to run an office, I had no argument. She's directed daily affairs in businesses ranging from financial investments to a string of pizzerias. She's efficient and reasonable, and customers love her. It was not her fault her job in an insurance office was about to disappear. Times are tough in Michigan, and it had come down to a lay-off for either the boss' sister or mine. You can guess how that ended up.

As for me, I retired young from a career as a lawyer, if you call the fifth decade young. I suppose my co-workers gossiped among themselves that I was disillusioned or burned out or whatever the current term is for it. While I hate gossip, they might have been right.

A *profession* is exactly what people in the Middle Ages meant by the term, a job in which one professes faith in something. The legal profession, like medicine and education, requires dedication to helping others, faith in the work that's being done, and commitment to the future of the field. Having lost both my faith and my sense of commitment, I'd retired from the law and most of the human race. I came home to Allport, the location of what was left of my family. It was quiet and no one expected anything from me. Rather, no one had until now.

"You're bored." My sister's voice interrupted my woolgathering.

"Not bored. Unsure what I want to do next."

"It's the same thing. If people could decide what they wanted to do, they'd never be bored." She has this disturbing tendency to be right, at least when it comes to other people's lives. In her own, Faye's faced plenty of problems worse than boredom. Hence the plan for the deer suit.

I *was* bored. After years of answering the alarm, in fact, anticipating its ring until the clock itself wasn't necessary any more, I'd had no plan for six months. Busy saving the world from criminals, I'd never married or had children. Now I found myself too young to be finished being useful but too old to start a family. I was fifty-two, alone, financially stable, and rather passively looking for something to catch my interest.

My sister thought we should open a detective agency.

"Who's going to ask two inexperienced women detectives to track down a missing spouse or prove a neighbor set fire to his house?"

"People who need us," she replied calmly. "There isn't a detective within an hour's drive of here, and I can think of three friends right off the bat who need a professional investigator."

"Does even one of them have money with which to pay such a person?" Faye Problem Number One: she collects strays and losers like a cocker spaniel collects burrs. My sister has the softest heart in Michigan, and her head is sometimes squishy, too. She's Mom to the world; I'm Mom to nobody. We're an odd pair, but we love each other too much to admit our differences.

***

Fast forward several months. No need to list all Faye's arguments or recount how she wore me down over time. My sister wouldn't think of nagging, but she'd slip in a reason here and an enticement there, answer an objection with a well-considered argument, and generally encourage me to come to the right decision.

The fact that I finally agreed stemmed from two considerations. First, I was concerned about Faye finding a job. She's almost fifty, which is a disadvantage in job-hunting, no matter what the Equal Opportunity people say. Her husband's disability check wasn't enough to support them, so a job was essential. Running a business together would provide money Faye was too proud to take as a gift. Secondly, I was interested in working again, this time as my own boss.

We got the necessary certifications and registered with the appropriate agencies. Some eyebrows were raised at the prospect of two decidedly mature women becoming private investigators, but we pretended not to notice. I even took a refresher course in self-defense, which I'd had years ago as an assistant DA. I paid more attention this time, not because I planned to get into situations where I had to defend myself, but because the instructor scared the hell out of me with demonstrations of how to hurt someone. I didn't remember being that impressed by violence at twenty-six, but then, what do babies know about reality?

I had one big problem with the whole thing. In order to be a P.I., I'd have to deal with people again. In twenty-five years of law, I'd seen more than enough human stupidity, and I was decidedly unexcited about inviting people into my presence to confess their lack of brain-power and ask me to fix whatever they had screwed up.

Still, I'd never seen my sister so excited. To her, the whole thing was a big fairy-godmother trip. We'd swoop in and make things better for people life had dumped on. She's hopeless, but you have to admire her optimism. Besides, she was right about it being good for me to have a goal. At the very least I'd have lots of idiots to make fun of.

Less than a year after the subject was first broached, Faye opened the door of an office we'd set up in the front parlor of my home one block off of the main street of Allport. We'd worried a little about what my neighbors would say to a business operating out of a residential area, but we weren't the first in our neighborhood d to do it. Just the strangest. A discreet sign and some classy ads in area newspapers, Internet sites, and the phone book, and we were ready to undertake our first case.

There followed a series of exactly the type of experiences I had feared. Our first clients were a long way from the drama of TV detectives: no hidden fortunes, no long-lost spouses, no suspected embezzlement. That first month we took two cases and turned two away. We located a deadbeat dad for one of Faye's friends, who paid for our services with the title to a junk car that smelled like pot but was worth five hundred dollars. Well, according to the owner, it would be "if you put in a new solenoid and redo the interior." We turned it over to Faye's husband Dale, who accepts hopeless mechanical cases much the same way his wife does human ones.

We also tracked down a runaway teen who had run off with a good-looking young truck driver from Texas. We found her mostly by luck, but the parents were grateful. The police hadn't taken much interest since the girl was over seventeen, went voluntarily, and was already out of the state. Faye called some trucker friends (in one job she'd shipped Michigan cherries all over the country) and they put the word out to watch for the couple. We located them in New York, and police there stopped the truck and sent the girl home on a Greyhound. Faye charged them $75.00. I have no idea how she arrived at that amount.

One might wonder what we turned down, given we could hardly afford to refuse work. First, a rather odd fellow came in wanting protection from the aliens who were stalking him. Since they'd planted incendiary devices in his clothing, he'd removed it. All of it. I also refused to help a woman looking for her ex-husband and his new wife so she could "tear that bitch's bottle-blond hair out by its black roots." She struck me as the type a man deserved to get away from. I'm not a bottle blonde, but I've been to that bottle a few times myself.

So that's where we stood when Faye came into the office at the end of Month One. I put aside the newspaper article I'd been working on—not writing, but correcting. I know small towns can't hire the cream of the crop for writers and editors, but they could at least find someone who knows what a subordinate clause is. I figured I was doing them a favor by sending, anonymously of course, a corrected copy every once in a while. Free grammatical instruction, if they were smart enough to make use of it.

Faye settled onto a chair with what I call the old lady noise, half sigh and half groan as her weight shifted from feet to rear. "Nothing new and/or exciting out front?"

"We have to give it time." She spoke with more hope than conviction.

"One decent case would show people we're for real," I muttered. Although reluctant to start the venture, I was now loath to accept defeat.

Faye looked at me once, looked away, and seemed to come to a decision. "There's someone who could help us get started." Her too-casual tone said I wasn't going to like the suggestion. Reading my body language, she began arguing before I could speak. "Who has connections all over the state? Who has friends that could actually pay our daily rate?" She groped for the traditional third supporting argument for a debatable point, but words failed her.

"Who'd insist on 'helping out' and drive us both crazy within a week?" I asked.

Faye's expression said she got my point, but she forged ahead anyway. "Maybe she wouldn't. I mean, she's smart, and she's got more nerve than both of us put together."

I glared at her. "Your sister is superficial, bossy, and impulsive. We'd be sorry."

"She knows everyone, from the governor to the county animal control officer, and they all think she walks on water."

"Your sister makes me nuts."

"Stop that. She's your sister too."

Knowing it sounded childish, I said, "Not if I don't let her be."

Faye backed off, letting me roll the idea around in my head for a while. The worst of it was that she was right. Our only other sibling, Margaretta, was the widow of a state cop killed in the line of duty. That tragic event had become a cause célèbre in Michigan. Margaretta had been on the news, in magazines, everywhere for over a year, pushing for better body armor for police officers. It was an idea whose time had come, and Retta served as spokeswoman with both charm and tenacity.

It didn't hurt that she was gorgeous. At forty-eight, Margaretta still looked like a CNN anchor. With her looks and kittenish charm, she usually got people to do exactly as she wanted them to do. The smart ones, once they walked away, might have realized they'd been manipulated. Most never figured it out. It's a gift Hitler had too, they tell me.

Faye often hinted I was jealous, and it was true, at least a little. I'd succeeded in life by using my brain. Faye had spent her life working hard. Margaretta prevailed because she was pretty and because she went after things like a Labrador diving for a duck. Somehow, everything just fell into the pond in front of her.

Not that she was evil. She had no idea how irritating she was, and I recognized that. Retta simply believed she knew what was best for everyone else. In order to remain sane, one could either avoid her or become resigned to accepting her version of his happiness.

"If we let her anywhere near our business, she'll 'suggest' and 'hint' until it's no longer what we want," I reminded Faye. "You and I do okay together, but she's impossible."

"I know." Faye sounded reluctant. She's always been more accepting, which is her weakness, just like rejecting the majority of the human race is mine.

"You can't argue with Retta, because her conversations are round. You make point after point, but eventually she gets them to curve back around to what she wants."

Faye sighed. "I know."

"Remember when we were in high school and she was in junior high and she somehow talked Mom and Dad into letting her go to Cedar Point with us? She ruined everything."

"I know, but she's our sister."

I gave Faye a hard look. "*Your* sister is not welcome in *our* detective agency."

That ended the discussion, because in her heart Faye knew I was right. Besides, Baby Sister was wintering in Florida, which I'd taken into account when setting the opening date for our agency. I'd figured on three months to get up and running before she came home. The plan had been we'd be established by then, able to tell her thanks but no thanks when she offered to help. That wasn't working out well at all.

I opened my datebook with more than necessary force. Although the question was temporarily settled, I knew that when Retta came home, she'd immediately stick her nose in. If we didn't have some cases—even *a* case by then, Faye would argue we had to include her.

No, I promised myself. I'd lay down the law. Two detective sisters, not three.

***

The next week we located an Allport heiress.

Actually, that's stretching the term. We found a woman who'd inherited a bar in town that would have fallen down except it was between other buildings slightly less decrepit. When we informed the lucky inheritor of her uncle's bequest, she shook her over-cooked black hair until her earrings bounced. "Do you know how much money it's going to take to demolish that wreck?" she rasped.

"I won't even be able to sell the lot in this economy. Thanks for nothing."

Despite the clever work we'd done to locate our quarry, the result was less than satisfying. She wrote a letter to the editor of the *Allport Press* about how we'd invaded her privacy and ruined her life.

We turned down three more cases that were either spiteful or spooky, like the guy who wanted us to find his "dream woman" for him. He'd seen her riding around in a classic convertible and was sure she'd given him a come-hither look. I was sure he'd watched *American Graffiti* one too many times.

Faye watched me for two weeks, waiting. I knew we'd discuss the prospect of inviting Margaretta into our business again, and I dreaded it. I'd sunk quite a bit of money into this enterprise, insisting Faye be an employee with a regular paycheck until we got established. Once we had a client base, we'd form a true partnership.

I had also invited Faye and Dale to move into my house. The place was huge, built by some timber baron in the late 1800s, but it had been cut up into apartments in the '70s and rented to young families. I was undoing all that, ditching the grungy shag carpeting, tearing out flimsy dividing walls, and replacing the orange appliances in the large downstairs kitchen.

The top floor was plenty spacious for my needs, and the ground level had a large front parlor we turned into our reception area. A second parlor behind that became our private office. At the back was a kitchen, a dining room, a full bath and two small rooms we made into a den and a bedroom. It was bigger than the house they'd been renting, and living there made it possible for Faye to work with me and keep an eye on Dale at the same time.

Upstairs, I knocked out walls and made five dinky rooms into two large ones with a generous-sized bath. Center front was an all-purpose dining/kitchen/living area with a huge window that looked

down on the street. In the back was my bedroom, just the right size
for a woman alone who intends to stay that way, pretty much. A
nice, wide staircase on the west side led down to the front entry, so I
came and went through the same door our clients did. But if I
needed it, there was a cramped, skinny, twisting staircase at the
back of the house, once used by servants. Those stairs ended at my
sister's kitchen, where the back door opened onto our large, fenced
back yard, which I fully expected Faye would take over and carpet
with flowers.

I was happy with the setup, being close to Faye and Dale but
not tied to them. I was happy to have returned to Allport, to my
roots and a relaxed way of life. Still, I had a sense of urgency now
that we'd launched this enterprise. Anxious to get a real start, I
wasn't sure how far I was willing to go to get clients. There was no
halfway with Retta. Anything she touched became hers, and I was
unwilling to let her share the dream Faye and I had created.

CHAPTER TWO

Faye

Opening a detective agency is a dream I had for years. I just didn't see for a long time that it was possible. All my life I'd read mystery novels, which helped me relax while raising a family and working for bosses, some nice, some not-so-nice, but all a little crazy. About the time my kids turned into adults, life turned crappy. Dale got hurt, our sons floundered in the lousy economy, and we all slipped farther and farther away from the American Dream. I could never get the medical bills caught up, and at least one of the boys always needed help. We just barely kept up.

Then, with a fake smile and a rotten deal, my job disappeared. With nothing to look forward to, I asked myself, "What do I want from the rest of my life?" I came up with three things: I wanted a job where I was my own boss, I wanted to help people, and I wanted something more exciting than counting boxes loaded onto a truck.

My sister Barb had recently retired. Successful, financially secure and well-respected, she missed the people part of life somehow: no husband, no kids, not even a long-term lover. She came home ready to be done with the politics of the legal system, but after a few months she was restless and vaguely unhappy. I pulled her into my scheme, knowing we'd work well together. My organizational skills would extend her intelligence, and my desire to make a difference would be expanded by her awareness of how things get done.

After a month in business, I realized we needed one more thing to make our agency take off: connections. Retta has those, but Barb and Margaretta remind me of the Green Bay Packers and the Detroit Lions, alike in background but unable to come together without a fight. As the middle sibling, I knew it was up to me to see that things worked out between them.

Once I'd mentioned Retta's possible value to Barb, I let the idea settle into her mind. After two more disappointing weeks, I began trying to think of a way to bring Retta up again. Without her, our agency seemed likely to fail. Barb pretended to be busy, and I spent my time sharpening pencils. We avoided talking about the nothing we were facing.

As soon as Retta returned from her second home in Florida, I vowed to talk to Barb again about enlisting her help. I wasn't looking forward to it.

One Thursday I'd taken the pencil sharpener apart and was examining its insides to see why its growl had turned to a crackle when the phone rang. A few minutes later, I was in better spirits. We had a client.

A few hours later she showed up, right on time. Judging by the car she parked out front, Madison Bowers was able to pay our fee. She shook hands like an adult and sat in the chair opposite my desk with prim propriety, clasping her hands in her lap. Barb explained I'd be taking notes on the meeting, and Madison gave permission with an almost regal wave.

"What can we do for you, Ms. Bowers?" Barb was searching her pockets for an oft-needed tissue, and I pushed a box of them toward her before sitting down in the third chair in our office, ready with notepad and pencil. I have an iPad, but I prefer paper for a first draft.

"I'd like you to locate my brother Rob. He's been missing for some time now."

"I'm sorry to hear it. Can you tell us the circumstances of his disappearance?"

"Of course." She shifted in her chair. "On the night of February sixth of last year, I went to my brother's home to visit. His wife informed me he had left her and the children."

When she didn't go on Barb asked, "You don't think he left voluntarily?"

"Oh, no!" Madison took a photo from her purse and passed it to Barb, snapping the clasp closed again quickly, as if it held Pentagon secrets. "Robert's a devoted father and husband."

Barb examined the picture then passed it to me. A tall, slightly flabby man, a blond woman with glasses too big for her face, and two little boys with resigned look-at-the-camera smiles. "Were the police called in?"

"Sheryl, Robert's wife, insisted he ran off. The police say there's no evidence he didn't."

"And why don't you believe her?" I leaned forward, eager to get to the good part.

Ms. Bowers bit her lip, her emotions getting the better of her for a moment. "She said the most awful things about Robert. It's terrible what they did to that woman."

I kept my expression blank. "Who, Mrs. Bowers?"

"Why, Congress. They took Rob away to one of their reeducation camps. I thought he might be released by now, but—" She smiled through her sadness. "He's held out all this time."

Barb's gaze never wavered, but I read her thoughts like there was a news crawl rolling across her forehead. She stayed professional, promising to look into the case. Our visitor left with her head held high, but I couldn't help picturing it filled with bats.

Barb pushed her bottom lip up into the top one. "This shouldn't take long. I'll put it on speaker."

The call yielded one positive and several negatives, delivered in a definite, rather nasal tone. Ms. Bowers indeed had a brother named Robert, but he was neither missing nor a victim of Congress, at least, no more than the rest of us. "What he is," Robert's ex-wife Sheryl reported, "is uninterested in being a husband or a parent or a homeowner. Grown-up stuff like that."

"Do you know where he is?"

"Oh, yeah. Once I got two hundred in cash and a note: *Tell the boys I love them.*" She sniffed dismissively. "If he really cared he'd visit once in a while."

"And the authorities are aware of his whereabouts?"

"Yup. He lives in Gaylord, works at The Home Depot. If I wanted my kids exposed to that loser, they could visit Dad and get new bedroom lamps at the same time."

"Why does his sister think he's missing?"

"Did she give you the brainwashing story?"

"Well, yes."

A sigh on the other end signaled exasperation and pity. "Maddie practically raised Rob. I guess their parents were real boozers. She can't accept that he turned out shiftless, and she can't believe he doesn't want to see her. She came up with this fantasy that it's not Rob's fault. It's the Evil Empire. Don't send her my way, okay? I'd rather live without both of them."

Barb set the phone down with a gentle click and rubbed the frown lines between her eyes. "No one's ever going to take this agency seriously, not anyone sane. People expect detectives to be retired male cops whose outdoor plumbing proves they've got crime-solving skills."

I couldn't decide if I should tell her we had a second prospective client due in an hour. Would the next person to sit in our guest chair be broke, spiteful, crazy, or all of the above?

After a suitable interval I called Miss Bowers, telling her we were unable to take her case. She hinted "they" had gotten to us but didn't seem angry. Maybe part of her, the tiny little sane part, sensed that what we discovered about her brother wouldn't have made her happy.

Madison Bowers was followed by Meredith Brown, and the unfortunate similarity of their initials made Barb's left eyebrow rise. I don't even think she knows she does it, but it's a sure sign she's ready to dismiss an argument, a possibility, or a person.

My sister appears brusque, even uncaring, but honestly, she's just so focused she has a hard time coming out of her bubble to notice the world around her. Daily stuff doesn't matter to her. For example, you could feed her chicken and mashed potatoes every night for the rest of her life and that would be fine, not because she loves those things so much, but because she doesn't care about food--or clothes or movies or Facebook. Barb goes along with the world because it's expected, but what concerns the world doesn't really concern her.

When she does let herself care about something or someone, however, Barb is whole-heartedly involved. Unable to turn her emotions off, she holds back from most people. It's simple self-defense.

Meredith Brown didn't appear crazy, but neither had the woman who an hour before had insisted her brother was being re-educated by the government. Miss Brown was about twenty-three, cute in a well-scrubbed way, and dressed in khakis and a light sweater. I guessed elementary teacher, and I was right. Of course the magic marker stain on the heel of her right hand was an important clue, and I am a practicing detective.

That was the good part. The bad part came after we finished the preliminary introductions and offered coffee, tea, or water. Once that was settled she began, "My brother is missing."

Barb's eyebrow went up again, and I stepped in quickly. "Was he kidnapped?" Barb's gaze shifted to me, but I looked at Ms. Brown in what I hoped was an encouraging way.

"Oh, no, nothing like that. He left several years ago, but now I need to find him." She made an obvious decision, and the process by which she came to it was easy to follow in her expression. There was uncertainty, pain, and finally determination. "He was accused of a crime, and he took off to avoid getting arrested. I'd like you to find him and prove he's innocent."

Now Barb's forehead puckered. It was a step up from alien abductions and Congressional plots. We were capable of doing a search for someone missing, but proving someone didn't commit a crime when the police thought he had might be a tricky proposition.

"Ms. Brown, what makes you think your brother is innocent of this crime?"

"He told me so." She smiled at the ingenuousness of her own statement. "Can I tell you the whole story before you decide I'm nuts?"

"Please do, Miss Brown." Whatever it takes to grab my sister's emotions, this sweet young thing had it. I put my head down to hide a grin. We had a real case at last.

"It happened six years ago," Meredith Brown said after a sip of water. "I was eighteen and my brother was twenty-five when he married Carina Wozniak."

Brown hadn't struck a chord in my memory, but everyone in Allport knew the name *Wozniak*. The story had been in all the papers that year, even big ones like the *Detroit Free Press*. I tested my recall as Meredith Brown gave her version.

"Even then I knew it was a disaster, but Neil never had a chance. Carina was gorgeous and different from most girls he knew."

"How was she different?"

"My sister's been out of state." I hitched my chair closer so I could rest an elbow on the desktop. My right shoulder goes numb if it doesn't have something to rest on.

Meredith sighed as if she'd thought about that question a lot. "Carina was the type of girl Neil had never imagined would look twice at him. She'd gone to some expensive school, and she looked like a model. I think at that point in his life she was irresistible." Barb was frowning, and Meredith tilted her head in a question. "Her family has lots of money."

"You remember the Wozniaks."

"Oh," Barb said, catching on. "The stone quarry people."

"Right," Meredith said. "Except Carina's father took over the family business in the '90s and diversified. Now they have interests in just about everything you can imagine."

"WOZ Industries," I told Barb. "Remember, I drove you out to see the Pit?"

"Yes," Barb said, nodding. "Much bigger than I remembered."

Meredith returned to her story. "Carina and Neil met when the contractor he worked for did some expansion on their house on Pierce Lake. You should see it!" Her tone revealed awe and a hint of disapproval. "Neil was dazzled. My parents tried to tell him it would be tough for a working guy to marry into that family, but he wouldn't listen."

"He saw things differently after the marriage?" Barb asked.

"Mr. Wozniak—his first name is Stan—wanted Neil to move to Detroit and run one of his subsidiaries. Since he offered two choices, he thought Neil was ungrateful when he refused them both. But both the so-called choices involved things Neil hated: inside work, lots of travel, and public speaking." As Meredith ran a hand through her taffy-colored hair, I noticed a small, partially healed incision on her scalp.

"When he asked Carina to marry him, Neil thought she understood they'd stay in Allport and live on his income. If you ask me, her plan was to get him then change him into the kind of husband she wanted." A turn of Meredith's lip revealed her opinion of her sister-in-law.

"So the marriage was in trouble?"

A flush began at her neck and rose to her face. "It was, but not like they said. Neil wanted to work it out, but Carina only spoke in ultimatums. They had some pretty intense arguments."

The media had reported that a neighbor actually went to their door one night, fearing the young couple had come to blows. I decided to wait until Meredith was gone to mention it.

"What did your brother do?"

"He moved out." Meredith wiped her palms on her pant-legs. Even after several years, reliving the events was harder than she'd thought it would be. "Neil insisted he and Carina could work things out." She grimaced. "I wasn't so sure."

Despite not knowing where this was headed, Barb seemed to sense that background was important. "So the wife was staying in the couple's apartment alone?"

"Well, no. Her brother Carson was visiting from California. After a few days at the family's house on Pierce Lake, he moved into Carina's spare bedroom." She licked her lips. "When…it happened, people said she asked him to stay with her because she was afraid of Neil."

"What happened?" Barb's tone was gentle.

Meredith literally squirmed in her chair, and though her mouth opened and closed a couple of times, nothing came out. Guessing what it would cost her to put it into words, I stepped in. "Carina and Carson were both murdered. All the evidence pointed to Neil Brown."

Barb looked from me to Meredith and back again, her eyes wide. If we took this case, we'd be chasing down a double murderer, at least someone the police thought was guilty.

And of course we were going to take it. I knew my sister, and she already wanted to find out what happened that night. Two people dead, a third missing. It was what we'd been hoping for since the doors to our agency opened: something that made a difference.

Barb scribbled a note on the legal pad in front of her, and again I smiled. For a lawyer, taking notes is like a boxer taking off his robe.

"Tell us what you know about that night. And tell us everything."

Meredith's eyes moved to the left as she searched for a beginning point. They say left is good; it accesses the brain's recall. Liars look to the right, accessing creativity.

"Neil was working down in Lincoln. He called a little after one and said he had to leave Allport."

"Try to say it exactly as he did."

Again her eyes turned to the left. He said, 'Hon, it's me. Something bad has happened, but it isn't like he says. I've got to leave town for a while. If I can, I'll contact you, but even if I don't, I'll be okay. I'm really sorry. There's nothing else I can do.'" Meredith swallowed hard. "I tried to ask questions, but he just repeated he was sorry and hung up."

"He never said he didn't kill them." When Meredith simply sat there looking sad, Barb went on. "'It isn't like he says.' Whom did he mean by that?"

"I think he meant Mr. Wozniak—Stan. He insisted Neil killed Carina and Carson. For years after the murders, he spent every free minute and a ton of money trying to find Neil. He even moved his main office from Detroit back up here. He was like a bulldozer, pushing the police, offering rewards for information leading to Neil's capture, and giving TV interviews where he claimed Neil was abusive. He made my brother sound like a Neanderthal."

"And what is he really like?" Barb's tone was casual, but I heard a test in the undertone. In her career she'd probably heard every excuse family members give for errant relatives.

Meredith's demeanor softened. "Neil's a normal Michigan redneck: tough, hardworking, and not very demonstrative. But he had a creative streak, too. He could always think outside the ordinary." Taking her wallet out of her purse, she removed a picture from the plastic file and passed it across the desk. "He's very good looking. I guess that's what attracted Carina."

Barb studied the photo then gave it to me. It had a dog-eared corner and looked like it had bumped around in there for a long time. I rose and went to the scanner, listening to the conversation as the machine buzzed, chugged, and spit out a copy.

"What were your brother's hobbies and interests?" Barb asked. Most missing people are found because they continue some activity they enjoy. They don't realize their subscription to a stamp collecting magazine or their passion for Farmville can help locate them, even if they move away and change their name.

Meredith touched the incision near her temple lightly but turned the gesture into grooming, smoothing her hair. "The usual: hunting, fishing, music, softball. I know he doesn't sound sensitive, but—" She groped for an example. "When I was thirteen I got strep throat just before Junior High Prom. As soon as I was better, Neil got all dressed up and took me to a fancy restaurant for a nice dinner, to make me feel better about missing the dance."

Barb seemed unimpressed. Even a double murderer might take pity on a little sister as cute as Meredith and give up one evening of cruising Main Street looking for action.

"May I ask why you're pursuing this now? It's been years."

Meredith straightened her spine and returned the photo to her wallet before answering. "First, my parents are dead, Mom five years ago and Dad last fall. They always thought Neil was better off wherever he is, since it isn't prison. Second, I have a job now and can pay your fee." Barb gave me a quick glance. Would we take money from a girl just out of college, with her first job and a load of student loans to pay off? Just enough to save her pride, I guessed.

"Next, it's not fair to Brooke to have these lies continue."

Barb frowned. "Brooke?"

"The baby." I spoke without conscious intent.

Meredith nodded. "Carina was pregnant, and they were able to save the baby. Neil doesn't know it, but he has a six-year-old daughter who looks just like him."

"You have the child?"

She smiled. "Grandpa and Aunt Meri, we did it together. But now I—" She swallowed. "I have to have surgery in the very near future." Her hand started upward, toward the incision, but she set it back in her lap. "It's, um, serious, and the doctors don't give any guarantees. Even if I—even if it goes well, I'll be incapacitated for a while. Brooke needs her daddy."

Barb scanned Meredith's face but didn't ask for details. "What if he's guilty?"

"Find him first. Then help me prove he's innocent."

Barb was firm. "You know we can't guarantee that. He could face life in prison."

"Ms. Evans, Neil didn't kill his wife. Even if—" She hurried on, seeing Barb's face. "Even if he'd accidentally killed her, he wouldn't murder Carson to cover it up, like they say."

Barb didn't argue. "We'll look into this, but we won't waste your money. If it doesn't look like we can locate your brother, we'll charge you only for expenses incurred."

"I hope you can find him." With an embarrassed flush, Meredith pulled an envelope from her purse. "I never shared this with the police."

She handed Barb a newspaper cutting of about two by two inches. After a quick scan, Barb handed it to me. "Buck Lake Resort?"

"I didn't really hold out on the police," Meredith defended herself. "I found that a long time afterward."

"Why do you think this is significant?" I asked.

"It was in a book I loaned Neil shortly before Carina was killed. He's a big-time hunter, and he'd been looking at rentals in the U.P." Meredith looked from me to Barb. "Wouldn't a remote place like that come to mind when he needed somewhere to hide?"

"The whole Upper Peninsula is remote." My sister sees Allport as the absolute end of the civilized world. She won't camp, refuses to hike, and sees no difference between the tree outside her bedroom window and the gazillion trees on the north side of the Mackinac Bridge.

"Was your brother familiar with the U.P.?" I asked.

"Not really, but he wanted to try hunting up there."

"And the police didn't know about this?"

"Just me. Neil asked if I thought Carina would be okay with him being gone for a week." She smiled. "I told him he should forget it, especially with a baby on the way."

"So it's a place no one knew to look for him."

Barb cut in, her tone businesslike. "Miss Brown, you need to understand we can't guarantee results. If you need someone to care for the child, you should talk to other relatives."

"The only other relative Brooke has left is Stan Wozniak, and he has nothing to do with her." Meredith twisted her purse strap. "I've been thinking of people who might help out."

My eyes got kind of prickly, and I had to look down at my notes for a minute. A nice girl like her, who'd gone through so much, shouldn't have to face health trouble, too. It wouldn't be a big inconvenience for me to take the child for a few weeks. And Dale would—

I looked up to see my sister sending a firm "No" with her eyes. She was right. We had to be professional. Still, I could call some people at church. They'd help her find care for the girl.

Barb returned her attention to Meredith. "What sort of man is Wozniak?"

Meredith passed a hand over her mouth as if to stop her first response. "I shouldn't speak badly of the man, but he was so sure Neil killed Carina that he went a little crazy. He hired detectives to find him. He said terrible things about my brother to the police and the media."

"You understand he'll probably do his best to have your brother arrested if we locate him," Barb said. "Nothing we can do will prevent that."

"I understand." Meredith picked up her purse and set the strap on her shoulder. "All I can hope for is that Neil has some way to prove he isn't a killer."

If he'd had that kind of proof, Neil Brown wouldn't have fled. Barb's glance told me she was thinking the same thing. It was probable this case wasn't going to go in the direction Meredith Brown wanted it to.

When our client had gone, we laid out a course of action. I volunteered to visit Tom Stevens, Allport's acting chief of police, and get his take on the Wozniak murders. Tom's been on the job for years, and I knew him from high school. His superior had died suddenly, and the city was in the process of finding a replacement. Apparently it wouldn't be Tom.

Barb pulled out her phone. "I'll call this Buck Whatever place."

When I have to tell Barb something she doesn't want to hear, I've learned to tread carefully. One wrong move, and she'll refuse to listen to further argument. "We could drive up there, talk to the owner, and be back in a couple of days."

The idea of going to the U.P. made her brows pull together. "Why? We send them a photo; they tell us whether they remember seeing Brown or not."

"Think about it, Barb. Neil knew he was the subject of a police search. The first thing he'd do is alter his appearance: his hair color, his clothes, maybe even theatrical makeup. He'd start a beard, which isn't unusual for hunters and changes the shape of the face."

"A picture isn't enough." It was a reluctant admission.

"Unfortunately, time is not on our side."

"Right. Who knows if they'll remember a guy who rented a cabin years ago and probably kept a very low profile?"

"But it's a clue the police didn't have."

She slid open her desk drawer and began rummaging. "I don't blame Meredith for not ratting on her brother, but the police need to know where he went."

I wasn't happy with betraying Meredith's confidence. "When we know he's up there."

Barb retrieved the object she'd been hunting, a Michigan map. "I guess you're right. We'll check out the Outer Boondocks ourselves."

"I'd sure like to hear Neil's side of the story."

Barb shut the desk drawer with a thump. "Faye, if this guy has avoided the police for this long, he's clever. And if he did what the police think he did, he's dangerous."

"I get that. But he probably missed the media coverage. If we tell him his daughter's alive, he might come forward and explain what really happened."

Barb lowered her eyes, and I sensed how naïve my argument sounded to an experienced attorney's ears. Neil Brown's innocence wasn't likely. I had to face that.

"Our job is to find him," she said. "Then he can tell his story to anyone who'll listen."

"Do you think the police will give him a chance?"

She shrugged. "You know Tom Stevens better than I do."

"Tom isn't the most original thinker I ever met." Saving the file *M.Brown,* I turned my iPad off. "Wozniak was a big factor, and the local police pretty much did what he told them to."

"Money talks, huh?"

"Well, that and the fact he actually saw Neil leaving the apartment. He didn't think anything of it until he went in and found his son dead and his daughter dying."

"So public sympathy was for the Wozniaks?"

I waved a hand. "You know how it is. The media focuses on the people who make good sound bites. Some people I talked to said privately that Carina wasn't the poor, abused wife her father insisted she was, and lots of people said Carson was shiftless and spoiled, but Neil's DNA was under Carina's fingernails, he left her dying, and their marital problems were well known."

"I see." Barb's tone hinted at regret for having taken the case. I, too, hated the thought we might have to tell Meredith, dealing with a deadly disease, a young child, and a family scandal, that her brother was what the rest of the world thought him: a double murderer.

***

In my high-mileage Volvo, I rattled my way to City Hall the next morning to see Tom Stevens. Our acting police chief graduated from Allport High School a year after me, and as I followed him into his office, I took note of the trophies and photos from those days when he was a basketball star. Judging from his hula-hoop waistline, he didn't play much ball these days.

Tom was a good small-town policeman. He worked hard to keep the public safe and contented, supported every humanitarian organization in the area, and had a fatherly approach to law enforcement well-suited to the many juveniles he dealt with. Most Allport crimes required a ride home, a conference with Mom and Dad, and a stern reprimand.

The Wozniak murders were the biggest case Allport ever had, and the only unsolved murder. We had instances of violent death, of course, but the killer usually called 9-1-1, tearfully confessing to the crime and desperate to tell what happened. Even the ones who didn't confess weren't much of a challenge. They were usually found cowering in their parent's garage or in a cousin's house in the next county. Before Neil Brown, not many felons had eluded capture for more than a week.

I'd have bet Tom and K, the old police chief, began work on the Wozniak case thinking it was a golden opportunity to look good. As the trail grew colder, they must have become frustrated. Local police agencies have neither the time nor the resources to track a clever criminal. Of course, the Michigan State Police contributed significant expertise, but no trace of Neil was ever found. Many believed he'd escaped to Canada on the VIA Rail, though there was no record of him boarding a train.

"Probably used an alias and changed his appearance," Tom told me once I'd introduced the reason for my visit. He rocked back in his padded plastic chair, not a flattering position, since his belly rose like a blue moon over the desktop. "Nobody expected a guy like Neil to fool every lawman in Michigan, but he did, and you can throw in the OPPies and the Ohio, Illinois, and Indiana State Police, too."

He watched my face to see if I understood the reference to the Ontario Provincial Police, and I did, having once observed Barb in a spirited discussion with a member of that organization over her possession of a radar detector. She'd contended since it was unplugged he couldn't confiscate it. My sister the lawyer lost that roadside case.

I offered a plate of fresh oatmeal cookies. No harm in minor bribery, and a few more couldn't make much difference to Tom's waistline. "Why were you so sure he went south?"

Tom took a cookie, bit off half of it, and talked around the mouthful. "Found his truck in Port Huron, near the train station. After that he just disappeared." Tom sounded half-admiring, half-rueful. The fact that Brown had eluded all cops, not just those in Allport, Michigan, had probably made losing the prime suspect of their biggest felony case a little more palatable.

I'd made a list of questions, and Tom and I covered all of them. Neil had no prior record, his friends and family had been questioned and re-questioned about possible hideouts, and none of them appeared to be holding anything back.

"Mostly what we got was shock." Leaning forward, Tom clasped beefy hands on the desktop. "No one wants to think somebody they like is capable of murder. His people said Neil wouldn't hurt anyone. The sister especially." He paused. "She the one that hired you?"

"I can't say." Even a novice crime fighter knows clients' names shouldn't be revealed.

His round face showed amusement. "You don't have to. Meredith Brown had a big case of hero-worship for her brother, which means you can't take her word for anything." He took on a manner that no doubt worked well on teenagers caught with a trunk full of beer. "I'm helping you out, here, Faye. You're wasting your time and her money."

Not being a juvenile delinquent, I wasn't required to sit through the whole lecture. "It's up to us how we spend our time and up to the client how she spends her money." I rose and gathered my things. "Thanks, Tom. I'll let you know if we find anything."

"You do that." Taking a second cookie, he leaned back in the chair again, signaling he wouldn't hold his breath until we broke the case.

As I left, I pictured Tom telling his coworkers about the two women on Bentley Street who were playing detective. I could even imagine the chuckles that followed.

CHAPTER THREE

Barb

While Faye visited what she called the "cop shop," I tracked down Byron Sparks, the state police detective who handled the Wozniak case. When I reached him and gave a brief overview, there was a pause before he spoke. "You're hired to prove Brown's innocence?"

"To find him. The client expressed hope that he'll be proven innocent, but I made it clear we couldn't guarantee that."

Sparks snorted. "That's good, since he's guilty."

"You have no doubt of that?"

I pictured Sparks' lips tightening at the audacity of my question, and there was irritation in his voice. "There was a fight. He killed the wife and brother with what was probably a softball bat. Brown's DNA was all over, his blood was on the brother's shorts. The place was a mess. No way the guy's innocent."

I kept at it, looking for a crack that might let out a little hope. "Could there be extenuating circumstances? Maybe Carson and Neil argued, and Carina got hurt by accident."

"The two men hardly knew each other. The Wozniak kid went to some fancy school in California and ended up living out there." He paused, apparently letting the details come back to him. "Brown was separated from his wife, but she called him that day and asked him to stop by."

"Why?"

"Her father said it was because she'd decided to file for divorce." His tone had grown more irritated, and I decided not to interrupt again. "However it started, things got violent. The father came along in time to see Brown leaving the house. He saw him, and he went inside to find his son dead and his daughter dying."

I heard little thumps and imagined Sparks punctuating his points on the desktop with his index finger. "Neil had a temper. He was there. His softball bat wasn't anywhere to be found. We searched the apartment, his truck, and the place he was renting." Sparks spoke confidently. "The guy had motive, means, and opportunity. He did it."

I couldn't think of anything to say. It sounded bad for Neil Brown, and for Meredith.

"If you find him, that'll be great," Sparks said, "but don't expect a happy reunion between Brown and his family. It isn't going to happen."

He was more correct than he knew. Even if Brown were innocent as a lamb, Meredith's illness would be devastating if he turned out to be the person his sister thought he was.

Did Neil Brown want to know he had a six-year-old daughter? Faye hoped he did. She also hoped he had an explanation for what happened. Had Carina fallen during an argument? If she had, why hadn't he called for help? Why had he attacked her brother, beating him bloody and crushing his skull? I wanted to pose those questions and more to Neil, wherever he might be.

I suddenly remembered I hadn't asked Sparks about Stan Wozniak, whose dislike of his son-in-law might have colored his story. As an outsider, Sparks was the best person to judge how truthful the old man had been. *Old man?* He was probably my age. *Father*, I corrected.

I hit *Redial* and got the switchboard operator again. "It's Barb Evans again. I just spoke with Detective Sparks, but I'd like to ask him one more question."

"One moment." As I waited, I walked around the desk and studied the map of Michigan Faye had attached to a bulletin board. When the woman came back on the line, there was a false note to her voice. "I'm sorry, but Detective Sparks is gone. He'll be out for the rest of the day."

I thanked her and hung up, guessing Sparks considered more contact with me a waste of his time. I'd have to go at things from another direction, and sadly, that direction had to be north.

***

Faye was excited about driving to the U.P., and before I knew it, she'd mapped our route and made a list of what to pack. "I don't want to sleep at a place called Buck Anything," I groused. "Nor do I want to hobnob with deer-killers."

"It's May," she reminded me. "We won't run into any hunters."

"Good." I didn't even try to curtail my grouchiness. "They spend one day hunting and the other fourteen playing cards, drinking, and walking around town in orange camo."

"That doesn't mean they're bad people," Faye scolded.

"They take over and treat the town like their personal back yard. People who don't shave, bathe, or brush their teeth should stay away from those of us who do."

"Do you go with me, or do I go alone?"

"I can't let you go into the wilderness by yourself, but I won't like it. And there's the bridge, too." I hoped that would give her second thoughts. Faye's greatest fear is being anywhere there's air beneath her: bridges, elevators, and airplanes.

Faye sighed. "The Mackinac Bridge has stood since nineteen-fifty-something. I suppose it'll bear the weight of two middle-aged women."

"But what about the half-dozen semis, assorted campers, and fully-laden passenger cars bound to be on it at the same time?" I was teasing now, and she knew it.

"Fine, don't go."

"I'm going," I said. "I'm just not happy about it."

Dale came into the room at that point, moving deliberately, touching furniture for stability as he passed. A head injury several years back had left him unsteady on his feet and unable to work a normal job. He got vertigo from standing or moving too suddenly. Light bothered him so much he wore dark glasses inside and out, and anything above conversation-level noise was torture. Luckily, his mishap had not destroyed his sense of humor, and he said, "I'm told that tomorrow morning I become the Smart Detective Agency's Man Friday."

"If you don't mind," I replied. "It's just overnight, but you'll be in charge."

"Okay, but no brawling with the Yoopers."

"Maybe we could Skype the owner of the lodge."

"Go pack a bag," Faye prodded. "One night of misery and you can return to the civilized side of the Bridge." As I left the room she added, "And bring lots of tissues. It's spring, so your allergies will really kick in up there."

CHAPTER FOUR

Faye

If you haven't seen the Mackinac Bridge, you should. Laid across the Strait of Mackinac, a full five miles of suspension bridge hangs from lofty towers footed deep in the waters where two Great Lakes, Michigan and Huron, meet at the tip of the mitt. Despite admiring its engineering, I hate the damned thing.

US 23 took us to Mackinaw City, a pleasant drive that often skirted the shore of Lake Huron, providing great views. We got admiring looks as we passed through towns along the way, not for ourselves, but for the car. Barb drives a '57 Chevy, Matador Red with white side panels. It might sound odd for a person who can afford all the modern bells and whistles, but as a kid she was obsessed with Uncle Carl's car. Having no children of his own, he left the car to Barb when he died. All the years she lived on the Pacific Coast it was stored in a barn, on blocks and drained of fluids. When she returned to Allport, she spent a sizeable chunk of money to have it refurbished and modernized to meet present laws. The surprisingly comfortable bench seat and flat dashboard left lots of room for two mature women. At my age I appreciated things like that.

As we approached the bridge, I got antsy. A feeling of dread always hit me as the land receded. Images of the car lunging over the side or the bridge collapsing under me came to mind. I could almost feel the car plummet into space and after a few terror-filled seconds, plunge into the icy water. I heard the bubbling as we sank beneath the surface, unable to escape as pressure increased and light faded. If I dwelled on it, I became unable to function. Aware of this, Barb maintained a conversation, no matter how inane it became.

"How long do you think it'll take to get there?" I sounded just like my kids used to. *Are we there yet?* I tried to keep my voice steady, but the choppy water far below moved like a living thing, waiting like a terrible fish to swallow us alive.

"Frau GPS says we'll arrive at 3:55." According to Barb, the GPS voice sounds like a Nazi housewife. She described the route we'd take in detail to keep me from focusing on my fear. "We'll take US 2 for a couple of hours then head north on a paved road that turns to dirt. After that it's a bunch of twists and turns. I hope the Frau knows what she's doing."

At the northern end of the bridge, we stopped at the tollbooth, paid the friendly attendant, and exited the "Mighty Mac." Thrilled to be back on dry land, I tried to paint a rosy picture of our destination. "The guy at the Chamber of Commerce didn't know a lot about Buck Lake Resort, but he's driven by it lots of times. He says it doesn't look bad."

Barb raised that brow. "He's a Yooper. What does he know?"

"It might be nice."

"Hampton Inn is nice. Buck Lake Resort is mice, I guarantee it."

We left I-75 and turned west, stopping for drinks at the last McDonalds we'd see until the return trip. The U.P. of Michigan was beautiful but a little desolate. US 2 crossed it and continued all the way to the Pacific if a person wanted to go that far. The towns along the way were small, the permanent homes mostly modest, with signs proclaiming businesses from computer repair to pasties, the delicious meat pies whose invention is claimed by both Brits and

Finns. Peeps of the big lake provided beautiful views, but mostly there were trees. Lots of trees.

Just before the town of Manistique the Frau ordered a right turn, and we headed north on a county road that quickly turned from pavement to gravel. As the Chevy chattered over washboard bumps, Barb grumbled about the dirt she'd have to wash off her baby. Now the forest closed in on us from both sides, opening infrequently to reveal no-frills houses with multiple sheds, trailers, and vehicles huddled around them as if for company. Some were hunting camps, introduced with signboards over the drive with fanciful names like "Deer Jane" or "Hunters' Home." Many had a padlocked gate, though I never saw one that looked worth breaking into.

At each turn the GPS called for, the road got narrower. "What are those?" Barb asked, indicating tall willow sticks stuck into the shoulder of the road at irregular intervals.

"Snow sticks," I answered. "Without them, plow trucks might go off the road in the winter when all the drivers can see is white."

Barb snorted. "The best thing about this trip is it didn't happen in February." No argument there. Spring comes late to the U.P., but there aren't a lot of blizzards in May.

My companion's griping aside, the drive was beautiful. We passed a dozen small lakes, some still hung with fog left over from the cool morning. The Chevy climbed small hills and wound frequent curves, and more than once we surprised animals—a waddling porcupine, two deer, and a shy, side-stepping coyote.

It seemed to take forever, but finally we turned west again, onto the road given as Buck Lake's address. It was a hard-packed, arrow-straight path over-arched with trees whose tops were just turning green. In a month it would be a leafy tunnel, and in the fall, a kaleidoscope of color. Barb slowed even more, both to look for the resort and because the ruts had gotten even worse. At one point the GPS told us we had reached our destination, but since there were only trees and more trees, we kept going.

Finally, I pointed left. "There!"

Barb pulled into a circle drive running past a cedar-shake building. Over the door a hand-painted sign said, OFFICE, and on the door itself another sign said, COME IN. "Exactly as expected," she said. "Hardly palatial."

It was, I had to admit, the most rustic of rustic structures. There were antlers mounted on either side of the door. At one side of the building was a buck pole, thankfully empty.

"I can just picture that thing hung with gutted deer carcasses." Barb's grumpy mood was rapidly getting worse. You'd think someone who grew up in northern Michigan would accept the whole hunting mind-set, but she'd lived too long in the big city.

"Don't start," I told her sharply. "It's one night." We'd agreed (one of us reluctantly) we should stay at the resort in order to speak to anyone who might recall a guest from years ago.

We got out of the car, greeted by the piney scent no commercial cleaner can truly re-create. Barb went inside while I waited in the drive, smoking and surveying the place. There were five rustic cabins behind the main building, each with a metal number tacked to the door. Each was about ten by twenty feet, and I shuddered to see a small outhouse behind the last of them. Trees circled the resort, making it seem crowded against nature rather than nestled into it.

In a few minutes Barb returned with a key and a bemused expression. "The owner isn't here right now. There's a note that says to check yourself in, take a key, and make yourself at home. He'll be around in the morning."

"This isn't the peak time of year for U.P. vacationing," I responded. "The guy didn't expect company, so he went off to do whatever men like him do in the off-season."

Barb shook her head in disbelief. "Trust lives in Michigan's Upper Peninsula."

"I kind of like it."

She gave me a look then headed for the first cabin, remarking, "I figured we might as well be Number One."

The cabin was neat, though sparsely furnished. It smelled a little musty, and I saw Barb's nose twitch with distaste. In one corner was an icebox that would have brought a nice price from any antique dealer in Saugatuck. Next to it was a hand pump. On another wall a lumpy-looking couch sat under a window with glass so old it made the trees outside look wavy. In the center of the room sat a table and four rickety chairs. To my great joy, there was a bathroom with the required amenities, though they were jammed into a space hardly large enough for Barb, much less a woman of my size. The toilet apparently flushed by gravity, and I explained the buckets lined up against the wall. "You pour water from the pail into the bowl, and whatever's in there goes away." The look she gave me spoke volumes.

I opened a door opposite the bathroom to find a small bedroom with two bunks along one wall and a folded cot against another. There were gas lights, and we read the instructions while daylight made that possible. I suggested we light the one in the main room and leave it burning, first to make sure we knew how, and second so we could see to light the others when it got dark. It wasn't as scary as I'd imagined, and the friendly glow of the mantle was comforting. When that was done, there seemed to be nothing else to do but haul in our stuff.

I'd brought along two sleeping bags, and we'd stopped at a grocery and bought enough deli food for several meals. In fact, we'd over-bought, the way people tend to do when they know they'll be unable to shop for a while. You think you might need everything in the store.

Oh, yes, the mice. There were none visible, but there was plenty of evidence. You couldn't really blame the owner. Mice can get in almost anywhere, and they abound in woodsy areas. The fact there were no tiny skeletal forms lying around indicated effort, but I was sure we'd hear the skitter of little feet in the night. I was pretty sure Barb wouldn't sleep a wink.

Once we unloaded the car, we explored the property. A pathway behind the cabins had an arrow-shaped wooden sign that said simply, LAKE, so we went there first. The path slanted gently downward, and about a hundred feet into the trees we found it, not a large body of water but certainly scenic. It was almost perfectly round, and there were only a few other buildings along its murky edge, all of them far removed from us. At our feet were two aluminum rowboats, overturned and pulled back from the shore, and a primitive launch site, gravel dumped into a rectangular frame and edged on one side by a wooden dock.

The lake was quiet in that way that gets your attention because it's so deep. An occasional bird-call echoed over the water, but mostly there was only stillness.

"Pretty," Barb murmured. It seemed wrong to use normal tones.

"Yes," I agreed, waiting for the *but* that threatened: *but* there are mice, *but* it will be cold tonight, *but* we have no TV, no cell phone reception, etc. She didn't say it, and I realized she was trying not to be a party pooper.

I lit a cigarette. The great thing about the great outdoors was it provided guilt-free smoking. While I enjoyed my drug of choice,

Barb explored the lakeshore. I contended there wasn't much to see, but she had to look.

She went left until swampy ground cut off her progress, then returned and did the same the other way. Same result. Sadly for her improved mood, she stumbled into a hatch of black flies, which are at their best in the springtime U.P. Bugs don't like the smell of cigarette smoke any more than other non-smokers, so they circled Barb like a moving halo and left me alone. I tried not to look smug.

We finally retreated to the cabin, bug-free but dark and dampish. Our one gaslight put out heat as well as light, so we lit the others. Following instructions on a hand-lettered sign, I elicited water from the pump, refilling the bucket after we each flushed the toilet. A stove made from an old oil barrel stood in one corner on skinny metal legs. Four uniformly cut logs lay beside it, but there was no kindling, no paper, nothing with which to start a fire. I had my cigarette lighter, but fire-starting doesn't work without the in-between ingredients. "Maybe the lights will be enough," I said hopefully. Barb's silence was eloquent.

North of the 45th parallel, May doesn't always mean spring, and the sun had sunk below the tree line, leaving behind a definite chill. As we ate coleslaw with cold beans and chicken, the temperature in the cabin dropped, and we both began to shiver. Neither of us had brought enough clothes, and I pictured a miserable night huddled in our sleeping bags, noses red with cold. There wasn't even room on the bunks to bundle and share body heat like we had when we were kids.

Barb got quiet, and I figured she was kicking herself for coming here. "Just because I don't like it doesn't mean it's going to kill me," she said, rubbing her hands together. Either she was trying to make me feel better or convince herself she'd survive.

"When I said one night, I forgot how long that can be when you're miserable," I said.

Just then there was a knock on the door, a hard three-count that meant business. "Yes?" Barb called, shooting me a wary glance.

"You want help building a fire?"

I sprang to the door, muttering, "I wouldn't need help if I had the materials!" Opening the door brought both relief and shock. A man stood on the pallet porch with an armload of wood that ran the gamut of appropriate sizes, from kindling to all-nighter. From one roomy pocket of his red-and-black plaid jacket a rolled catalog, presumably tinder, protruded. The other pocket bulged in the shape of a thermal bottle, which also boded well for us.

Despite the anticipation of warmer times, I was hesitant. The bearer of these gifts was so scary I had to make an effort not to stare. Tall and muscular, he had flat-brown hair and an untrimmed beard that lay on his chest like a dead animal. His eyes were hazel, or at least one of them was. The other was clouded with a white haze, probably blind and definitely disconcerting. His teeth were crooked and discolored, and his right arm hung limply at his side. It was hard not to register pity at the sight of so many physical deformities visited on a single human being.

"I can have you a fire in a few minutes."

"That'd be great. Come in," I invited, trying to look directly at him without flinching.

"Didn't expect anybody, so I didn't fill the wood-boxes yet," he said, entering and setting down the carefully balanced load. It made quite a clatter, since he had no way to control the landing of the various pieces of wood. He set to work nimbly enough, opening the firebox door and piling the makings of a fire inside. Within minutes, the metal of the old stove began to smell hot, which our host assured us was fine. As he encouraged the fire, leaving the round, grated door open a little, he offered gruffly, "There's cocoa in the bottle. Warm you up some." The protruding teeth made it hard for him to enunciate clearly, and he spoke with a halting cadence. At times I had to think about what he said for a few seconds before it registered.

Barb accepted his offer without mentioning we'd have drunk hemlock at that point if it was warm. Placing the bottle between his thighs, the man removed the cap and stopper with his good hand. I found two cups (who remembers Melmac!) on a shelf, and he poured, drinking his own portion from the bottle's cup-top. We sipped surprisingly good cocoa silently, Barb and I avoiding each other's gaze and our host watching the fire. When he was satisfied it would live, he closed the door, secured it with the coiled metal handle, and turned down the draft.

"Roger Kimball," he announced, turning to us. "I own the place."

Barb offered her left hand. "Barbara Evans, and this is my sister, Faye Burner." I shook left-handed too, a little self-consciously.

Kimball regarded us with his good eye narrowed. "What you looking for up here?"

Barb offered a professional smile, perfected over years of difficult interviews. "You, Mr. Kimball." When his dark eyebrows rose she explained, "We're hoping you can help us with a case we're working on."

"Have you owned this place for long?" I asked.

Kimball's lips moved slightly before he was able to form a reply. I guessed he didn't have many conversations with women, maybe with anyone. "Four, almost five years."

Disappointment showed on Barb's face as she wrapped both hands around the warm cup. "I guess you won't be able to help us."

"Before I bought it, I worked here."

"You worked for the person who owned the lodge before?"

"Haike Makala, my uncle. I came over from Munising when he got crippled up with arthritis." Kimball nodded to himself, pleased to have formed such a long string of words.

"Your uncle."

"He needed help putting boats and the dock in, dressing deer, like that. I'm pretty strong." Almost defiantly he glanced at the arm, lifeless as an ax handle.

"So how did you come to own the place?"

Kimball spoke in the peculiar sing-song quality of Yooper speech, a leftover from the area's Scandinavian settlers. "Haike went to live in Arizona. Drier climate." He dragged out the "o" in the state's name and seemed to think of it as a foreign land. To him it probably was.

He went on, his voice betraying fondness for the old man. "He sold it to me cheap, wanted somebody that would live here, not some club that leaves it empty most times." The odd face changed subtly. "I like it, away from people."

It was easy to understand the choice to avoid the curious stares and pitying comments he'd probably dealt with daily. Here Kimball could forget his physical problems, adapting to his disabilities until he didn't have to think about them much. His uncle had done him a real favor.

"In November six years ago," Barb prompted, "a man might have come here from the Lower Peninsula who wasn't equipped very well for hunting. His wife and her brother were murdered, and the police think he did it."

Kimball bit a rather grubby fingernail, looked at it, and rubbed it on his flannel shirt. "November's busy. Lotsa guys come."

"This one was new, hadn't been here before."

"Why would he come here?"

I pulled a copy of the newspaper ad and a picture of Neil Brown from my jacket pocket and passed them to him. "His sister found your ad in a book. The police thought he went south at the time, but we think he might have had this place in mind."

Kimball looked at the picture for some time. "I don't know that guy."

I stuffed the papers into my jacket again and sighed. "A long trip for nothing, I guess."

"Is there anyone else around here we might speak with?" Kimball shot Barb a look and she added hastily, "I'm not saying we don't believe you, Mr. Kimball, but he would have interacted with as few people as possible. Kept to himself, you know?"

"Yeah." Kimball thought about it. I got the sense he thought things over carefully before saying them, a luxury afforded to those who deal mostly with deer and squirrels. "Most people been here all their lives. Ask anyone."

Barb seemed disappointed at the generality of the suggestion. "Okay, thanks."

Kimball rose to go. "Anything else you need?"

"No, we'll be fine, thanks," I answered, not allowing Barb the chance to suggest a better mattress, a microwave, and water that didn't require physical effort with a hand pump.

Kimball emptied the remains of the cocoa equally into our two cups and replaced the stopper and cover. He seemed to sense that leave-taking pleasantries were required but couldn't quite get the phrasing. "Fire's good for the night." With that he left, pulling the slightly warped door closed behind him with a scrape.

We sat silent until we heard the door of the main house close a few seconds later. Barb raised her cup in salute. "Our gracious host!"

"He isn't so bad," I countered. "Just not used to being in the company of ladies."

"Being in company, period. The guy can barely put a sentence together."

"Can you blame him? People treat him like he's a freak, so he avoids them. He was actually quite concerned for our comfort."

She glanced around. "This won't rank with a stay on the Riviera, I can tell you that."

"The only Riviera you even got close to is the hotel in Vegas," I countered.

"True." Draining her cup, she set it down. "We'll stop on the way home tomorrow and show the picture around. Maybe someone at a gas station or a party store will remember Brown."

"Okay, but the person most likely to remember him was Kimball. During hunting season, he could have stayed here for weeks without raising suspicion."

Barb looked around at the shadowed knotty pine and shivered at the thought. "I suppose you're right. This was the perfect place to plan his next move."

"We can't be sure he came here."

"But I think he did."

"His truck was a couple hundred miles south of here, in Port Huron."

"Up here, no one questions strangers during hunting season. Who'd know where he came from or where he went when he left?"

"How'd he get the truck down there?"

"Drove it there and backtracked, maybe. Or he paid someone else to do it."

"Who?"

"I'm just theorizing," she said impatiently. "Meredith might have a guess. Let's see if anyone remembers Brown being up here. That would help."

After a not-too-uncomfortable night we left Buck Lake and started for home. On the way we stopped at several businesses, but everywhere we showed the picture we got shrugs and negatives. Barb was clearly disgusted, whether because she'd really thought we'd find Neil or because she'd driven to the U.P. for nothing.

Something odd happened that had nothing to do with Mr. Brown. We entered a party store/gas station with our photo and our questions, and as we went in, I elbowed Barb and snickered at a sign taped to the counter. PUPPY'S FREE TO GOOD HOME. I'm not the world's best speller, but I caught that one.

We showed the photo to the girl behind the counter, got nowhere, and turned to leave. "Go ahead," Barb said. "I'm going to get a water."

"You've got one already."

"It's warm."

At the car I remembered I was almost out of cigarettes. I went back inside, got a pack, and went to the counter to pay. The sign now read, PUPPIES FREE TO GOOD HOME. Heavy black letters had been written over the incorrect ones with a marker.

"Did you point out the spelling error?" I asked Barb as we left the store.

"I never correct people." She uncapped the water bottle. "She must've caught it herself."

We continued our quest, stopping periodically to show Neil Brown's picture. Nothing. I stared out the window at Lake Michigan's beautiful, rocky shore. "It was a faint hope, I guess."

Barb concentrated on navigating the always-tricky traffic. Despite plentiful passing lanes, there's a constant game of Involuntary Chicken on US2, initiated by idiots too impatient to wait for the next one. At the same time, a second game called Pass-Then-Slow-Down is played. Drivers pass via the extra lane then slow to fifty miles per hour when it disappears. Barb made some decidedly un-lawyerly comments about being an unwilling participant in both games.

"We'll go home and start again," she said as she passed an ancient Ford pickup for the second time. "We'll find something the police missed."

"Neil must have had someone he could ask for help."

She pulled in just as the passing lane came to an end, and I tried not to cringe. "What if Neil traded cars with someone and had him leave the truck where the police would find it?"

"But then he'd have the other person's vehicle."

"The guy picks it up later."

"Then that person would know where Neil went."

"Initially, but Neil severs contact, maybe takes a bus from wherever he leaves the car."

"Could it have been Meredith?"

"I doubt it. It sounds like Brown didn't want his baby sister involved in his troubles. Besides, she'd have told us. If she wants to find him, she has to be completely honest."

"So we find out who his friends were."

"Right. Especially his best friend. That's who he might have turned to."

CHAPTER FIVE

Barb

Back in Allport, a call to Meredith gave us three names. "Neil called them his Musketeers," she told me. "Amos, Portly, and Hairless." She chuckled, explaining. "Amos is Amos Carroll, who worked with Neil in construction. Portly is John Mason, who is a little . . ."

"Portly?"

"Yes. The last guy, who is of course bald, is Rick Waller, who's in real estate. They played ball in school and stayed connected like guys do: softball, poker, and golf foursomes."

"Who would Neil call if he needed someone he could trust to keep his mouth shut?"

Meredith considered it for only a second. "John is a guy who'd take your secret to the grave. But the police really put him through the ringer, and they got nothing."

"I'll start with him. Are they all in the book?"

"Yes, but there are a dozen John Masons. Neil's friend owns the Party Stop on Main."

I called the number listed for the Party Stop and got John. When I explained my purpose, the voice changed from cordial to distant. "I've got nothing to say about Neil."

"Mr. Mason, Meredith hired us to find her brother and try to prove he's innocent of killing his wife and brother-in-law."

"Shouldn't be hard, because he *is* innocent. I told the police that at the time."

"They didn't believe you?"

"They weren't looking for the truth. They swallowed everything old man Wozniak said."

"What might the truth be?"

Mason paused. "I don't know. But Neil wouldn't kill anyone, especially Carina."

"He still loved her?"

Mason seemed uncomfortable with analyzing emotions. "He'd never hurt her."

"Do you mind if I stop by, so we can talk in person?" I wanted to see Mason's face when I mentioned Buck Lake, wanted to watch his expressions as he talked about Neil.

"There's nothing I can tell you."

"Probably not, but I have to do what I can for my client." I figured he couldn't refuse to help Neil's little sister, and I was right. He gave me directions to his store.

Fifteen minutes later I pulled up alongside the Party Stop, a cement-block building with products listed on every conceivable surface: the windows, the roof, the side wall, and even a movable posting board out front. It was the usual mix of goods: beer, fishing licenses, hot pretzels, ice, and, of course in a town on a large lake, bait. I noted with approval that everything was spelled correctly. No midnight visit from the Grammar Police needed here.

The store was claustrophobia inducing, with shelves along every wall and even overhead, like looming eavesdroppers. The aisles were filled with objects, some of them dusty from long occupancy. Coolers lined one whole wall, giving off an eerie, bluish light. The sales counter was at the back, a mistake in my opinion, but I soon saw the reason. In a room behind it, a television flickered.

Mason probably spent a lot of time there between customers. At least he'd had the sense to install convex mirrors in the corners and two strategically placed surveillance cameras.

"I always work Friday nights," Mason told me. The guy had probably once been athletic, but all the muscle had melted into his middle and he looked soft. His dark hair was already speckled with gray and his mouth turned downward, either from genetic predisposition or life's accumulating disappointments. "I didn't hear about the whole mess until the next day."

"When did you last see Neil?"

"He came over that week for Monday night football. Amos was here too."

"And the other guy? The one Neil called Hairless?"

"Rick's wife was pregnant. She had the kid that Friday, the day Carina died."

A guy whose wife was in labor was unlikely to help with an escape. "Where was Amos?"

"Home alone. Amos is divorced, at least he was then. He's had a wife and a half since."

"Meaning?"

"A two-year marriage and a bride-to-be in the wings." He grimaced. "When Amos gets the urge, he should just find a woman he doesn't like and buy her a house."

"Amos was a good friend to Neil, though?"

Mason saw where I was heading. "Amos would be the last person to call if you need someone to keep his mouth shut. The guy couldn't keep a secret if you put it in a vault for him."

"But you could if it was important to Neil, right?"

He looked me straight in the eye. "I could, but I didn't."

"Have you ever heard of the Buck Lake Resort?"

I watched as he considered it. "I don't think so. There's something called Buck Lodge down by Pinconning, I think."

Sensing no falsity, I moved to the next question. "Are you married, Mr. Mason?"

"Yeah. My wife works at Emergency Services. Lousy pay, but she gets benefits."

"Important," I allowed. "Was she with you that Friday?"

His expression turned irritated. "She got home around seven fifteen and found me minding the store. Does that satisfy you?"

"Yes, thanks." I bought a soda and a can of Pringles as a conciliatory gesture. Mason rang it up and handed over my change without further comment. I left feeling he was angry about losing a friend, about being questioned and re-questioned on the subject, and maybe about being left out of Neil Brown's life for the last six years.

As long as I was out, I decided to locate Amos Carroll. Even if he hadn't gotten a call from Neil that night, I wanted to see what I could learn from a guy who didn't understand the concept of secrets. I planned to leave a message, but Amos answered my call. When I asked if he was busy, he laughed. "Nobody in the construction business is busy these days. We ain't building nothing but birdhouses."

Putting the address he gave me into my GPS, I drove out of the city until ordered to turn right. The house, situated at an angle to the road, was obviously a labor of love. Carroll saw me coming and stepped onto the porch wearing jeans, a faded Michigan sweatshirt with the sleeves and neckband cut off, and grungy white socks. He was under average height but stocky, and I could imagine him easily hefting a bundle of shingles onto a roof. His hand was scratchy with calluses, and his grin furrowed deep lines in his face. Lots of hours in the sun, lots of smiles.

Carroll seemed okay with being questioned, even happy that someone wanted to listen to him. "Neil," he said, wagging his head sadly when I told him my purpose. "Neil was the best."

"You don't think he killed his wife?"

Amos shook his head as if I'd said something silly. "Neil loved that girl. And to tell you the truth, none of us could see why. I mean, yeah, she was pretty, but it ain't worth it, y'know? Puttin' up with all that sh—uh, stuff."

"What do you think happened?"

"I s'pose some drifter noticed her, y'know?" He flushed. "Like I said, she was pretty."

"Right."

"Anyway, her brother probably tried to help her and got killed."

"But Neil's skin was under her fingernails."

"I figure he came in and tried to help Carina. She was hurt, and she scratched him."

"Then why did he run?"

"Her old man hated Neil. If Wozniak wanted him arrested, it woulda happened."

I tried to put myself in Neil Brown's place. His wife was dead; at least he thought she was. Her brother too. His father-in-law was on the way. If I were innocent of the crimes, would I stay and try to prove it or run, as he had?

The thought was still with me that night when I left the house in my black running suit. Since coming to Allport I'd come to understand the desire to hide one's activities—one's crimes—and the panic that rises at the thought of apprehension. Fear makes one do odd things.

Of course, I wasn't murdering anyone. My crimes stemmed from a need for correctness and other people's lack of caring about it. For years, sloppiness in English language usage had bugged me, and of late it had taken me over the line. I knew my forays into vandalism were illegal. Despite the fact that I acted for a good cause, I was breaking the law when, late that night, I crept up to Allport's Medicine House Pharmacy and went to work on their sign.

My work took longer than planned. First, cars kept going by and I had to retreat into the shadows until they disappeared. Second, I had to fix three errors, turning "magizines" into *magazines*, "greeting card's" into *greeting cards*, and "candys" into *candies*. The last one took some doing, since I had to squeeze in the correct letters. It felt really good when I finished, and I stood back to take a look at the sign, which was now, if not perfect, at least correct.

I screwed the lids on the paint jars, sealed my brushes in plastic bags, stowed it all in my backpack, climbed from the porch roof to the shed to a trash barrel to the ground, and started for my car. I was more than surprised when I collided with another person at the corner of the building. What the heck was he doing here at this time of night?

"What are you doing here at this time of night?" The man, who had grabbed me to prevent us both from falling, released my arms and stepped back.

"Walking." I'd thought about this moment, about the possibility of getting caught at my little game, and decided that an old excuse was the best one. "I couldn't sleep."

His answering grunt indicated neither belief nor disbelief. "Are you okay?"

"I'm fine."

A car passed, illuminating us in its headlights. He was about my age, tall, dark hair sprinkled with silver, and crow's feet around dark eyes. Native American ancestry, maybe. Other than a slightly thick waist, he looked fit. What conclusions was he was drawing about me?

I got no indication from his next comment. "It's probably not safe to be walking the streets alone at this hour."

"I'm on my way home now." My voice sounded false, but the guy had nothing to compare it to, so how would he know? I thought about saying he wasn't safe either, but I sensed he'd laugh at that. His manner indicated certainty of his ability to handle just about anything. Muttering an apology, I continued on my way.

He watched me go, which meant I had to go all the way around the block to reach my car. A woman out for a walk has to walk. I was thankful the guy hadn't come along a few minutes sooner and caught me with paint and brushes in hand. How would I have explained that?

My crusade was a little crazy and I knew it, but somehow I couldn't stop myself. My life as an attorney had brought some successes, a lot of failures. In my night-time ventures, I always won, even if I was the only one who noticed. The Grammar Guru, the Spelling Star, the Punctuation Perfecter. That was me.

CHAPTER SIX

Retta

I'm used to being left out of my sisters' plans. They got stuck in the older sibling thing and never learned to see me as an adult. Honestly, Barbara Ann is the smartest woman I know, but like a lot of smart people, she's kind of cold. Faye says it just seems that way, but what seems to be is usually what is, in my opinion. As a lawyer Barbara did well, but in life, not so much: no marriage, no family, not even a long-term commitment. I'll tell you right now, she's no lesbian. Just really, really reserved in the emotional department.

Faye is the classic well-intentioned woman who, with all her street smarts, never figured out how to use the brains God gave her to help herself. It's great to serve your fellow man, but Faye takes it to the point where she's left with just enough to get by. That's just crazy.

When I came along, some weird bonding thing had already happened with my sisters. They think each other's thoughts and finish each other's sentences. Still, I was surprised to hear they'd started a business together. A detective agency, no less.

It's wrong from so many angles, even dangerous. Two fifty-something women taking on wife beaters and bail-jumpers! It's not something a small town will take to, either, women doing the work police forces are created to do. Those forces are going to dismiss their efforts as a joke.

Add to that the fact that Faye and Barbara haven't spent significant time together for decades. I don't wish them ill, but it will be interesting to see how they fare in a business relationship. With all that going against them, if they were going to have any chance of making it work, they needed me. They just hadn't realized it yet.

Let me say right now that I do not interfere in the lives of others. It never works, and furthermore, it makes people dislike you. However, once I heard about the private detective thing, I knew I had to help. In the first place, I had the exact qualities and experiences they needed to succeed.

When I dropped by Barb's house on my return from Florida, a sign on a post out front said *Smart Detective Agency*. Their so-called office was deathly quiet, and Faye was playing Skip-Bo at her desk. It was obvious nothing was going on, but there was no way either of them would ask for their baby sister's help. I either had to make an offer or wait around until it was too late to save their little enterprise.

Setting up shop in Barbara Ann's house was a good move financially, but the location was wrong for a business like theirs. Too residential, too wimpy. I envisioned a more modern office, maybe in the new building the bank planned to build this summer, but of course that would be once I got them moving in the right direction so they could afford the rent.

On Faye's desk were business cards that said *Smart Detective Agency*. Who'd patronize a business with a name like that? It brings to mind all sorts of bad connotations: smart aleck, smart ass, smarty pants. I'd have to be subtle, of course, but I'd come up with something better.

The decor was tasteful and professional: cream walls with walnut-toned furniture and polished oak floors warmed by Persian rugs. The windows were corniced, the wood the same tone as the floor, and jade-green sheers filtered light from the spring sun. Near the windows were two chairs upholstered in green and cream stripes, and centrally located was Faye's desk, which contained, besides the basket of business cards, a phone, a computer, and a stack of books, on top her dog-eared copy of *The Poor Speller's Dictionary.*

As I closed the door behind me, Faye's eyes widened. "Retta! What are you doing here?" The game slid into a drawer with a discreet clunk.

"I came to see you," I told her, raising my arms for a hug. Faye rose and embraced me, and I noticed it was harder than it had been last time to reach around her. "And Barbara Ann too, of course." I looked around. "Where is she?"

"She's...out." Could they actually be working on a case?

I pointed at the desk. "What's this? I go away for a while and you two start a business?"

"We put a lot of thought into it, Retta. We made a business plan and did the research."

"You thought about it."

Faye blushed, realizing she'd admitted they left me out of their plans on purpose. "It's an income for me and a way for Barb to use her expertise. And we both can use our brains."

"I have a brain, too." I get exasperated with them sometimes. As a kid I was "too little" to be in on their exploits. As an adult I wasn't neglected; birthday cards, recipes, family holidays, all the required sister stuff was there. When Don was killed, they were supportive, helping me through it and almost as sad to be unable to relieve my grief as I was bereft at the loss.

But it was only when I needed them that they came around. Otherwise they hung with each other, even when Barbara Ann lived in Washington. I was across town, but Faye called her when she needed someone to talk to. Those two thought they only needed each other.

"Did you ever think your little sister might help steer clients your way? My husband was in law enforcement, and I know most of the cops in northern Michigan."

Faye was a bit sheepish. "We did think of that, Retta, but it didn't seem fair to ask you to use your friendships for business purposes."

"That's why you won't succeed at this," I told her. "Of course you use your family *and* your friends *and* your postal worker *and* your trash collector if they can bring in clients. You use whatever you've got, because that's business. It isn't about exchanging recipes."

Faye flinched, but I knew *she* knew I was right. I pulled a chair up close so we were knee to knee. "Now tell me what you're working on."

Her answer was uncharacteristically firm. "I can't do that, Retta. As you say, it's a business. We can't talk about cases."

"I'm here to help, you goon! How can I do that if I don't know what you know?"

"I can't."

"Barbara doesn't have to know. You tell her you dug up the information yourself." I let her think on that. "How much money has Barbara Ann sunk into this private eye thing?"

She bit her lip. "She won't tell me, but I think it's a lot."

"And are you getting the cooperation you need from law enforcement?"

"Well, Tom Stevens was nice but condescending, and Barb ran into a state cop who pretty much told her to play with the other girls and leave the men to do the work."

I took Faye's hands and leaned in so she couldn't turn her eyes away from mine. "So tell me. What are we working on?"

She took a deep breath, as if she were about to jump off a dock into frigid water. "Do you remember the Wozniak case?"

I was a little taken aback. "Of course I do. Murder, escape, old man Wozniak screaming for his son-in-law's head, it was crazy. Don worked day and night for weeks."

"Did he ever say the husband might not have done it?"

"Oh, no. His trace evidence was all over the room: blood, fingerprints, skin under both the wife's fingernails and her brother's. He was there, and he attacked those people."

"What was Don's take on it?"

"It appeared the guy came to see his wife, maybe to try to reconcile, but they got into a fight. The brother must have been in the shower, because he was wearing just boxers. He evidently heard the ruckus and came out to help his sister. They fought, and Brown killed him."

"Could it have happened another way? The brother attacks Neil and Carina gets in the way and gets knocked down in the struggle?"

I shook my head. "From the way the police recreated the scene, the brother was bending to help his sister when he was struck from behind."

There was a long silence as Faye took that in. "I hadn't heard that part."

"You've been hired by the family to prove Brown's innocence, then?" It was a guess, but not a stab. If someone was reopening the

Wozniak murders, it had to be either old man Wozniak, who'd have told them that little detail, or the Browns. "Neil's dad?"

"He died. It's the sister."

A vague image of an earnest teenager formed in my mind, but I couldn't dredge up any details. "Why does she want to find her brother at this point?"

"She's sick. She's hoping to clear Neil so he can take over for her."

"How awful! That family's been through a lot, but I wouldn't count on Brown being able to take care of his daughter. If you find him, he's going to prison."

"Barb told her that finding him and proving his innocence might not go together."

"Good advice, though she probably made it sound like a threat. So what can I do?"

Faye's eyes swept the room, trying to decide what to do, but finally she said, "The state cop who was in charge of the case doesn't seem interested in helping us."

"Name?"

"Uhhh, Sparks."

"Oh, yeah. Byron is a bit full of himself. So he stonewalled Barbara Ann?"

"He gave her the basics but implied she should stick to finding runaway teens."

Faye sighed. "You say there's no doubt Neil Brown was at the scene. That makes our job harder, since it's not what the client wants to hear." She tapped on the desk with a pencil. "The only other thing we can hope for is extenuating circumstances. Maybe one of them attacked Brown. Maybe husband and wife were arguing and the brother joined in. We need to understand the relationships better." She looked at me speculatively. "I don't suppose you know Mr. Wozniak?"

I couldn't help but smile. "As a matter of fact, we serve together on the Tourism Council. Stan isn't a very active member, but he lends his name to several local organizations as a way to give them legitimacy and state-wide cachet."

"Then he'd recognize your name if we mentioned you?"

"Better than that. I have a standing dinner invitation I haven't yet taken advantage of." I leaned back in the chair, pleased with myself. "If you want me to, I'll give old Stanley a call."

CHAPTER SEVEN

Barb

I was eager to meet Stanley Wozniak, but my call requesting an interview resulted in a dense-sounding secretary promising only to relay the message. Within ten minutes she called back with a negative. Apparently he wasn't curious as to why a detective wanted to discuss the case.

Faye had asked around about Wozniak, and despite the fact that some waxed eloquent about his civic contributions and the state-wide prestige he'd brought to Allport, the image I got was of a self-important, stubborn man who got away with being arrogant because everything he touched turned to gold. Without many millionaires in northern Michigan, people tended to be a bit in awe of them, forgiving them their faults in return for a share of the profits.

Unable to meet Wozniak face to face, I turned to the problem of who had driven Neil Brown's truck to Port Huron. The principal candidates for such a favor were accounted for, which left me stymied. If someone had driven the truck downstate and left it, that person had been stranded there. Who wouldn't have been missed by the police?

Checking my notes, I found the name of the contractor Neil had worked for. When I called the number in the phone book, I got a voicemail that asked me to leave a number. He'd get back with me as soon as possible. At least he didn't tell me how important my call was to him.

It took about twenty minutes, but Ralph Torey returned my call, his voice hopeful until I explained the reason for contacting him. He'd obviously hoped it was an offer of work.

"Yeah, Neil," he said. "I liked the guy, but you just don't know people. I mean, I knew they was having trouble, but nobody thought it would ever go that far. The wife was hard to take, the screechy type, but he always acted like it didn't bother him. I guess it was different at home, though, from what the neighbors said later."

I heard a clunk as he apparently moved the phone from one ear to the other. There was the scratch of a lighter and a sigh as that first puff of inhaled poison was released. "He wasn't happy when she called the job site that day," Torey said around the cigarette. "I told him his wife wanted to talk to him and he said something like, 'She can wait till I'm ready to talk to her.' Maybe not his exact words, but close enough, I told the cops."

"What I wonder, Mr. Torey, is if there was someone on the job Neil might have asked to drive his truck to Port Huron. Someone who went missing for a day or so."

"The cops asked that back then. Only guy missing was a Mexican I fired that morning."

"One of your crew?"

"Yeah. Those people got no sense of time, y'know? He was always late and always with an excuse. I'd had it that day so I said, 'Adios.' Even watched him walk down the road to make sure none of my tools walked away with him, y'know?" He waited for me to agree. I didn't.

"Anyway, they found him in Saginaw, where his family lives. He didn't know nothing about Neil's problems, said he hitched a ride south with a semi driver."

"Did this man work with Neil?"

"Yeah, same crew, but like I said, I sent him on his way first thing. He ended up in Saginaw, but he coulda kept going south, y'know? Take his friends--that'd be even better."

I kept my voice level. "The police checked his story out?"

"I guess so."

It was a possibility. "What's the man's name?"

"Guillen, like the baseball player, except his first name was Juan."

Pretty much like looking for someone named John Williams in Rhode Island. I tried all the Guillens in the Saginaw phone book, but no one answered to Juan. Some spoke no English and I spoke no Spanish, so it was hard to tell if I was getting through.

Still, I had a scenario. Neil had worked with a guy from Saginaw who'd been fired that day. If Guillen had still been around Allport, he might have driven Neil's truck to Port Huron, allowing Neil to take a different direction.

I was pleased to have found a possible explanation of how the truck got to the train station, but it was another dead end until I had a way to prove it. I cast about for other ways to learn more about the case. As I scribbled nothings on a notepad, my computer signaled an arriving email. I was surprised to find a cordial note from Detective Sparks with an attached file on the Wozniak murders. He hoped the information would get me started and ended by gently chiding me for not mentioning I was Margaretta Stilson's sister.

The file was great, but it irritated me to find that Retta didn't even have to be around to interfere with my life. Although the guy had apparently heard about the connection and decided to be nice to the sister-in-law of a former cop, I'd have preferred it if he helped because it was the right thing to do. Still, the file was a gold mine: Sparks' notes on the case.

He told the story succinctly:

Police called by S. Wozniak to his daughter's home, where they found the daughter badly hurt and the son dead. SW said he saw his son-in-law, Neil Brown, leave the apartment building in a hurry. SW reports the couple was separated. Brown was abusive to his wife and had possibly been unfaithful. Neighbors don't confirm that but say the Browns had noisy arguments accompanied by various things apparently hitting the wall.

Brown was last seen at the local bank about fifteen minutes after the murders were discovered. He went to his safety deposit box then left the bank quickly, saying little and acting nervous. No one admits seeing him again.

Reading Sparks' words, I realized we'd begun with only Meredith's version of what had happened. In our eagerness to tackle a real case, we hadn't done the background work good detectives need to do. I began to remedy that by noting the names of the people Sparks had interviewed. The neighbor who reported violent quarrels between the Browns was Jasper Conklin. The EMT who had discovered that Carina Brown still breathed was Annamarie Bailey. I copied the names onto a sheet of legal paper.

In the phone directory I found a number for Jasper Conklin listing Windswept Drive as his address. He hadn't moved. There was no listing for Annamarie Bailey, but there were lots of Baileys. I called fourteen of the eighteen before I got somewhere.

"She's my niece," a squeaky voice informed me. "Got married and moved to Wisconsin."

"Do you have a number for her there?"

"Sorry. I don't even remember what her husband's name is. Von something-German."

"Does she have relatives left in the area who might get me in touch with her?"

"Her mom's still here, but she's not a very trusting person, you know?"

"And no one else knows her married name?"

"I don't know who. He wasn't from here, so why remember it?"

"For class reunions?"

"Maybe. I don't know who's in charge of Anna's class, though."

I thanked the woman and ended the call. Since Annamarie's mother wasn't a trusting type, I decided to ask Faye to handle that interview while I talked to the neighbor and a Wozniak employee the papers had mentioned. My sister looked like someone you could ask to hold a purse full of hundred dollar bills in perfect confidence they'd all still be there when you come back for them. The reason she seemed that way was because it was true.

CHAPTER EIGHT

Faye

I was thrilled when Barb asked me to do an interview. Technically, I'm a partner, but I'm afraid she thinks of me as the office person, not one who goes out and tracks down leads. As things go on, I hope she'll let me do my share of the legwork. I have a sense for those who've been kicked in the teeth by life, the type of person who doesn't often trust easily.

Putting together what the cousin said with the trailer park address, I figured Nancy Bailey wouldn't answer the door to just anyone. To people like her, strangers mean trouble, and the best way to avoid them is to be out, or appear to be. To combat her distrust I took a bouquet of flowers along. How can trouble arrive at your door holding a handful of lilacs?

The trailer park was—well, who doesn't know about trailer parks? Steering around four small children whose game seemed to require screeching, I found Nancy Bailey's rental by means of a wooden pylon out front that had been knocked crooked, apparently by someone backing into it. The number painted on it had faded from sun and weather. As I pulled into the drive there was no other car, but a shadow moved at the window.

The trailer was battered and ugly, but attempts had been made. Weeds around the concrete slab had been pulled, and fresh digging indicated recent plantings, maybe flowers, maybe vegetables. The trailer's exterior was scrubbed clean, unlike the one next to it, which had enough mold to manufacture penicillin.

I knocked briskly on the door, and after a few moments, a woman opened the door a crack and peered around it as if she might need it to stop a bullet. Or an alien death ray.

"Yes?"

"Mrs. Bailey? I'm Faye Burner. I hope you like lilacs." I held the bouquet just far enough away that she had to open the door to accept it. "I picked them from my yard." Actually I'd taken them from a vacant lot near our house. They say stolen flowers smell the best.

"For me?"

"A get-acquainted gift."

Mrs. Bailey didn't seem anxious to get acquainted, but she liked the idea of flowers. She opened the door an inch wider but didn't invite me in. I held onto the flowers.

In her mid-forties, with dark hair and pale skin, she would have been attractive except for two things: her grooming habits and her eyes. *Grooming* might not be the right word, for no attempt had been made to groom anything, not today, not yesterday either. She wore a grimy housecoat bought before the century changed. Her hair was a parody of the "uncombed" look that was so popular. Her hands were grimy. Yesterday's yard work hadn't been washed away.

The woman's gaze telegraphed madness: not raving lunacy or hysteria, but madness she'd lived with for a long time. Her eyes moved constantly with no apparent purpose, not registering anything specific. When she briefly made eye contact with me she seemed confused, not quite sure what was going on. Drugs? Long-term mental illness? Stress? I had no idea.

"May I come in while you put these in water, Mrs. Bailey?" After some thought, she moved back.

"Nancy. Just Nancy."

Once inside, I felt like Shrek in an elevator. The place was claustrophobia-inducing, over-heated, closed-up, and stuffed with furniture and knick-knacks a second-hand dealer wouldn't have given twenty dollars for. Everything was covered with a thick coat of dust, indicating that once an item arrived, Nancy paid little attention to it. The Room That Time Forgot.

She seemed unsure what to do with a visitor, but when I handed over the flowers she went to the kitchen and began rummaging through the cupboards.

"Mrs. Bailey, I work for a company that tries to find out what happened." Instinctively I avoided the words *crime* and *investigation*. "I need to speak with your daughter."

She paused, and her eyes sought whatever it was they were unable to find. "Annamarie?"

"I need to know about a woman she helped."

Pride raised her chin half an inch. "Annamarie helped lots of people." She opened a door, took a plastic cup that said ARBY'S ROAST BEEF from the cabinet, and filled it with tap water.

"I heard that."

Nancy stopped fiddling with the flowers. "She don't want me giving her number. There's nobody here she wants to talk to." Her tone changed as she parroted her daughter's words.

If I'd endured this depressing environment as a child, I'd have moved away, too.

Nancy touched her chest, fearing I'd misunderstood. "She calls Fridays to see I'm okay."

"Will you ask her to call me?" I handed her one of the business cards Barb insisted I carry. "It's about an emergency she handled."

"Annamarie didn't do nothing wrong. She scored real high on the test." Nancy's face had grown suspicious again.

"That's right," I said. "Annamarie found a mother who was dying. She saved her baby."

Again Nancy's roving eyes found mine for a second. "I know who you mean. The husband hurt her bad and killed her brother." She paused. "Brown. Neil Brown."

I'd said too much. If this woman could figure out what our case was, anyone could. Reiterating that it was important Annamarie call as soon as possible, I moved to the door. "Annamarie saved that baby," Nancy repeated, holding onto a bright moment in her past.

"I hope she'll tell me about it. Will you call her, please? Today?"

I left, keeping my smile bright as I closed the trailer door behind me. The deep purple flowers on the counter contrasted starkly with the rest of the place. I hoped she liked them, but for me they only made Nancy Bailey's home more depressing.

CHAPTER NINE

Barb

Jasper Conklin, Neil and Carina Brown's neighbor, had a doctor's appointment in the afternoon but agreed to see me that evening. With several hours to wait, I went to the library and read old news stories. The local paper fairly dripped with excitement over having something to report besides city commission proceedings. There was a little purple prose, but mostly the reporter kept to the facts. What I'd been told so far was more or less confirmed. Though the bereaved father had declined to be interviewed, Eric DuBois, spokesman for Wozniak Industries, said the company would do everything possible to see that the killer was brought to justice.

Digging my phone from the bottom of my bag, where it always seems to end up, I called Wozniak Industries. Despite protests from the secretary that Mr. DuBois was a very busy man, I managed to talk my way into a ten-minute interview at two-thirty in his office.

There was plenty of press on Wozniak, but it revealed little about his personality. Ubiquitous in business circles, he guarded his private life jealously and seldom spoke directly to the press. In articles about him dedicating a building or contributing to a cause, there was only standard biographical information, couched in identical terms, meaning it was handed out on a press sheet. Reporters could use what they were given or say nothing.

In the years after the murders, a reporter occasionally took an interest in Neil's daughter Brooke and wrote a story on her progress. She was always referred to in terms of tragedy, but the candid photos snapped from far away, obviously without permission, showed a little girl playing happily in the park or splashing in the community pool. Whatever traumas she had experienced coming into the world had been eased by the obvious love and care she received from her aunt and grandparents. She didn't look like the child of a crazed killer.

One reporter had written a series of human-interest stories to serve as Sunday fare for a month: What would life have been like if the tragedy hadn't occurred? He covered the possibilities for Meredith one week, Stan Wozniak the next, then Brooke, and ended with Neil himself. He considered two scenarios, what might have occurred if Neil had been able to control his rage in the first place, and how it might have gone if he'd "accepted as a man" responsibility for what he'd done. Nowhere was there any suggestion Brown wasn't guilty of the crimes.

When I got back to the office, Faye told me about her visit with the trailer-park lady. After congratulating her on getting into the house, I told her I was meeting Mr. Conklin at seven.

"Go slowly," Faye said with that look she gets when she feels compelled to instruct me. "Old people want you to talk to them, or even better, they want you to listen to them."

"I'll listen as long as Mr. Conklin wants me to," I promised.

"I'm hoping Annamarie calls us, but here's one for you." She handed me a note that said JUAN GUILLEN and a phone number. "He wouldn't talk to me. I told him you'd call back."

In the office, I located my phone and made the call. A man answered with a terse, "Yes?"

"Juan Guillen? It's Barbara Evans from the Smart Detective Agency."

"You say you want to help Neil Brown." His English was softly accented but precise.

"I'm working for his family. Once I find him, I'll do what I can to help."

"What do you want from me?"

I wished I could see Guillen's facial expressions and let him see mine. Lacking that, I tried to inject honesty into my voice. "Neil's truck. How did it get to Port Huron?"

There was a pause, a very long one. I'd begun to wonder if he'd hung up the phone when he finally answered. "I was not a citizen then. They could have deported me."

"If you'd told the truth?"

"Yes." A pause. "I don't want to go to jail."

"Mr. Guillen, I won't make trouble for you. I just want to know what happened."

"I don't know where he went."

"Tell me about the truck."

Guillen sighed. "I got fired that morning. I was late, but it was not my fault."

I didn't want to get into employer-employee relations. "So where did you go?"

"I had to walk back to town, which took an hour. I went to the motel room we were renting and packed up my stuff. I hung out for a while, trying to decide what to do. Then I started for the highway, to hitch a ride to Saginaw."

"What time was that?"

"Early afternoon, maybe one o'clock."

"But you told the police you left town that morning."

"Like I said, I was scared it would mess up my citizenship to be involved in a crime."

"What really happened?"

He sighed as if preparing to jump off a cliff. "I was hitching, like I said. Neil came along and picked me up. I could tell he was in trouble. He said he could get me close to Saginaw. He drove for a while, kinda quiet, then all of a sudden he pulled off the road. He said he was getting out, and I should take the truck and keep going south."

"So after he picked you up, he got the idea of planting a fake trail."

"I guess so. He said I should leave the truck somewhere public. When I got to Saginaw, I called a friend with a car who followed me to Port Huron, and I left Neil's truck near the train station. I figured they'd think he went to Canada, and that would make it tough for them to find him. My friend took me back to Saginaw." He paused. "Neil was good to me, you know?"

Guillen's tone spoke volumes about how guys like Ralph Torey treated him as opposed to people like Neil Brown, to whom he was a person, not just another unwelcome foreigner.

Allport is a lake-side city, which means it's T-shaped. Lake Huron forms its eastern boundary, and two highways cross at city center. US 23 runs north and south, skirting the lakeshore. M-9 serves as Main Street until it ends at 23, just a few hundred yards from the lake. Along M-9 are most of the businesses of Allport: restaurants, gas stations, and a just-barely-thriving mall.

A few stores occupy the west side of US 23 as well, but the east side is residential with a capital *R*. Timber barons, shipping magnates, and other men of wealth built houses along the lakeshore, flaunting wealth that had now pretty much deserted the area. The houses were unique, barn-sized, and romantic. Some had turrets, others Victorian gingerbread, and still others cutting edge architecture of former times. These days they were often second homes, maintained by people who visited northern Michigan a few times a year to escape the city heat or to enjoy the snow for a weekend. I loved driving along the stretch and imagining the original owners' lives. I hoped they'd appreciated living in houses that didn't look exactly like the one down the block.

About a half mile from town, US 23 was forced inward as the land rose steeply. There, between the lake and the highway, a huge deposit of limestone had been quarried for decades, accessible raw material easily loaded onto freighters and taken anywhere on the Great Lakes.

The mining operation was simply called the Pit. A huge, ugly hole in the earth, it was impressive for its sheer size and its evidence of how Man shifts Nature around to suit his desires.

Because the Pit interested tourists, a viewing point had been constructed, complete with cyclone fencing to keep the overly curious from falling a hundred or so feet to the quarry floor. One day Faye had taken me to see how the Pit had grown in my absence. It had expanded along the shoreline like a monstrous horse nibbling its way across a grassy field, and I'd gone onto the platform to stand in the lake breezes and enjoy the panoramic view. Of course Faye remained in the car the whole time. No way she'd go near that edge.

WOZ Industries headquarters was a half mile or so past the turnout for the Pit, about four miles out of town. Due to its presence, the secondary road was wider and better-maintained than most in the area. I followed the signs to the main building and hurried through the front doors.

Because of Guillen's call, I'd almost forgotten the meeting I'd talked so glibly to arrange. I had to hurry to get to WOZ on time, but my haste was for nothing, since DuBois was later than I was. Perhaps by way of an apology, he came out himself to the reception area where I sat pretending to be interested in *Software Horizons*. (It was that or *Industrial Business.)* I looked up at the sound of a pleasing baritone voice. "Ms. Evans? I'm Eric DuBois." He pronounced it *doo-boys*, and I guessed it was impossible to teach most Americans to say *doo BWA*, as in Blanche.

I rose and shook his hand. "Nice to meet you, Mr. DuBois."

"Eric, please. This town's not big enough for formalities." He frowned at me briefly. "Aren't you the one I see running every morning when I am on my way to work?"

I grinned. "That's me, but I don't run. I walk fast."

"Still, it's a good habit, and you seem pretty faithful about it. Wish I were more active." He looked fine to me, but then, couch-potato, computer-squash behavior often doesn't catch up with a person until later in life.

DuBois led me to an elevator and from there to a well-appointed office on the second floor. Inviting me to sit he asked, "Would you like something to drink?"

I chose coffee, using the time it took him to arrange it to get an impression of the man. He was good-looking in a Tom Cruise kind of way: direct gaze and confident manner. I guessed his age at forty, but he could have been five years older.

The door opened and coffee entered, not just coffee, but choices. A woman pushed a cart toward us that held three thermal bottles, the kind with pumps on top. There were also little cups of extras to add in: whipped cream, raspberry cordial, even chips of chocolate. Despite my years near the crazy-coffee capital of the world, I stuck with a basic brew, two sugars. I sipped cautiously. It was just the right temperature, and delicious.

"I understand you're trying to find Neil Brown."

It was a little surprising that word had gotten around so quickly, but Allport isn't that big a town. "Yes. We've been hired to try, anyway."

His expression indicated concern, but I thought I detected a smirk behind it. Was it female detectives he found laughable or the idea of us finding a man who'd remained hidden for years? His next words belied my impression. "I always liked Neil. I'll certainly do what I can to help." I decided I was probably a little defensive, imagining criticism where there was none.

"How well did you know Brown?"

DuBois sat back in his chair and ran both hands through perfectly barbered hair. "Not well, actually. Of course I knew Carina, since I've worked for the family my whole adult life."

"How did that come about?"

He grinned. "Luck, but hopefully skill as well. I started as an intern while I was still at Eastern Michigan. When I graduated, Stan offered me a job, and we've worked together ever since." Something buzzed discreetly on the desk. DuBois didn't even look at it, which scored points with me. A face-to-face visitor should come before cyber-sounds.

"What is it that you do?"

He put up a hand in comic pantomime of a stop sign. "We've just met, and I don't want to bore you this early on." Gesturing at a stack of files on his desk, he went on. "If Mr. Wozniak wants to buy a company, I do the initial research. If he wants to go fishing somewhere in South America, I arrange it. And if he needs someone to act as proxy or agent or scout, I do that too."

"Jack of all trades?"

"In this day and age, you'd better be if you want to keep a job." He shrugged. "I'm not complaining, not even a little bit. I'm very well paid for what I do."

Looking at the suit, I guessed he wasn't fibbing. "So you knew Carina?"

DuBois' face revealed a brief conflict. "She stopped in a couple of times a week."

"What was she like?" The conflict deepened, and I leaned toward him. "Look, Mr. DuBois, I'm not here to smear anyone's memory of her. I'm trying to understand the players so I can get a fair idea of Neil Brown's situation at the time of the murder."

DuBois fingered a Petoskey stone paperweight before letting out a huff of decision. "Carina was all about Carina. I think she cared for Neil, but she wanted to control him, too."

"How did he react to that?"

"Neil didn't come around here much, so I hardly knew him. Carina came by fairly often, mostly when he was at work. I guessed it was easier if he didn't know how often she visited."

"She came to see her father?"

He shrugged. "She liked the business, liked seeing how it worked. She'd ask me questions, and she'd pick out of Stan what he had planned for his next project." Eric chuckled dryly. "Looking at her, you'd never have guessed she had anything going on in that pretty little head, but she understood a lot more about finance than she let on."

"Why do you think she was like that?"

"Well, Stan likes his women beautiful and not too liberated, and I guess she went along." DuBois glanced away. "She was an attractive woman, and she liked men to notice."

"And did you notice?"

He grinned. "Sure. I was single. But once she met Neil, she didn't want anybody else."

I left the subject of Carina. "What can you tell me about the day of the murders?"

His expression turned serious. "Stan and I were out most of the morning, working on a proposal. When we got back, the secretary said Carina had stopped in. She wanted her father to come to her place as soon as he could because she had something important to discuss with him."

"What time was that?"

"Around eleven."

"He didn't go right over? The paper said he arrived just after one."

DuBois looked slightly embarrassed. "Carina was into drama." He stared at the corner of his desk. "I guess Stan thought what she had to say could wait."

I wondered how many times in the last six years Stan Wozniak had regretted that decision. "He told you he wasn't going there until later?"

Raised brows and a shrug excused the decision to put family after business. "He had a lunch date with the mayor and some council members. He said he'd stop at Carina's after that."

"And what did he find when he got there?"

DuBois clasped his hands and set them on the desk before him. "All I know is what he told me, and what I read in the papers." His chair let out a discreet whoosh of air as he settled back, letting himself remember. "Stan said he pulled up outside Carina's apartment around twelve forty. As he got out of his car, he saw Neil hurrying away from the building. Neil didn't see him, but he seemed agitated. He wore a hooded jacket, one of those sweatshirt type things. It had stains the boss swears were blood."

"How could he tell from a distance?"

A single vertical line appeared between his brows. He'd asked himself that same question. "He was pretty adamant about it, but we know what he found when he went inside."

"Tell me."

"Well, the door was open. He called out to Carina, but no one answered. He went inside and saw Carson, sprawled in front of the couch, face down, with the back of his head caved in. Carina was under him, lying on her back. She'd been struck on the side of the head, and a ball bat that had been sitting beside the door was missing."

"Terrible." The scene would have been difficult for anyone, but for a father? I understood Wozniak's anger at Neil Brown, even as I hoped it was misplaced.

"When Stan called for help, he thought they were dead. The EMTs saw she was still alive and went to work--"

"What's going on, Eric?" We both jumped at the voice from the doorway.

"Mr. Wozniak." DuBois seemed to grow smaller, paler, and tighter before my eyes. He rose, sending his chair backward, where it hit the wall with a soft thud. "This is Ms.—"

"I know who she is. What I want to know is what she's doing here."

I rose and stepped toward the man in the doorway, though it was rather like moving toward a growling Doberman. "Mr. Wozniak, I was interviewing Mr. DuBois about—"

Wozniak's malevolent glance stopped me cold. "Didn't my secretary tell you I would not be interviewed about your so-called case?"

I made myself answer calmly. "No one said I couldn't speak to the others involved."

"Eric wasn't involved. And we have more important things to do than chat with a nosy female who's been scammed by the Brown family." Wozniak was tall, with deep-set eyes, a large Adam's apple, and working man's hands, even after decades of financial success. I decided he wasn't equally successful as a human being.

"I am trying to get at the truth of your daughter's death, Mr. Wozniak."

"The truth is that her husband killed her. But that wasn't enough for him. He took my only son, too." His voice rose. "Go ahead and find Neil Brown, lady. I'll see he never takes another breath outside a prison." He took a step toward me, and I had to force myself not to retreat in the face of anger that pulsed like a force field around him. "Now leave this property before I have you arrested for trespassing. Eric, see Ms. Evans to her car." His tone hinted that if I didn't have an escort, they'd be less a ficus or two.

I was as angry as I'd been in years, but Wozniak held all the cards. Gathering as much dignity as I could muster, I left the room.

As I searched for the stairs, unwilling to wait for the elevator, DuBois caught up with me. Gently, he led me to the elevator and pressed the call button. "He had no right to be rude. I told him I intended to apologize."

"I'll bet he was thrilled." The elevator doors opened with a muted chime and I stepped inside. DuBois followed. Neither of us said anything. He was apologetic; I wasn't yet ready to accept. We both knew the person who should have offered the olive branch wouldn't do so.

When the elevator doors opened, I headed for the exit. DuBois stayed beside me, and I had to give him credit for standing up to his boss, at least a little. I slowed my pace in recognition of his attempt at atonement. We left the building, stepping into a breezy but mild afternoon.

As I got out my keys and headed toward my parking space, DuBois whistled. "Nice car!" His tone was so boy-in-love-with-power that I had to smile as he opened the door for me. I answered the obligatory questions: what size the engine was, how much horsepower, how I'd kept it cherry. Once I was inside the car, DuBois bent down so that his face was level with mine. "Stan isn't a bad guy, Ms. Evans. He's just touchy on the subject of his children's murders."

"I guess a father would be," I admitted grudgingly.

"I didn't know he was coming in today or I'd have suggested we meet somewhere else." He glanced back at the impressive building. "I also didn't realize he'd get so upset."

"I'm sorry if I got you in trouble."

"Don't worry. Stan's tough, but he treats me like a—" He stopped, embarrassed. "When he lost Carson and Carina, I was just an office away. We do okay together."

Probably because DuBois did everything Wozniak told him to. Stan would need a nice guy like Eric to smooth the feathers he ruffled. "Thanks for the information."

Sweeping his wind-ruffled hair off his forehead, he hurried back into the building. I imagined his boss standing in the window of his office, watching to make certain I left. I imagined it because I refused to give Wozniak the satisfaction of looking up to find out for sure.

CHAPTER TEN

Retta

It took a while to figure out something else I could do to help Faye and Barbara. The call to the state police was good, but I wanted to show them I could find information as well as open doors. As I thought about the Wozniak case, it occurred to me that what I have and they don't (well, one of the things) is connections in the community. Barbara was gone for decades and no longer has any idea who anybody is. Faye stuck to family and work her whole life. I know a lot of people, especially those on the higher social levels. Why couldn't I use that to help them?

Questioning Faye until she used the word *badgering,* I refreshed my memory of the crimes. Using the file Detective Sparks had sent them at my request, she listed the people who'd been interviewed for background information about Neil and Carina Brown. When she got to John and Susie Mason, I knew I'd hit pay dirt. Susie I knew personally.

John Mason's wife is a dispatcher for the city's emergency services. She has been at it for years, and she's good at her job. At best I thought she might know something that wasn't public knowledge. At the least she could paint me a picture of what the local police heard, did, and concluded in those first few days. Susie and I were, if not friends, friendly acquaintances, thanks to Kiwanis. The year I'd been president of the club, she'd been secretary, which necessitated a lot of working together. It was time to do lunch, and I knew just where to look for her.

McPub is the trendy eating spot in the tiny old-town section of Allport. It's one of those dark-paneled eateries with classical music in the background and art posters on the walls. They serve over-priced salads, sweet-potato fries, and twenty different kinds of beer. On any Friday between twelve and one, the local gentry gather, celebrating the end of the work week. Knowing I'd be welcome, I invited myself along for this Friday's lunch.

The table was almost full when I got there, and Susie was elbow-to-elbow with two other women. Someone invited me to sit on the opposite end, and I spent a pleasant hour catching up. It was good to see everyone after my winter stay at my condo in Florida, and I love McPub's food. The noise level was high as one person after another told stories to entertain the group. We all laughed even though we'd heard most of them before.

When lunch was over, I caught up with Susie just outside the place. "Suze, can I walk back to the station with you? I need your help."

"Sure." She balanced her take-out carton on her purse for a moment while she dug in her pocket for sunglasses. "I'm starting to get frown lines, so I'm fighting back."

Checking to see that no one was near us I said, "I understand you knew Neil Brown."

She turned to look at me for a moment, but the dark glasses kept me from reading her eyes. "We were in school together. It was terrible what happened."

I didn't ask if she thought he'd killed his wife. "Were you on duty when the call came?"

Her gaze slid in my direction. "Yeah." There was a question in it.

"My sisters are trying to help Meredith find him."

She sighed. "I heard about the brain tumor. Poor kid."

Faye hadn't known the specifics of Meredith's condition. "Brain tumor?"

"Yeah. They say it's benign, but they have to remove it. The tricky part is getting it all so it can't grow back."

"That's awful." We paused for a while, reflecting on the fact that you're fine one day and not fine the next. "If there's anything you can tell us that might help, we'd appreciate it."

She blew out a breath. "I took the call, that's it. Wozniak was shouting they were dead."

"Then later you heard Carina was still alive?"

"She lived till they got her to the hospital, but I don't think she really had a chance. It gave the doctors time to save the baby, though. Have you ever seen Brooke?"

"Not that I know of."

"She's a doll. Looks just like Neil, and she's got his temperament, too. Not like Carina."

"Carina was difficult?"

"Humph." That was it for a few moments, but she added, almost to herself. "She did not deserve him, and I don't care if that's speaking ill of the dead. Neil did everything to make their marriage work, but Carina was a selfish, scheming brat."

A note in her voice sent three clear signals. First, Susie Mason had feelings for Neil Brown she couldn't quite hide. Second, she'd seen Neil and Carina's relationship the same way Meredith had, and finally, she'd said all she was going to on the subject. I switched to questions about how her daughter was doing in track, listened for a few minutes, then watched her disappear into the dispatch office, heels clicking on the sidewalk like military drumbeats. There was something more than a friend's outrage at work. Susie was hiding something.

Returning to my car, I sat for a few minutes wondering who might tell me about any relationship Susie and Neil might have had prior to marrying other people. I couldn't think of a person, but another inspiration hit: high school yearbooks. If I looked to see who'd graduated with Neil and Susie, I might find someone I knew well enough to ask.

I am a member of the Allport Alumni Association, called "Triple A" with no attempt at originality. Our main function is to provide a party once a year for alumni at the last home football game, but we beautify the school grounds and give out scholarships too. We had an archive of every yearbook from the '30s to the present, kept in the library at the high school.

It took some digging to find what I wanted. Neil Brown was pictured only twice in the book, his posed senior photo and a group shot of the baseball team. In his sophomore year, however, I found pay dirt. He'd served as escort to Homecoming Queen Candidate Susie Wexford. The picture showed a boy two inches shorter than his date, who of course had chosen heels. The extent of his dressing up for the occasion was black slacks and a long-sleeved white shirt. His hair was a mess of unruly curls, his expression one of extreme discomfort.

That was what I wanted to know. Susie and Neil had once been close. Barbara and Faye had considered his buddies as possible helpers, but had they looked at Neil's old girlfriends?

Faye was excited when I called to tell her. "That could be important," she said. "I've been looking over the file, and some kids saw a blue truck parked at the dispatch center. Neil's truck was blue, but it turned out someone passing through town stopped for directions."

"Who told them that?"

After a prolonged hum of concentration, she read from Sparks' notes, "*Dispatcher reports a man in a blue Chevy stopped for directions.* Neil's pickup was a Ford Ranger."

"Susie was the dispatcher on duty. Maybe you should talk to her."

"Maybe I should."

"Keep my name out of it. I don't want my friends thinking I'm a snitch."

Faye coughed the smoker's version of a chuckle. "You got it, Retta. And thanks."

I hung up, feeling that Faye was starting to lean to my side. If I kept this up, I'd soon be part of the Needs-a-New-Name Detective Agency.

CHAPTER ELEVEN

Barb

Jasper Conklin was an old guy who looked like his legs wouldn't hold him up but his ears might. Windswept Apartments were not nearly as whimsical as the name indicated, but Jasper assured me it was a good place to live. "Lots of kids," he said, ushering me in and indicating a blanket-shrouded couch. "I like to watch them." He pointed at the sliding glass door, where the dying daylight revealed an overturned trike and a slightly deflated soccer ball. I could hear a child crying a floor above us, but there was no sign my host did.

He recalled Carina and Neil Brown. "They was a beautiful couple. Out of the world."

"Happily married?"

"At first." He shrugged. "Later on, they had fights, but everybody does."

"What did they fight about?"

"Money, mostly. One time I heard her say her dad could help them and they could have a real house before the baby came."

"And what did he say to that?"

Conklin frowned. "I never could hear much of what he said. But I heard her real good."

"She was a screamer?"

"Girls, they're different when they're, you know, P.G."

I hadn't heard anyone use that euphemism in decades. "They sometimes threw things?"

"I wouldn't say *they*. I think she did the throwing and Neil, he just did the ducking." He laughed at his own joke, snorting a little. "He did the ducking."

I sat with the old man for an hour, letting him talk, as Faye had advised. He was thrilled to have company, and I ended up drinking tea from a poorly-washed cup (bad eyesight) and eating slightly stale cookies from the dollar store. ("You get two packages for a buck.") I heard stories about his kids, too busy to visit very often, and his neighbor, the object of pity because of her failing health. "Osteo-arthritis," Jasper said, lowering his voice to emphasize the seriousness of it. "When she drives me to the doctor's she can barely see over the steering wheel. I do the shifting 'cause she can't raise that right arm hardly at all."

When I finally bid Mr. Conklin goodnight, it was after nine. Once I left the reach of the parking lot's lamps, it was as if a blanket had dropped over my car. There was no moon, no stars, and the street lights were swathed in mist so that I moved from black to light to black again.

Conditions were perfect for some night work. A billboard at the edge of town needed my healing touch, a bedding ad that read, A PERSON NEEDS THEIR REST. Holy mixed numbers, Batman!

My paints and a change of clothes were always handy in the trunk of my car, so I was ready. The problem with the task was the billboard's position. Situated on poles sunk deep in a ditch and rising far over my head, I didn't know if I could reach the spot that needed fixing. At least it hadn't rained recently, so the ditch would be dry.

At an empty house a hundred yards or so down the road from the billboard, I pulled my car far enough up the driveway that it wasn't visible from the road. I turned it around, difficult to do with the lights out, but it makes for a quicker getaway if things go bad.

The night was cool, not cold, but I wore gloves anyway. No sense leaving fingerprints, no matter how unlikely the possibility of CSI. Hiking back to the sign, I ducked down when a car appeared, letting the darkness hide me. When I reached the sign's base, I was pleased to see foot pegs leading up a post, supplied to facilitate changing the message. That was precisely my intent.

Climbing to the platform, I tested my reach. I couldn't get to the top line, "A person needs," but the last two words were accessible. I had a decision to make: "her rest" or "his rest"? The picture showed a woman, but of course masculine pronouns are understood to refer to both sexes. I decided to take the easy way. Taking out my white paint, I began doing away with the *t* and the *i* in *their*. No complaints, no outrage—just another Correctional Event.

CHAPTER TWELVE

Faye

Before I approached Susie Mason, a woman I didn't know at all, I decided to check with Meredith to get the facts straight. It's not that I don't trust Retta. Well, maybe it is. She sees romance everywhere, probably due to her reading choices.

Meredith had just arrived home when I got there. The big cloth bag every teacher in the world seems required to carry sat on the kitchen table along with her purse, an umbrella, and something that looked vaguely like a ceramic ashtray I once made at summer camp.

"It's a bird feeder," she explained, following my glance. "They want to give you things."

"And you'll find a place for it."

She raised her brows in a what-can-you-do grimace. "Have you found him?"

"No." The look on her face made me wish I'd called first and avoided getting her hopes up. "I have a few more questions."

Just then a kid who hadn't yet got the hang of girl-walking clattered into the room. Her feet moved around each other clumsily, as if each wanted the other to fail. She stopped when she saw me, head tilting to one side in curiosity. The two looked a lot alike, right down to the tilt.

"Brooke, this is Mrs. Burner. She's helping me with some work."

"Hello."

"Hi, Brooke." I kept it short. To a kid, an adult is just someone they have to be polite to.

"I'm going to go over to Allie's for a minute, okay?"

"Sure, hon, but watch the time. Supper's at five."

"What is it?"

Meredith appeared to think. "I can't remember. It has something to do with pasta, I think. Maybe something with red sauce and cheese. What do they call that?"

"Lasagna!" Brooke's face lit with delight. "Cool. Can Allie eat with us?"

"If her mom says it's okay."

Brooke was gone in a flurry of scuffs, rattles, and a bang as the door slammed behind her. Meredith frowned and smiled at the same time. "She always moves at full speed."

"It's the age," I replied. "When they get a little older, you can't speed them up."

Her eyes stayed on the window and the disappearing child for a moment before she turned to me. "Allie's mom says Brooke can stay with them when I go into the hospital. At least I've got that off my mind."

I touched her arm gently. "It's going to turn out all right. I just know it is."

"Thanks." She shook off her thoughts and asked, "Now, what do you need to know?"

"First, tell me how Neil and Stan Wozniak treated each other."

"They were complete opposites. Neil doesn't care about money and boardrooms and plaques from the Chamber of Commerce."

"And Wozniak does."

Meredith looked at her hands. "He cultivates this image of a self-made man who can run with the big dogs or walk with the common man. Some people eat it up."

"So Neil didn't like his father-in-law much."

"He never said it out loud, but I sensed it." Her sweet expression hardened. "After what he's done to my brother's reputation, I can't say I like him much, either."

"Sometimes in-laws make an effort for the sake of the person they both love."

Meredith answered obliquely. "A while back I got Brooke two cats, thinking they'd be company for each other. One cat refuses to let the other anywhere near Brooke."

"Neil's father-in-law resented his influence over Carina."

Opening the refrigerator, Meredith pulled out a casserole dish ready for the oven. "Stan resented her choosing a guy with a mind of his own."

I was wondering if I had time to make lasagna for dinner. Hers looked really good. Sliding the dish into the oven she closed the door and twisted the timer button. "It wasn't just that Neil didn't have money. It was also that he wasn't impressed by Stan's wealth."

A son-in-law who refused his offer of employment and his advice on how to get ahead in life. How much had that figured into Carina's choice of husband? Apparently it had backfired. Carina couldn't have guessed Neil would actually expect her to live on his paycheck.

Meredith wiped her hands on a towel. "I was afraid he'd wake up one day and realize she wasn't what he wanted in a wife. What would he have done then, with a baby and all?"

I was wondering how far he'd have gone to escape the marriage, but Meredith saw it in my eyes. "He hadn't come to that place, Mrs. Burner. Neil was still in love with Carina." Her smile was a little sad. "When she found out she was pregnant, he was so happy. He bought her this necklace with their names on it. Even with the pressure to move to Detroit, he wasn't mad at her. When she said he should get out if he wasn't willing to make a good life for their baby, he came to ask me if I thought he was being selfish."

Meredith wouldn't—probably couldn't—admit Neil might have come to the point of violence, so I changed the subject. "We asked you about Neil's male friends, but I wonder if there were any women he was close to in the past."

She thought about it. "The only other girl he ever dated was Susie, and that was over a long time before he married Carina."

"Might he have gone to her for help?"

She thought about her answer. "Neil was a little uncomfortable with Susie. He never said why, but I figured it was because he broke it off with her when he met Carina. I think she still had feelings for him, even after she married John."

"And that made things uncomfortable between them?"

She ran a hand down her sleek ponytail. "Neil pretty much steered clear of her unless John was around. I got the impression he was avoiding any appearance of wrongdoing."

"Even when his marriage went sour?"

Meredith's pretty face hardened. "Especially then. Neil wanted his wife back. He wouldn't have done anything to jeopardize that possibility."

***

Susie Mason was leaving work, which was perfect. There was no one around to hear our conversation, and the day was nice enough that we could stand in the parking lot chatting without seeming out of place. I hoped the warm, sunny spot would put her at ease.

"I'm Faye Burner, of the Smart Detective Agency. Could I ask you a few questions?"

"About what?"

"Neil Brown."

Her expression turned suspicious. "Did Margaretta send you?"

"Not exactly, but you probably know she's my sister. We were talking today, and she mentioned you graduated with Neil. I did some digging and learned you two dated in school." I handed her a business card. "We're trying to locate Mr. Brown."

"So you can throw him in jail for something he didn't do?"

"Just the opposite. We hope to prove his innocence."

Susie sighed. "There's nothing I can tell you."

"All right. Then can you give me your impression of Carina Wozniak?"

She made an ugly face. "You don't want to hear that."

"Actually, I do. If Neil didn't kill his wife, there must be another reason for her murder."

"Everyone in that family thought their money meant the rest of us should just bow down," Susie said, her eyes hard. "Carina thought she was better than everyone in Allport. I didn't know the brother, but I've heard the same thing about him."

"What about the father? Might they have had a family squabble that turned out badly?"

She shook her head. "Stan was crazy about his kids. Neil said Carson was a screw-up, and he and his dad argued about money, but the old man never held a grudge for long."

Interesting that Susie knew Neil's opinion of his in-laws. "Someone saw a truck similar to Neil's here around the time of the murders."

Her gaze shifted like my sons' used to when they lied. "It wasn't Neil's. I told them that."

"Yes." Moms know that if you want someone to say too much, shut up and let her talk. Susie was no gabby teen, though, and she remained silent. "Your name never has to come up."

Her gaze turned away from me. "I can't help you."

Guessing she was trying to decide whether it was best to help those who might prove him innocent or to let Neil remain hidden, I gave her a little nudge. "Brooke needs her dad."

Susie studied the concrete, repeating, "I can't help you." But before she moved past me to her car, she added, "If I was Neil, I'd have gone in the opposite direction the cops expected."

She left then, but I took the statement as confirmation that Neil Brown had gone north, not south, and somehow Susie Mason knew it.

I returned home, anxious to tell Barb what I'd learned, but she'd left a note saying she'd be in late. Dale and I go to bed early, but I often hear her come in after midnight. It's good she has a social life, though I'm not sure what it is. I hope whoever keeps my sister out nights knows she's one classy dame for the likes of Allport.

CHAPTER THIRTEEN

Barb

"I can't get over the idea he went to that lodge," I said the next morning when Faye finished catching me up. "It's isolated, and they're used to strangers showing up."

Faye tapped her pencil against her note pad. "Too bad we can't talk to that Mr. Makala. The owner might remember a guest better than a guy who just worked there at the time."

"Why can't we talk to him?" When she looked at me in confusion, I said, "How many people can there be in Arizona named Haike Makala?"

Only one, it turned out once we'd figured out how to spell the name. It took most of the day to find that Haike resided at the Sweet Air Assisted Living Facility outside Flagstaff. Once we'd located him, another problem arose. "He's able to talk," the receptionist assured us, "but he doesn't like to. Won't have a phone in his room."

"Let him know it's about Buck Lake Resort," I suggested.

We listened as the woman explained our call. There was a question, an answer, and grudging assent. Haike's voice came in the booming tones of the almost deaf. "Hallo?"

"Mr. Makala, I'm from a detective agency in Michigan."

"I don't fish anymore," he hollered. "Too shaky to bait the hook."

"Michigan." Faye raised her voice slightly. "I'm calling from Michigan."

"Oh, Michigan, ya."

"Mr. Makala, I'm a detective."

There was a pause. "Did you say detective?"

"Yes, sir."

"You sound like a woman."

Faye grinned at me. "That's correct."

"And you're a detective, eh?"

"Yes."

"Well, I'll be damned." The music of the Upper Peninsula's Finlanders' speech rang in every phrase. "What does a lady detective want with an old coot like me?"

"I bet the ladies out there in Arizona like having an old coot like you around." Faye's tone conveyed warmth and gentle flirtation, which was why she was better with certain people than I. Faye took her time, while I tended to accost unsuspecting individuals, demanding information without benefit of social pleasantries. I'd been told it was unnerving, but I couldn't help it if I preferred to skip the verbal silliness that passes for conversation. Faye said I was born impatient.

Faye let Mr. Makala flirt with her for a while, which was interesting, to say the least. There were misunderstandings and repetitions, but she spoke slowly and clearly, exaggerating her enunciation slightly. Finally she brought the conversation around to her purpose, explaining that we were hoping he would remember a certain guest. "But it was a long time ago."

The old man chuckled. "I remember them all, eh? Every one had something made him different. One guy came every year with his cats. Can you imagine? Two cats, he'd bring to hunting camp. Another one used to bring his girlfriend for a week of fishing in the spring. Then in the fall, he brought his wife for deer season. Did that for ten years or more."

Faye leaned her elbows on the desk as she asked the important question. "We're interested in a man who came in 2008. He'd have been unprepared for hunting, maybe didn't even have a vehicle." We'd theorized that Neil might have hitchhiked across the U.P.

There was a pause, and when the old man spoke, his tone had cooled. "I don't recall anyone like that. People come to a hunting lodge, they come ready to hunt."

"You don't remember one guy with no gear and no buddies?"

"Nope. Nobody like that."

"That's what Mr. Kimball said, but we thought your memory might be better than his, since you'd have registered the guy."

"How's Roger doing?"

Faye shrugged helplessly at me, brows raised. A man with one eye, one arm, and a hermit's disposition? How would he be doing? "I guess he's all right."

"Roger's a good fella." Haike had a coughing fit that sounded awful, and I grimaced as we waited for him to speak again. "I never had nobody like what you said, and Roger wasn't around then. He came down from Ishpeming the next spring."

I frowned. Kimball had said he was working at Buck Lake that November. It was possible Haike's memory was bad, but he seemed to have all his mental faculties. Why did they disagree on when Roger came to the lodge?

On impulse, I wrote Faye a quick note. "Mr. Makala," she said after a quizzical glance at me, "how did Mr. Kimball lose the use of his arm?"

Another pause. "Some kind of accident. I don't remember."

Faye chatted for a while, thanked the old guy, and ended the call. "What was that about?"

"Just a thought." I added stars to notes I'd been making. "If your nephew had an accident that left him severely disabled, you'd recall what happened, don't you think?"

"It's not something a person would forget."

"And do you remember the paper Kimball used for tinder to build our fire?"

Frowning over the memory, Faye shrugged. "I remember there was paper."

Tapping out a little fanfare with my pen, I said, "It was a guitar catalog."

Faye still looked lost. "So?"

"Last time I knew, it took two hands to play."

Finally her face showed understanding. "You're saying Kimball is a fake."

"Think about it. Brown somehow makes it to Buck Lake Resort and rents a cabin. He gets to know Makala, and they realize they can help each other out." I spoke faster as things fell into place in my mind. "Makala wants to get away from the cold winters of the U.P. Brown has a wad of cash but nowhere to go. They work out a deal, and Brown becomes Haike's nephew from Munising. The old guy gets to go to Arizona, and Neil gets a permanent place to hide."

Faye twirled the pencil between her fingers. "Right. Neil starts the story from the time he arrived, but in Haike's mind, it started later, when the character of Roger Kimball came to life."

"They'd have had all winter to figure out how to make it work."

"Brown changes his hair, gets a milky-looking contact lens, grows that awful beard, and fakes a crippled arm. It not only disguises him, but it keeps people at a distance, too."

"But when no one's around, he uses the arm. It's just too inconvenient not to."

Grinning widely, Faye leaned back in her chair. "You know what this means, don't you?"

"What?"

"It means, Miss Smarty Pants, that we're heading north again. Back to God's country."

CHAPTER FOURTEEN

Faye

After lunch, Barb went out to do some errands, so I was alone when the phone rang. The readout said UNKNOWN, so I used my business voice. "Smart Detective Agency. How can I help you?"

"My name is Martin Arnold," said a raspy voice. "I want you to find my wife."

"She's missing?"

"Um, yeah. She disappeared a couple of weeks ago."

"When?"

"Last Thursday. She went to Miami on business, but she didn't come back."

I checked the desk calendar. "That would be the twelfth?"

"Right." He cleared his throat. "The cops say she took off, but she wouldn't leave me."

"What do you think happened?"

"I think someone kidnapped her." His voice got louder. "You need to find her."

"Have you been contacted with ransom information?"

"Uh, no."

"Then why do you think she was kidnapped?"

"I told you, she wouldn't leave me. She loves me."

The guy's manner seemed off somehow, like he was making up the answers to my questions. Still, I pulled a notepad from my organizer, selected one of my very pointed pencils and asked, "Have you contacted the police in Florida to see if there's been an accident?"

"She isn't dead. I'd know."

I began a litany of questions we'd devised to get the idea of what a case would involve. At his hesitant replies, doubts as to Arnold's honesty crept into my mind. Still, I was reluctant to reject a potential customer since we weren't exactly charging Meredith Brown by the hour.

Despite my patience, the interview went from bad to worse. Arnold's answers became more and more vague, and I sensed no emotion behind them. "She was supposed to come back Wednesday night," he said, "but sometimes she stays to take 'em out on the town."

"She didn't call to let you know when that happened?"

"Uh, no. We aren't like that. When she comes back, she's back, you know?"

Peering at the chair opposite me, I tried to imagine the guy sitting there. No picture came to mind. "When did you realize she wasn't coming home?"

"Um, I guess on Friday. That's when I called the police down there and told them."

"Who took the information?"

"I don't know, some guy that wasn't very helpful."

"Was it a desk officer, or did they refer you to an investigator?"

"I guess it was the desk. I only talked to one person."

"And what did he tell you?"

"He said he'd look into it. He called the next day to say my wife never used her return ticket. She checked out of her hotel, got into a cab, and disappeared. We're in debt, so they decided she left me. The cop said there wasn't any more they could do."

"It's hard to believe the Miami police would ignore something like this."

He made an impatient noise. "They didn't ignore me. They just didn't sound concerned."

Either worry was causing the guy to act weird, or this was some kind of scam. When I didn't respond, the man's tone turned irritated. "I'm worried, and I want you to go there and look for her. Tell me what you charge and I'll send you the money right now."

"I'll have to consult my partner. We might not be able to take on another case right now."

"But aren't there two of you? One could go and the other could stay here."

Now he was managing the agency for us! "I'll let you know by the end of today."

"You aren't going to get many chances like this." He tried once more. "I really need your help." His jump from threat to pleading wasn't convincing.

When Barb came back I told her about the call, ending with, "I got the feeling he was making it up as he went. Not many details, and he kept calling her 'my wife.' No name."

"Somebody's playing games with us."

"Who would do that? And why?"

She blew a gust of air upward, her usual response to a hot flash. "Someone wants to make monkeys out of the 'lady detectives' maybe." Her tone put quotation marks around the term.

"But he offered to pay."

"Offered." She mopped her forehead with a tissue. "The other possibility that occurs to me is someone wants to distract us."

"Yeah!" That hit home. "Split our resources and keep us from proving Neil's innocent."

"Or guilty." I hoped she was simply trying to remain neutral. Wanting Neil to be innocent, I wanted Barb to want it, too.

I called Mr. Arnold back and told him we couldn't take his case. When I recommended a firm he might contact in Miami, he said he was writing the name down, but I doubted it. He hung up quickly in what seemed to me more a snit than real distress.

CHAPTER FIFTEEN

Barb

I have never minded eating alone. I don't look around at couples
dining together and wish my life were different. Used to the pitying
looks a lone woman gets from the hostess, I ignore the *just* in the
question, "Just one this evening?" Upon returning to Allport, I'd
insisted my sister had no obligation to feed me, and she'd insisted it
was no trouble at all. We eventually came to a compromise. I have
dinner with her and Dale once a week and breakfast on Sundays.
Who knows what Faye would do if she couldn't cook for people.

Caroline's Cafe is a trendy little restaurant in the old section of
Allport. The lighting is dim but not cave-like, and the waitresses are
personally friendly, not professionally so. I have yet to hear one of
them say, "My name is Allison and I'll be your server." They
apparently understand that I don't need to know their name to ask
for more butter.

It was Friday and the place was crowded. Something about the
layout keeps it fairly quiet, however, so it doesn't feel like one is
eating in a mess hall. I was awaiting an example of Caroline's
excellent panini when I looked up and saw a man enter. I'd only
seen him in car headlights before, but he was the man I'd met after
my Correction Episode at the drugstore.

His gaze swept the room as he waited for the hostess and
stopped when it came to me. His eyes lit with recognition and what
might have been humor, but he merely nodded. The uniform he
wore identified him as our new chief of police, which explained
why Mr. Midnight had been on the street so late. He'd been

checking out night-time activities, possibly suspicious ones, in his territory. And what had he found? Me.

To my distress, the hostess led him to the only remaining table, which was directly behind mine. As if aware of my discomfort, he sat down with his back to me. I decided ignoring him was best, though our chairs were practically touching. We'd have to meet someday, perhaps even work together, if the Smart Agency was to succeed. *But not now*, I told myself. A visit to his office and a formal introduction would be better.

It was awkward, though. I heard everything the waitress said to him and everything he said back. He ordered the fish, and I wondered if he was fighting that thickening waist, at least until he selected fried rather than broiled. He looked good, though. I tried to remember what I'd read in the paper. Retired from the Chicago Police Department, Chief Something-unpronounceable had returned to northern Michigan, the land of his childhood. His coming was hailed as a new day in law enforcement, when Millden County would be dragged into the twenty-first century. I doubted one man could do it.

"Have you got some sugar over there?" His voice, coming over my shoulder, startled me.

"What?" *Great*, I berated myself. *Now you appear to be deaf as well as creepy.*

"Sugar. She brought me coffee but nothing to put in it."

Careful to avoid body contact, I handed over the little ceramic box of sugar packets. "Thanks." Now I was sure there was humor in his voice. "Crowded in here tonight."

"Yes."

"Would it start a rumor if we shared a table and let that couple sit down?" He indicated the doorway, where a nervous-looking young man and his date stood waiting for a place to sit.

"Yes."

There was a challenge in his voice. "Can you handle it?"

I had to smile. "Rumors have never bothered me."

"Good." Picking up his place-setting and coffee cup, he moved opposite me, signaling to the hostess that his table was free. "Ruairidh Clellan Neuencamp. They call me Rory."

"I'm Barbara Evans, mostly known as Barb."

"Nice to meet you, Barb. Will sharing a table really cause a flap?"

"You're the new man in town. Everything you do will be evaluated over the next few months. And I'm a spinster. Anything I do with a member of the male sex will cause comment."

He passed on the spinster epithet. "I vote we resolve not to notice." How easy it was for a man to say "to hell with gossip"! After decades of trying, I was still aware of the effort it took.

"All right." I put out a hand. "Rory, you said?"

His palm was slightly rough as we shook hands. "One parent Ojibway, the other Irish through and through. Ruairidh is a proud old Celtic name, but Rory doesn't require glottals."

Our meals arrived almost simultaneously, which kept us busy for a while. Wishing I'd ordered something less messy, I cut the panini into bits rather than biting off chunks and ending up with cheese dripping down my chin. Rory talked easily, telling me why he'd returned to the area and what he hoped the next ten years would be like.

"Big city cops either get old or get out. I decided from the first to put in my thirty and then find a quieter place to finish." He lowered his eyes. "Twenty was too much for my wife."

"I'm sorry to hear it."

"I was too, for a while." His tone was light, but a shade across his eyes let me know her desertion had hurt. "Anyway, last year I put in my papers and started looking for a place up here that needed an officer. I found Allport or they found me, I don't know which."

Thirty years on the force put him at somewhere between fifty-two and fifty-five, I guessed. The job had aged him, but not in a bad way. He looked like a man who'd seen it all and decided to grin it down, like Davy Crockett with a bear. "You're willing to keep at it?"

"Yeah. I'm hoping this town will be just what I need, stimulating but not overwhelming."

"That sounds like my home town," I said. "Definitely not overwhelming."

"You've always lived here?"

"No. I came back after almost thirty years in Washington state."

"Doing what?"

Although I usually tell people I retired from the practice of law, somehow I didn't mind giving Rory a more accurate picture. "Assistant D.A."

He set his cup in its saucer with a clink. "You've had adventures of your own, then."

"Like you said, you get out or you get old."

His eyes met mine. "You're one of those people who'll never look old. High cheekbones, beautiful skin, the gifts of good genes." He grinned, adding, "And clean living, I'm sure."

How long had it been since a man told me I was attractive? I couldn't remember. My face warmed, and I took a sip of water to keep from looking too grateful. "Of course."

Through the rest of the meal, I waited for the question he had to want to ask. What had I been doing alone on the streets at midnight with a lumpy backpack? He didn't ask, and instead of relaxing in his easy company, I became more agitated. Rory was attractive, but there was a question between us. A truthful answer would bring surprise, maybe disdain. A lie would ruin any chance we had of being friends. I had to pretend there was no question, but it left an empty space between us we'd have to step around each time we met.

Oh, god. We'd meet again, and each time I'd wonder what he was thinking about the night when I'd obviously been up to something. I'd wonder what he thought that had been.

I wanted to get away from Rory Neuencamp, but I couldn't simply leave in the middle of dinner. Then he'd really wonder what I was hiding. I imagined the question lingering in his mind, moving toward the front, receding as I asked about his experiences, then resurfacing: *What was she doing, all in black and out at midnight?* I felt like the man in the Poe story, waiting for the cop to notice the beating heart under the floor.

Rory seemed relaxed as he made casual conversation about people he'd met in town. I, on the other hand, became more tense, almost spilling my water at one point and dropping a forkful of panini into my lap. When the main course was gone, I skipped dessert with the excuse that I was dieting, wished him well in the job, and hurried away.

In the car, I cursed myself for all kinds of foolishness. The first attractive single man I'd met in Allport and I had two strikes against me: first, I appeared to be some sort of night stalker, and now he'd think I was socially anxious, ungracious, and possibly bulimic as well.

Still angry at myself, I spent the rest of the evening working on a letter to the mayor of Allport, my next Correction Event. Wearing rubber gloves, I took a single sheet of paper out of the center of a stack in my printer tray. Placing it on top of the stack, I printed the letter I'd composed. I read it through once more to be sure it was clear and error free.

Mayor Gleason:

Several times in the months since you took office, you've been quoted in the local paper using incorrect grammar. Since I have no way of knowing if you were misquoted, I am sending a copy of this letter to the newspaper editor in hopes one or both of you will address the problem.

The word myself *is a reflexive pronoun that should only be used in certain instances. Therefore, please do not say that "the commission members and myself" took action. In addition, you are quoted as saying people may contact "my secretary or myself."*

You might recall from school that the key to correct pronoun use is to think how the sentence would be framed if no other person is mentioned. Since you would say "I feel" and not "myself feels," **I** *is the correct pronoun in the first instance. Since you would say "contact me" and not "contact myself,"* **me** *is the correct pronoun in the second.*

If you become more aware of your tendency to err with pronouns, you can avoid these unfortunate

mistakes and become a better example to your
constituents.

A Friend

Satisfied, I made a second copy, again using untouched paper from the middle of the stack, then addressed the envelopes the same way. Modern science can probably determine which printer created a document, but I doubted it would ever come to that. Both letters were likely to be thrown in the garbage with hardly a thought. Still, I had to try.

Putting the envelopes in a plastic zipper bag, I stowed it deep in my purse. As we traveled north tomorrow, I'd drop them in a mailbox somewhere. Feeling a little better, I went to bed, humming a song my grandmother used to sing, "Brighten the Corner Where You Are."

CHAPTER SIXTEEN

Faye

The next morning we again left Dale in charge and headed north. I lived through the bridge crossing, and Barb had resigned herself to driving her beloved Chevy over bumpy dirt roads a second time. Once we left US 2, I watched the two-track driveways disappear into the woods, allowing only glimpses of the homes at the end. Lacy-fingered firs lined the road, many with lower branches that had turned red-brown from distress. There was the general messiness of untamed lands: fallen trees downed by winter storms, some dragged off roadway just far enough for cars to pass. We saw several gas wells, some landowner's dream come true. Depleted woodpiles testified to the winter the residents had to hope was truly over. It would soon be time to start building them up again, however. Summer never lasted long at this latitude.

At a huge signboard listing upcoming camps, we turned right, passing a row of more than twenty mailboxes. Residents for miles around had to find their own way to them if they wanted their mail, no matter the weather. Several were painted green and yellow. Yuppers were often Green Bay Packer fans, no matter that they lived in the wrong state.

We braked for a dozen turkeys who chose that moment to cross the road, some geeking their heads as they hurried, others strolling as if they ruled the world. As we waited, Barb wondered aloud what would happen when we got to the lodge. We'd decided calling the police was premature, but now she seemed to question that. "What if Brown—if that's who Roger Kimball really is—gets violent when we show up again?"

"We tell him the police know where we are so it won't do him any good to attack us."

The last turkey cleared the road, and we started again. Barb gripped the wheel with both hands as a series of nasty ruts sent the car slithering sideways. "What if he wants to take his anger out on somebody? There we are." I figured her argument came from lawyer habit. Neither of us really expected the guy who'd served us hot cocoa to turn into a raving madman.

Reality was stranger than anything we'd imagined. We pulled in at the lodge and got out just as Kimball came out his front door, dressed in jeans and a flannel shirt. The arm hung limply at his side, and he wore a patch over the eye that had appeared milky. When he recognized us, his lips pressed together in stoic acceptance. "Figured you'd be back."

"Mr. Brown." Barb made it a statement.

He nodded. "You might as well come inside."

We followed him into the cabin. With an ironic grimace, he removed the patch to reveal a perfectly normal eye. Next he shrugged off the flannel shirt, revealing wrist weights wrapped around the supposedly lifeless arm. Velcro rasped as he removed them, remarking, "They make it hang stiff and remind me not to use it."

"And the eye?"

"Halloween supply companies have all kinds of spooky-looking contact lenses. The patch is a quick fix when people drop by unexpectedly." He dropped the weights onto the counter with a careless clatter as if glad to be finished with them. "Please, follow me."

Behind the reception area was living space, not large or elegant, but comfortable. I guessed the furnishings were largely unchanged from what Haike had collected for himself. Snowshoes and trapping gear hung on one wall. Another was lined with foot-square storage units stuffed with blankets, towels, and clothing. Atop them a battered guitar rested, probably good company on long winter nights. A third wall had a Murphy bed folded against the knotty-pine wall, its feet doing double duty as clothing pegs. Beyond the bed was a wood stove similar to the one in our cabin but raised higher with bricks to make loading it easier for an old man with arthritis. At the far end of the room, a door stood open revealing a refrigerator, pots and pans hanging from nails over an apartment-size gas range, and a wooden table with one chair.

The place smelled like a man who'd had no reason to pretend to be civilized for some time. Noticing Barb's unconscious sniff of disapproval, Neil opened the window beside him, inserting one of those expandable screens that let fresh air in and keep some bugs out. He moved to the opposite window, which resisted his efforts. He pounded at it with a palm and the frame accepted defeat, sliding upward as if it had meant to all along.

"Have a seat." We obeyed, me on an old rocker and Barb on the visibly lumpy couch. I felt awkward, and even my cut-to-the-chase sister seemed unsure how to start the conversation. We'd expected Neil to make some attempt to maintain the pretense, but it appeared he was at peace with whatever happened. After all, he'd had a long time to think about it.

He disappeared into the kitchen and after some vigorous pumping returned with a ceramic pitcher and three enameled cups. "Best water in the world." He handed us each a cup and poured as if we were welcome guests. The water was icy cold, chilling my fingers through the cup's bumpy surface. Using both hands and freed of his disguise, Neil seemed a different person from the shy, shuffling misfit we'd met before.

"How'd I screw up?"

"You didn't, really. We talked to Mr. Makala, and his story didn't quite match yours."

Brown seemed more pleased than upset. "You talked to Haike? How is he?"

"Deaf. Pretty much bed-ridden, they said."

"Too bad. He's a good guy."

"You said you were working here that fall. He told us you came the next spring."

"Shoulda got our story straight." He took a sip. "Six years, though. Can't ask for more."

I couldn't resist a gentle jibe. "Kimball?"

He actually grinned. "Lame, I know. A fugitive." He sobered. "I sure was."

Barb set her cup on a driftwood end table. "Want to tell us about you and Haike?" I sensed she was letting him come at things the easy way, how he came to own Buck Lake Resort, rather than why he'd left his dying wife and dead brother-in-law back in Allport.

"I arrived here that November, said my car broke down back in Manistique. I said I'd walked because I didn't want to miss a day of hunting. Haike knew it was bull from day one, but he just showed me to cabin number four."

"How'd you get here? Juan took your truck south."

Brown scrubbed a hand over his beard, reddish despite the dark dye job. "He in trouble?"

"No."

He nodded. "Good. I figured he'd play dumb and get by."

"He's a citizen now," I put in.

Neil nodded approval, curling his fingers around his cup as he took a seat on the raised hearth of his wood stove. "Seeing Juan hitch-hiking was the only stroke of luck I had that day. He agreed to take the truck in the wrong direction and save me the trip."

"Clever."

"Desperate," Brown corrected, shifting his feet uneasily. "We parted company at a gas station in Ossineke. I hung around there, waiting for a ride. After while a van pulled in from the south with Marquette Office Supply printed on the side. It was a good bet the guy was headed north, so when he went inside, I crawled in the back and hid behind some boxes."

"What if the driver had opened the doors and found you?"

Neil chuckled dryly. "Who'd expect some guy to come charging out of his van? I'd be half a mile away before he recovered enough to call for help."

"So he never knew you were back there."

"No." He smiled. "I had to listen to him sing along with his country music station for hours, but other than that it was easy enough." He paused, biting his lower lip. "The next time he stopped, we were in Munising. When the driver went inside, I crawled out."

"And headed for Buck Lake Resort."

"Not right away. I got a motel room for the night, used a fake name and made up the car information. The next morning I went shopping, bought hunting clothes, boots, and supplies."

"To fit in up here."

"Right. My ride in the panel truck overshot Buck Lake, but I didn't want to take a chance on somewhere else. What I knew about this place, single owner, remote location, made me think I could spend a couple weeks here without having to prove who I was or where I came from."

"How'd you get here from Munising?"

"Walked. It took a few days, but it was safest. I bought a compass and a map. I followed the least traveled roads. Around dusk I'd look for a deserted hunting camp and break into it." He shivered at the memory. "Those nights were miserable, just mice, squirrels, and me wrapped in every piece of fabric I could find in the place."

"You couldn't start a fire and invite curiosity."

He nodded. "In one camp there was a gun hanging on the wall. I took it to complete my disguise as a hunter." Brown smiled. "Later I returned it. Fixed the door, too."

It seemed odd that of all the things he was suspected of, Brown fretted over stealing a probably useless gun from a possibly abandoned camp.

Barb ignored his attempt at atonement. "You're pretty cool under pressure, Mr. Brown."

"Not really. I was a basket case the whole time." Setting his elbows on his knees, he sighed. "All I could think about was getting away from Stan Wozniak, where I'd be safe."

As if in rebuttal, the pitcher beside Neil shattered into a thousand pieces. We all jumped; I think I screamed. For a split second we stood looking stupidly at the pieces, wondering what had happened. Neil recovered first. "Down!" he shouted. "On the floor!"

We obeyed as an odd thud sounded from the log wall behind us. A third followed, and I finally got it. "Someone's shooting at us!"

"Stay down." Belly-crawling to a corner, he opened a knotty-pine door to reveal three rifles. Reaching up he took one then reached up again to get a box of shells. "Direction?"

Barb pointed. "That way, I think." How could she be so calm? I couldn't even raise my face from the rough plank floor.

"Stay where you are." Neil crawled to the front door, opened it a crack, and slid the rifle barrel into the opening. I watched with one eye, keeping the other shut and pressed against the floor. *Small target*, my mind said. *As small a target as a large woman can be.*

Suddenly the whole cabin rocked with a boom that seemed to come from inside my chest. I groaned with the pain of distressed eardrums. The echoes hung in the room, rolling around the walls and assaulting us several more times. I looked toward Neil, but he was gone. Steps sounded on the porch, and another shot rattled the windows. He'd gone on the offensive.

Silence. I wanted to say something, to hear Neil reply and know he was alive, but honestly, I couldn't think of a thing that fit the moment. *Did you shoot someone, Mr. Brown? Can I get off the floor now, Neil? Are we going to die?* Better to say nothing.

Finally, a vehicle started some distance away and took off, its engine growling. Someone called out in distress. Car sounds faded, and the voice stopped.

A few seconds later Neil reappeared, crossing the room and peering out the window with his back to the wall, like they do in old westerns. After a tense, silent minute, he relaxed a little. "I think he's gone. It was a black pickup. A Dodge, I think."

Barb rose, keeping away from the windows, and came over to help me up, dusting off my clothes before attending to her own. "Do you have enemies up here, Mr. Brown?"

He turned from the window with a wry smile. "I didn't until you ladies showed up."

CHAPTER SEVENTEEN

Barb

"We've got to get out of this place." Despite sounding like a '60s song, it was the truth.

"But who was out there?" Faye's voice was higher than normal, and tight.

"Who it was doesn't matter at the moment," Brown said. "What does matter is getting you away from here so you're safe."

I looked at him significantly, and he seemed to understand. "I'll turn myself in." He glanced out the shattered window. "If you found me, so can other people."

"It's pretty obvious they did," Faye commented.

"They followed us." *If I'd been as bad at the practice of law as I was in my new profession,* I was thinking, *I'd have been disbarred.* Aloud I said, "I'm sorry, Mr. Brown. I never considered the possibility that our finding you would interest anyone else."

"It would interest Stan Wozniak." Faye gave the shattered window a tentative push, sending brittle glass tinkling to the floor.

Looking to Brown I asked, "Would Wozniak sanction murder?"

He shrugged. "The guy knows how to hate."

"Why don't we go someplace where we can talk this out?" Faye suggested. "I'd like to hear the rest of Neil's story before we go back to Allport."

It wasn't a bad idea. There was a lot we hadn't had the chance to ask Brown and a lot we hadn't yet told him. When we returned home, the police would take him into custody. "Where?"

"Not south," he said. "Whoever shot at us might be waiting, and we'll be easy targets."

"So we have to go north. What's up there?"

"This road joins 123, which arcs north to Paradise then goes south, back down to I-75."

"Paradise has restaurants? Flush toilets?" Checking my watch, I added, "A motel?"

Brown seemed faintly offended. "Yeah, sure."

"Okay, we head north. Want to pack some things?"

Opening a cupboard over the door, Neil took out a ratty knapsack. As he stuffed garments into it Faye said, "I take it we're not going to tell the local police about getting shot at?"

"I don't see how it would help," I answered. "Our best bet is to tell our police and let them investigate."

Brown's packing didn't take long. Shouldering the knapsack, he put a hand-lettered CLOSED sign on the front door. "I'll figure out what to do with the place later." He paused to look around once before climbing into the back of the Chevy. "Haike's old car, too," he added, nodding at a battered Ford Taurus beside the cabin. "Doesn't look like much, but it runs good and starts every time." He sighed. "Maybe someday I can come back."

It wasn't the moment to begin a discussion of what awaited him in Allport. An ailing sister and a daughter he apparently didn't know about would complicate Brown's life, even if he could explain away the crimes he was accused of. We turned north, toward a town large enough to hide in for a while. There, all stories would be told.

CHAPTER EIGHTEEN

Retta

When I visited the house and found my sisters gone, I tried to get out of Dale where they were, but he closed down like a turtle. I left feeling grumpy. Barbara Ann and Faye Elizabeth had left me behind while they went on an adventure, just like when I was little. While part of me argued it was childish, another part of me vowed I'd find out something important while they were gone, so they'd have to admit I made a contribution. I decided to start with Stan Wozniak.

When I phoned WOZ Industries, the receptionist made a lunch date with Stan sound unlikely. "Mr. Wozniak's leaving town tomorrow, Mrs. Stilson. He's really busy today."

"Please tell him I called to take him up on his invitation." I flipped through a magazine for a few minutes, checking out the scratch and sniff fragrance samples. It wouldn't take long.

Stanley Wozniak had been after me since a few months after my husband died. Now by "after me" I don't mean for marriage. Stanley thinks in terms of conquests, and I was a woman he hadn't had a shot at yet. He got more interested every time I said no.

He was smooth, I had to grant him that. He never pushed, he simply let a woman know he found her desirable with a glance, a word, or a gesture. Still, I'd never met anyone else who could make helping me into my coat seem like a sexual act.

Stanley didn't interest me, mostly because I sensed a hardness beneath his courtly exterior. I'd heard stories of good employees fired for no reason except that things always had to go Stanley's way. People who worked at WOZ seldom quit, because jobs at the company were like gold, but many admitted there was a hovering fear that Stan would at some point turn his anger on them. If that happened, whatever they'd accomplished for the company meant nothing.

Another mark against Stanley was his attitude toward women, which was just a decade or so this side of medieval. Wife #1, mother of Carson and Carina, was a former model who'd died in a car accident somewhere near Chicago. Alcohol might have been a factor.

Wife #2 had spent one year in Michigan before returning to Las Vegas and life upon the wicked stage. I remembered Wife #3 only vaguely: big eyes, big boobs, and a big mouth. There'd been no fourth Mrs. Wozniak. For over a decade now, Stanley had contented himself with women who knew better than to expect alimony, palimony, or matrimony.

I had no intention of becoming a notch on Stanley's belt. Dating is a choice I make from time to time, but I haven't yet met a man who could replace my husband, who I miss every single minute of every day. Despite lots of friends, two grown children, and my sisters, I don't feel close to anyone, and that's a lonely place to be.

In light of that, though I wasn't interested in Stanley long-term, I looked forward to our evening out. He was attractive and sophisticated, at least according to Allport's standards. I wanted to help my sisters, and dinner with the head of WOZ Industries couldn't hurt my reputation. Though Stanley didn't know it, one dinner would be enough.

I let the phone ring six times, so he didn't think I was waiting for his call. "Hello."

"Margaretta. Stan Wozniak."

"How nice of you to call back so quickly. I know how busy you are."

"Not too busy to take the prettiest woman in Allport to dinner."

With a feminine purr, I launched into my story. "Mike Morland is entertaining at the hotel tonight, and I remembered you said you liked his singing."

"I think I suggested we see his show, but you were busy."

I hummed non-committally. "Anyway, he's there tonight, and I thought if you weren't otherwise occupied, we could go."

"I can pick you up around six. Are you at the same address?"

I had a momentary attack of conscience, knowing Stan would spend lavishly on me and go home disappointed. But that's the game, isn't it?

CHAPTER NINETEEN

Barb

"A kid?" Brown's face pinched with astonishment. "I have a little girl?"

We'd checked into a motel in Paradise that was nicely anonymous and, except for the philodendrons in the lobby, could have been located in Florida or Oregon or New Mexico. There was a breakfast room, and we'd taken a table in a corner, out of sight of the front desk. After getting each of us a paper cup of water, Faye had gently made the announcement.

"Her name is Brooke." She pushed his cup closer, and Brown took a drink without seeming to notice. "Carina was alive when help arrived. They were able to save the baby."

"But I heard the call. Stan said they were both dead."

"You were at the dispatch office?"

"Yeah." He couldn't get his mind to move onward. "I have a daughter."

"Your sister hired us to find you. Your parents are dead."

He bowed his head, taking that in. After a while Faye said, "She's a beautiful child."

With visible effort he put his parents' deaths aside for the moment. "You've seen her?"

"When I got there, Meredith was making lasagna for supper. I guess it's her favorite."

Neil smiled. "Mine too." He shifted in his chair. "Haven't had it in a while."

I came back to the point. "After the hue and cry died down, your sister found a pamphlet for Buck Lake. She thought you might have headed there when you needed a place to, um, relocate. She didn't do anything at the time, being unwilling to risk betraying your whereabouts."

"Meredith." He almost smiled. "How is she?"

I met Faye's gaze and got permission to edit my response. "She's a teacher now. And she's done a great job with Brooke."

"Not surprising." His eyes went soft. "Sometimes out there in the woods I missed her most of all. Carina and I had some rough times, and it was hard to get past them in my mind. Our parents were older, you know, great people, but Meri and I were—we had a lot of fun." He rose. "If you don't mind, I'd like to walk around for a while. This is a lot to take in."

He might run and leave us looking like the amateurs we still were. On the other hand, he had a lot to deal with. I checked my watch. "Shall we meet here in the morning, around 7:00?"

Faye chimed in with just the right touch of honesty and humor. "Over breakfast we expect to hear your version of what makes somebody mad enough to kill you."

Brown didn't reply, but his expression said he had suspicions, probably the same as Faye's and mine. Stan Wozniak was the only man I could think of who hated Brown that much.

CHAPTER TWENTY

Faye

As soon as Neil was out of sight, Barb started doubting him. She began pacing. "He could disappear, just like before." The room was so small I crawled onto my bed to get out of her way.

"He didn't have to come with us at all," I reminded her. "He could have taken off into the woods back at the lodge. It's unlikely either of us could have caught him."

"Yes, but now that he's alone, he might rethink his options."

"He'll be there in the morning."

"If he is, we have to get him back to Allport and turn him over to the police."

"You still think he did it?"

Barb gave me one of her patient looks. "He seems like a nice guy, Faye, but remember the DNA and blood evidence? He was there, and things turned violent."

"There has to be some justification. I mean, the place was all torn apart. Maybe Neil and Carson got into a fight and Carina somehow got in the way."

Barb stopped pacing and turned to me. "Somebody came up behind her and bashed in her skull with a ball bat. Don't delude yourself, Faye. Neither Carina nor Carson died by accident."

CHAPTER TWENTY-ONE

Retta

Stanley arrived in a jazzy little sports car that was so low-slung it felt like I was sitting on the ground. Though I prefer a car one can get into and out of with ease and style, I made "I'm impressed" noises, knowing men like cars for different reasons than women do.

Dinner was fine. Stanley talked mostly about his only real interest, himself. I learned the basics of limestone quarrying, software pirating, and employee shortcomings in the first half hour. As we ate, we sipped drinks, wine for me, Crown Royal for him. He easily outdid me in quantity with no apparent effect. His hand remained steady, his words clear. When I thought he was warmed up enough, I brought the conversation around to our personal tragedies.

"You certainly stay busy," I said, adding with what I hoped was charming honesty, "I do, too, so I don't think about the past too much."

He chose to focus on my tragedy. "Tough break, losing your husband so young."

"It was. Of course, having the children helped. You didn't have that comfort."

His face clouded. "No." Finishing his drink in one swallow, he set the glass down hard enough to catch the waitress' attention. Nodding understanding, she headed to the bar.

"At least you have your granddaughter," I went on. "How old is she now?"

"I've never seen the child."

"Oh." I tried to look embarrassed. "I suppose seeing her would bring awful memories."

His face seemed cut from stone. "I want nothing to do with the child of a murderer."

"But she's your granddaughter."

His lips barely moved as he said, "And her father killed my children. With my own eyes I saw him running away." The muscles of his face stood out as if he held himself together with effort. "I will not have anything to do with that man's offspring."

The waitress appeared with another Crown Royal and the dessert cart. I took a long time with my choice, giving Stan time to regain control and become the man he wanted me to see.

The show started then, and we turned to enjoy the music. Looking at Stanley from time to time, I thought of his innocent grandchild. Even if Brown was guilty, how could he reject her?

When the first set ended, Stanley asked politely if I wanted to stay for another. When I said we should go, he called for the check. Somewhat ostentatiously he added a large tip for the waitress, who urged him more than once to "Come on back."

Recovering his good humor as we left, he put an arm around my waist and pulled me close as he asked, "Interested in a nightcap, Retta?"

I knew if I said yes, the next question would be, "My place or yours?"

"If you don't mind, Stanley, I should get home. My son's supposed to call from Fiji."

The Fiji part was true, but the call was fictional, a gentle
negative on the possibility of sharing the rest of the night. He took it
well. At his age he'd learned to wait for what he wanted.

***

When Stanley dropped me off at home I went right back out,
because something he'd said bothered me. One day while Barbara
was out of the office, I'd convinced Faye to let me read the notes
Sgt. Sparks had sent on the Brown murder case. He'd made a
drawing of the apartment building where Carina lived, and I recalled
that the entry doors faced north. The parking lot was on the west, so
Stanley had parked there and walked around to the doors. I wanted
to know exactly how far away he was when he supposedly saw his
son-in-law leave the building.

Windswept Apartments consisted of three fifties-era buildings,
two-story, red-brick rectangles with flat walls and a row of
identically battered storm doors at each entry. Parking in the lot, I
walked around to the front, almost bumping into a couple clinging
to each other like a flood was imminent. They eyed me with
hostility as I hurried on, feeling like an interloper.

When I checked the angle of sight from several different
vantage points, I concluded that Stanley might have seen someone
leaving the building, but it would have been at some distance. And
if that person was heading away and hadn't turned back, he'd have
seen only the back of a man in a hoodie. His willingness to believe
it was Brown might have colored his judgment.

Another point came to mind. If the guy running away was
Brown, why had he left on foot? He'd been driving a truck,
according to reports. That left me with a possible plus for Brown—
Stanley's inability to actually see his face, and a possible minus. A
man planning to murder his wife might have left his vehicle some

distance away to prevent it being reported later. That might signal premeditation, which wasn't a good thing for Mr. Brown

"Are you looking for someone?" The voice at my elbow made me jump.

"Huh?" I turned to find a man leaning out of a city police car. I'd been so wrapped up in my thoughts I hadn't heard his approach.

"I asked if you were looking for someone." In the street light, we examined each other. What I saw was pleasing, but he gave no indication of his thought. I had to say something.

"I know everyone in the department but the new chief, so I guess that makes you him."

"Yes, ma'am." His tone was patient, but he wanted an answer to his question, which really was, "Why the heck are you wandering around here at this time of night?"

I put out a hand. "I'm Margaretta Stilson, Chief Neuencamp. I'm trying to determine if what someone said about a certain situation is possible."

He shook hands then asked, "This person has a truth problem?"

"No, but my husband used to say people's memories get funny when the police arrive."

He nodded. "It's up to the investigator to apply a healthy dash of doubt."

"Exactly. Someone told me tonight he saw a man running away from this building after a crime was committed. There's no reason to doubt him, but I wanted to see for myself how it would have looked." I explained my reasons, leaving out names in order to protect my sisters' client's confidentiality. I also implied I worked for the Smart Detective Agency, possibly to convince the new chief that I wasn't some lunatic. In the back of my mind I was aware it was partly to keep the interest of those direct brown eyes.

The chief relaxed somewhat, apparently concluding I was okay. He shifted the car into park, and the engine stopped growling and went to a purr. There were questions he wanted to ask. What newly-arrived peace officer wouldn't want to get a sense of the possibilities, good and bad, of a local detective agency? He'd probably heard of it in a wink-wink, nudge-nudge way, from Tom Stevens. I pictured Tom settling his belt around that eight-month pregnancy he calls a stomach and saying, "Yeah, some gals in town got a yen to be private eyes. Got the paperwork and all, but I don't suppose they'll give us any competition."

"Are you the head of the agency?" the chief asked.

"I just help out when I can. My husband was a police officer, so I know how things go."

"Maybe I'll stop in one of these days."

I wanted to ask him not to tell Barbara he'd met me, and I should have begged him not to tell her I'd said I was helping out. There was no way to do that without looking like a complete fool, however, and the last thing I wanted was to appear a fool to the best-looking newcomer Allport had seen in years. I had to hope if he did stop by to meet Barbara and Faye, he didn't get chatty about women he met out and about at midnight.

CHAPTER TWENTY-TWO

Barb

To my great relief, Brown was waiting when we came downstairs the next morning. The motel offered continental breakfast, and from the yeasty smell and the little pile of trash in front of him, I guessed he'd had toast and jelly. Now he was drinking coffee, and the little pile of sugar packets nearby indicated it was not his first cup.

"Can't remember the last time I had this many choices," he told us, glancing at the array. He seemed more at ease this morning, as if he'd worked through the revelations of yesterday, good and bad. He'd shaved away the uneven beard, and without it and his fake infirmities, he was an attractive man with a definite likeness to Meredith around the eyes and mouth.

Brown sat patiently while we made our own breakfast choices, oatmeal for me. Faye smeared a bagel with cream cheese, took two spoonfuls of egg casserole, and wedged a doughnut onto the plate as well. When we were seated, he said, "You want to hear my side of the story."

"We do," I said, sprinkling a sugar over my cereal. "When we agreed to find you, we gave your sister no guarantee you won't go to prison."

"I was pretty sure that's where I was headed," he said. "But I swear: if I'd done anything wrong, I'd have stayed and taken my deads."

The phrase from childhood struck me, and I remembered the shots fired at us the day before. By tracking him down, we'd put

Brown in danger. Someone wanted him dead, and I was determined to prevent that. "You promised us a story."

He looked around the tiny dining area before meeting my gaze directly. "I didn't kill my wife. Or her worthless punk brother, for that matter."

"But when you heard they were dead, you ran."

"I knew it was going to look like I did it."

I turned my best lawyer look on him. "Your blood was on his clothes. Your skin was under Carina's fingernails."

My accusing tone didn't seem to disturb him. "Carina pulled me off Carson. She probably scratched me in the process." He turned to Faye, who I guessed he thought was more sympathetic. "Do you blame me for running?"

"With a man like Wozniak pushing things, maybe not," she answered. "What do you know about what happened after you left?"

"Nothing." He gulped the last of his coffee and stared into the empty cup. "I, um, made arrangements to be notified if it was safe to come home, but I never heard a word."

"From Susie Mason?" Faye asked, and he looked up in surprise. "You and Susie were an item before Carina came along, right?"

He made a negative gesture. "We dated in high school, before I met Carina, but Susie married my friend John. There was nothing between us." His earnest expression was hard to doubt. He was telling the truth as he saw it.

"But she helped you out when you needed her."

Brown swept some breadcrumbs into his hand and emptied them into his napkin. "In order to say how she got involved, I have to tell the story from the start."

"That would be good." I rose and got the coffee pot for another round for all of us, spilled two packets of sugar into mine, and looked at him expectantly.

His sharp exhalation scattered the pile of empty sugar papers, and Faye gathered them up while he talked. "Carina and I had been separated about two weeks. The pregnancy made things hard. She'd fly off the handle about some little thing. Or nothing at all sometimes."

He paused, and I suspected he hadn't spoken this many words all at once in years. It must seem odd to talk about it, but telling the story might bring catharsis, too. Faye leaned toward him, eager to hear it, and though I sat back, I was just as interested.

"The morning Carina—that morning, Ralph, my foreman, said he wanted me to run to Gaylord in the afternoon and pick up supplies. Just before lunch, he came over and said Carina wanted me to come by the apartment as soon as possible." He bowed his head. "She'd been pretty rough on me the last time we met, so I told Ralph she could wait a while, I'd stop and see her before I left town." His voice softened. "I didn't know she had a real problem to deal with."

"What time did you get to her place?"

"I left the job site at eleven twenty. When I got there it was about twenty to twelve. I heard loud voices inside and let myself in with my key. There was Carson, standing over Carina. She was on the floor, crying. I was furious. I charged the little creep and knocked him down."

There was anger in his voice, all these years later. Whatever the end result, Brown had been protecting his wife in the beginning. "Go on."

"Carson fought back, which surprised me. We went at it hard for a minute or so, and he got in a punch that split my lip. Finally, though, I got him on the floor. That's when Carina stepped in, screaming I was going to kill him." He looked ashamed. "I was just so mad he'd hit his sister like that, and her almost due to deliver our baby."

"But you stopped?"

"Yeah. We all kind of got it together for a minute. Carina told me they'd been arguing about something she found out that morning. She said it was a family matter." Brown pulled on one earlobe. "Looking back, I think when she called the job site that morning, she'd meant to tell me about it. By the time I arrived, something had happened that changed her mind. Instead, she told Carson, 'You gotta make this right, or I will.' I had no idea what she meant by that."

I sipped reached for another sugar packet. "Why did she call you? You were separated."

He flashed a humorless smile. "Whatever you've heard, Carina loved me. She was spoiled, but she depended on me in a lot of ways." He paused, searching for an illustration. "One day she called the job site to ask how many t-shirts I thought we needed for the baby."

"Were you going to divorce?" Faye obviously wanted him to say the baby would have had two parents if things had not gone horribly wrong.

He stared into space. "I probably would have gone to work for Stan. For her and the kid."

"Okay," I said. "You and Carina and Carson quit fighting. How did it start up again?"

He met my gaze steadily. "It didn't. Carson got all weepy and said he'd do what Carina wanted. It turned out he hadn't hit Carina like I'd thought. She'd got mad and pushed him and he pushed back." Brown shifted his feet under the table, causing a wobble that made me grab my coffee cup. "Pregnant women don't have the greatest sense of balance."

"He said he'd make it right, whatever he had done to upset her?"

Brown nodded. "I believed him. He was all sorry, said he'd never really wanted to do it."

"What did he mean by that?"

"I don't know. Carina shut him up and ordered me out of there. Her dad was on his way, and she said it was a family matter they had to handle together."

"You weren't family?"

"Not to Stan. Carina said if I was there when Carson faced his dad, Stan wouldn't like it."

"So you're telling us you left?"

"Yeah."

"And they were both alive and well?"

"Carson was a little bloody, but yes. Alive and well."

Faye was listening carefully. "What time was this?"

"Noon. I heard the clock downtown chime as I was getting into my truck."

"Wozniak said you left at twelve forty. He called the EMTs at twelve forty-two."

"I heard."

"How? How did you hear what he told the police?"

Brown began tearing his empty coffee cup into pieces. "I didn't have to be in Gaylord until two, so I had lots of time. I went down to the lake shore, ate the lunch I'd packed that morning, and thought about all the stuff that was coming between Carina and me. I sat there for a long time, letting the adrenalin from the fight wear off. When I finally got calmed down, it was time to head for Gaylord and pick up the stuff Ralph needed on the job."

"What time was that?"

"Around twelve thirty, twelve thirty-five."

"So you were still in town when they died."

He sighed. "Yeah. If I had—" He thought better of that and returned to the story. "On the way through town, I remembered I was supposed to have dinner with John and Susie that night. I had to pass the dispatch office, so I stopped to tell her I didn't feel like coming over."

"Then it *was* your truck someone saw there."

"Yeah. I'd barely said hello when the call came in." Neil's facial muscles tightened. "It was awful. Stan was screaming into the phone, and I could hear every word. 'That bastard killed my children! Neil Brown killed them.' Susie tried to calm him down, but he kept saying over and over again that I'd killed Carina and Carson. He saw me running away."

"Susie knew he was mistaken?"

Brown shrugged. "I'm not sure what she thought. I had a cut on my lip from where Carson punched me. First thing, she sent police and EMTs to Windswept. I was a wreck. I wanted to go there, but Susie stopped me. 'Wozniak will have you arrested,' she said. I told her I hadn't killed anybody, but she said it didn't matter. I'd just had a fight with Carson, so it would look like I'd done it. Susie kept saying Stan would see I went to prison for the rest of my life."

It could easily have gone exactly as Susie Mason feared. He looked guilty. The evidence proved his presence and his struggle with the victims. Who'd believe he'd left that apartment minutes before someone else came in and killed two people? Only Meredith and his parents.

"So you decided to run."

"Wozniak was a guy people listened to." He put a hand to his forehead as if the pain of it had gathered there. "I couldn't think. I kept saying Carina couldn't be dead, but Susie pointed at Carson's blood on my shirt. She said I had to get out of Allport."

"She offered to help you elude the law."

Brown came to Susie's defense. "If I'd stayed, I'd have spent the last six years in prison."

"What did she tell you to do?"

"She said I should turn my shirt inside out then get all the money I could get my hands on and go hide somewhere. If they found proof I didn't kill them, she'd put an ad in the Sunday *Detroit Free Press* saying, 'Son, come home on your birthday, Love, Mother.' Corny, but we were both pretty rattled." His face turned grim. "I've combed the personals every Sunday all these years, but there was nothing."

"How much money did you take north?"

Neil collected the bits of his demolished cup in one hand. "On our wedding day, Stan gave us fifty thousand dollars in cash, all wrapped up in a cardboard box with a bow. It was the kind of thing he liked to do, and when we opened it, everyone saw all that money. To me, it said I'd never be able to give Carina what he could." He swallowed. "That was the first time we argued. I didn't want it; she said it was a sweet gesture. In the end we put it in a safety deposit box till we could agree what to do with it." He dropped the Styrofoam shards into the trash. "That was our first fight, but not our last. The money was still there, so I took it."

Sparks had noted Neil's visit to the bank around one that day. Wozniak's money had given his son-in-law the means to escape. But was Brown guilty or falsely accused?

I found myself wondering what Rory Neuencamp would think. Would he conclude I was an idiot for wanting to believe this pleasant young man had not done the horrible things almost everyone in Allport believed he'd done? I didn't want him to.

Hardening my heart, I resolved to be objective, to question everything Neil Brown told us and ignore his innocent demeanor.

CHAPTER TWENTY-THREE

Retta

In order to speak to the employees at WOZ Industries and find out what they thought of the murders, I needed a cover story. Stanley was out of town for two days, his secretary had told me. If my purpose seemed innocent, he'd never know I'd visited. In my desk, I found exactly the thing: a book of tickets to the Fireworks Benefit Picnic. While some might consider it cheating to hit people up for money at work, where they can't get away, it happens all the time in small towns. Most folks would be good sports and buy my tickets, if only to get rid of me.

I started at the desk of the receptionist, Bambi, according to her nameplate, and I'm not kidding. Bambi looked a little like a deer, all eyes and soft brown fur—I mean hair. I did my bit about the tickets and, while she dug her knock-off purse out, asked if she'd ever met Neil Brown.

"Who?"

"The man they say killed Mr. Wozniak's children. I hear he might be found soon."

"Oh." It took a while for thought to get past all that makeup. "I wasn't here then."

"Who was Mr. Wozniak's secretary at the time?" Since Stanley talked about his "girl," I guessed she didn't expect to be called a personal assistant.

Again, her thought was slow. I waited. "I don't remember her name. She was nice, though. She showed me where stuff was." In a few seconds a name fought its way through the cosmetic wall. "Patricia?" She didn't like the sound of it. "Pricilla? Something with a P."

Thanking her, I moved on, guessing Bambi hadn't been chosen for her wits. Maybe something that rhymed. Stopping a woman in the hallway, I asked for directions to Eric Dubois' office in order to make a courtesy announcement of my purpose.

Eric and I had met a couple of times at civic events. He had a reputation as a good second in command, efficient, loyal, and patient with Stanley's demanding personality. Cheerfully ordering five tickets, he agreed to let me solicit further contributions in the building.

"I hear you met my sister, Barbara Evans," I said casually.

"I didn't know she was your sister." He dropped his fashionable black-rimmed reading glasses on the blotter, rubbing his eyes. "I hope she's able to find Neil Brown, so Stan can finally get past his children's deaths. It's been really hard on him."

"I know you were working here then."

"Yes, but I'm afraid I couldn't tell Ms. Evans much."

"You never know," I said. "You might say something that eventually leads to the killer."

Eric's brows rose, but his surprise turned to gentle admonishment. "I think the police already know who's guilty. I liked Neil but, sad as it is, likeable people can do terrible things."

I couldn't argue. I went on with my ticket sales, targeting people who'd worked at WOZ Industries for a long time. Scanning name plates displayed on the walls next to office doors, I located the company accountant, Miles Bonworth. Knocking twice, I invited myself in. He turned with a frown and regarded me balefully as I made my pitch for the fireworks benefit.

"I went to that picnic once," he said when I finished. "Too many bugs."

"Some people who don't plan to attend buy a ticket anyway, to support the city's efforts."

"I went to the fireworks once," he said with a sneer. "A lot of expensive noise."

"It brings a lot of people into town, though. Tourists are good for business."

"Tourists? I call 'em Cidiots!" He made a nasty snort. "Can't stand 'em."

I hovered, trying to find a way to segue to the Brown case. A picture on the shelf behind his desk gave me inspiration. "Is that your daughter's softball team?"

"Yes."

Your only child? sprang to mind, but I asked instead, "Which one is she?"

He pointed to a somber-looking child with arms too skinny to hit more than a single.

"What a doll." Having created my opening, I asked, "Didn't Mr. Wozniak's son-in-law play ball in school? I heard he could have gotten a scholarship."

"Don't know." His tone said he could not have cared less.

I lowered my voice. "They say he killed his wife with a bat."

"That's what they say."

Men fall into categories, and a clever woman can get what she wants by recognizing the category and working with it. Bonworth obviously enjoyed taking an opposite view of whatever was said, so I offered a comment he could disagree with.

"It must be a hardship on the company now that Mr. Wozniak's son is dead."

He looked surprised. "On the company? Not at all."

"Really? I assumed the son would take over when his father retired."

He snorted again, which was apparently his version of laughter. "That kid never took a minute's interest in this place except to subtract from the profits."

I threw another challenge at him, guessing he couldn't abide a misconception. "The papers said he was looking for ways to expand the business."

Snaky eyes slid across my face. "That just shows you what reporters don't know!" I'd hit the right button, and he was on a roll, forgetting I had no right to know what went on at WOS. "Expanding the business--what a joke! About every six months he'd come wanting Stan to 'invest' in some scheme." He made sarcastic quotation marks with his fingers. "Jet-packs for commuters. Biodomes in the desert. Some independent movie that was the next *Good Will Hunting*. I was always in the middle, trying to keep Stan from throwing away good money."

Bonworth seemed to resent losing control of funds, even if they weren't his. I shrugged delicately. "Stanley must have thought they were good ideas if he invested in them."

"For a while he gave the kid the benefit of the doubt, but then he said no more."

Again I let disbelief show in my voice. "How would you know that?"

One brow rose self-righteously. "You wouldn't ask if you'd heard them go at it the week the girl got married! Carson had another idea, but Stan said no more. He told the kid to either get a job out in California or come home and go to work here." Adjusting his tie, Bonworth added in a mumble, "Don't know what we'd have done with him. Kid couldn't balance a checkbook."

No one had mentioned that at the time of the murders. "Did this happen at the wedding?"

He shook his head. "In Stan's office. Just me and them." True to form, he added, "I skipped the wedding. Can't stand to see money wasted on a bunch of drunks."

Refusing to be diverted by Bonworth's dislike of everything, I asked, "Do you think the boy was really on his own? Maybe Mr. Wozniak gave him money from his personal funds, even if he didn't invest any more money from the company."

He went from terse to rude. "That would be his business, not mine or yours."

Accepting the rebuke, I said, "I don't want to seem nosy, but I spoke to Stan a few days ago, and it struck me that he's still dealing with the deaths of his children."

Bonworth regarded me, distaste evident in every wrinkle on his Shar-Pei face. "It had nothing to do with money. The girl's husband killed her during one of their famous fights, and Carson was unlucky enough to have been present—collateral damage, I believe they call it."

With that, he turned to his computer, dismissing me from his number-crunching mind.

I went on, selling a ticket here and there, asking my hopefully innocent-sounding questions. Everyone agreed, some sadly, some with gossipy delight, that Brown was the only possible candidate for murderer of the wife he hadn't been able to get along with. Some knew Carson had exhausted his father's patience with his money-making schemes, but no one even hinted Stanley would have laid a hand on either of his kids. Much less a softball bat.

My last stop was the computer tech's room. It was in the basement, as they often seem to be, a windowless square stuffed with devices I don't understand and don't really want to. They hummed and blinked, and oddly enough, so did the tech. He was humming as he removed the slightly dented back of an elderly-looking computer with a tiny screwdriver. He blinked when I called out a greeting, a mole unused to visitors in his natural habitat. Probably he was more accustomed to desperate summons by phone from the computer-deprived upstairs.

We did the ticket thing, and the man, whose name was Art Chalmers, dug out a battered wallet and handed me a five-dollar bill. Since computer people are in on many secrets of the businesses they work for, I pretended interest in the equipment in order to get him talking. Eagerly he explained in terms of gigas and metas and whatever. I was lost after the first sentence.

When he paused for breath, I asked, "Were you working here when Mr. Wozniak's children were murdered?"

He smiled, revealing crooked bottom teeth. "Yup. Came on board at nineteen with an associates from ACC and a ton of experience in World of Warcraft."

I'd been thinking of what Miles Bonworth said. Carson had gone back to California after Carina's wedding, apparently charged with getting a job and earning his own way. The news reports had called him an *entrepreneur*, which could mean almost anything, including nothing.

If the boy had come home that last time to try to change Stanley's mind about turning off the money spigot, they might have come to blows. Maybe Carina had been the collateral damage.

Guessing Art was the male type that responds to flattery, I looked around the room appreciatively. "I'll bet Stanley's glad to have someone here who knows all about computers."

"Yeah. He's great at business, not so great at technology." Art's smile indicated patience with clueless non-techs. "My generation's the first ever to be smarter than the ones before it."

That surprised me, but I'm good at hiding my opinions—and the fact that I have any. Turning up the brightness on my smile I asked, "What do you mean by that?"

"Well, we grew up with computers, so they're second nature to us. For older people, trying to understand them's like reading a book through muddy glasses." Raising pale eyebrows, he repeated his point. "First time ever, the younger generation is smarter than the old one."

Back in high school, I was on the debating team, and I'd always enjoyed destroying the cases of opposing teams who looked at me and thought, "Isn't she cute!" I saw all sorts of flaws in Art's logic, starting with his definition of the word *smarter*.

Gulping back the urge to argue, I asked, "Did you know Carson and Carina well?"

Art scrunched one side of his face in a move designed to push his glasses back into place. It was a gesture he'd repeated several times already. "She never looked twice at me, but Carson and me were kinda tight. He'd hang here sometimes when he was in Michigan."

Some people use words like "kinda" and "sometimes" to imply more than truth allows, and I guessed that "sometimes" meant once, twice at most. What I'd heard of Carson Wozniak didn't jibe with him "hanging" with a nerdy computer tech. I played along. "The two of you were interested in the same things?"

His brow furrowed. "Yeah, movies and stuff like that. And he liked watching me work on the computers." He chuckled. "He had a million questions."

"About how they work?"

"Yeah, like that." His thin chest puffed. "He said his dad was kind of a dinosaur with technology, and I told him how I'd got him to stop using family birthdays for his passwords."

"Mr. Wozniak used birthdays as passwords?"

Art's smile was smug. "For some he used Carina's, and for the rest he used Carson's. I told him to make a different password for each one, with numbers and special characters."

"I don't use birthdays, but I do use the same passwords a lot."

He nodded as if he could have guessed it. "They all gotta be different. If you can't remember them, make a file to keep them in. That's what I showed Mr. Wozniak how to do."

"I don't know," I said doubtfully. "If the file's on my computer and someone hacks it, all my information would be right there."

He pointed a finger at me. "He said the same thing, but you call the file something nobody would look at. 'Electric Bills' or 'My Favorite Poems'--something boring."

"That's clever."

"That's what Carson said, too."

"You told Carson about the new passwords?"

Art caught the tone of my question. "Nothing specific. I wouldn't do that."

I smiled my "How nice" smile, but if Carson had at some point hung out with Art, it wasn't because he found the tech's conversation scintillating. He'd been cut off from Daddy's money for a year, and he might have been desperate. Had he tried to dip into his father's accounts and found the passwords had been changed? That would explain Carina's anger at him, her demand that he make things right with his father.

"When did you tell Carson you'd helped his dad out?"

"That last time, just a few days before he got killed." Peering through dust-specked glasses, Art said, "Some people didn't like Carson, but he looked out for his old man, and he died trying to save his sister from that maniac she married. That shows he wasn't so bad."

Carson might have convinced a guy like Art Chalmers that his motives were pure, but I was a bit skeptical. While Art was smarter than I'd ever be about computers, I guessed he was clueless about the plotting a greedy son might do in order to get at his father's money.

CHAPTER TWENTY-FOUR

Barb

As Faye questioned Brown about his years at Buck Lake, I glanced out the window overlooking the parking lot. A man got out of a familiar-looking white Ford and started for the motel entrance. He stopped momentarily by my car, peering into it. He might have been in town for a convention at the casino, and he could have been checking out my Chevy, but I doubted it.

"Look out there."

They looked. "Haike's car," Neil said. Quickly we cleared our table and moved to the back of the dining area, out of sight of the front desk. After a few seconds Faye whispered, "I'll go see what's going on. If it's our shooter, I doubt he'll recognize me."

She was right. Today's outfit was flashy but not screaming like the lime green and pink from yesterday. In three minutes, she was back. "He's gone. The clerk told him she couldn't confirm or deny the presence of a guest."

"He accepted that?"

"Maybe." Faye peeped cautiously out the window. "He could wait outside until we leave and catch us on the open highway."

"We need to call the police."

Faye glanced at Brown, knowing what that meant. He nodded. "No more chances."

"I'll call," Faye said. "Go up to the rooms, get our stuff, and check out." Pulling out her phone, she headed outside. I guessed the call would accompany the second cigarette of the day.

I wasn't gone ten minutes. Brown was waiting for the elevator, knapsack slung over one shoulder, and we rode down together. Faye wasn't in the lobby. I went outside, but she wasn't there, either. I asked the clerk, "Did you see where my sister went?"

"She went outside. Then that guy said something to her and she left with him."

"What guy?"

"The guy that was looking for the three of you."

I felt my chest tighten. "She left with him?"

The clerk picked up the ringing phone and held it to her chest. "That's correct." Putting the phone to her ear, she began the Good-morning-and-thank-you-for-calling spiel.

My cell vibrated in my jacket pocket. Checking the screen, I saw it was Faye. "Hello?"

"Ms. Evans." The speaker's voice was breathy, as if he was on edge.

"Who are you?"

"That doesn't matter. Who I'm with is more important."

"Is my sister all right?"

"I think the term 'fat and sassy' works."

"If you hurt her—"

"I have no desire to hurt her. Once I speak with Mr. Brown, we'll see what happens."

I turned to Brown, who watched with concern on his face. "He wants to talk to you."

He took my phone, holding it as if it were a foreign object, which it probably was. "Hello?" After a few seconds his expression turned angry. "I don't know what you're talking about." Listening again, he shook his head, frustrated. "I can't give you something I don't have...Don't hurt her, she hasn't done anything."

I heard a change in the tone of his voice. "Okay, where shall we do this? ...No way. I'm not going back there so you can wait around in the woods and shoot me... How about a restaurant here in town?... I don't care who sees me... Okay, okay. Somewhere out of town, then? Do you know the area at all?... That makes it more complicated." His gaze searched the lobby and landed on a display of pamphlets near the doorway.

"How about the park at the falls? It's easy; you just follow the signs. There won't be a lot of people there this time of year." Brown glanced at me, nodding toward the rack. Scanning quickly, I pulled a glossy brochure on Tahquamenon Falls from the array and turned to the map on the back. Tahquamenon, just a few miles away, showcased one of the largest waterfalls between Niagara and the Mississippi. Skipping the tourist information and pictures of rushing water turned brown by tannins, I studied the map, committing it to memory. Brown continued to argue with the caller. "I need more time. But—" He looked blankly at the phone. "He hung up."

"What does he want?"

Suddenly we became aware of the clerk, who was leaning so far over the desk she was in danger of toppling onto the tile floor at our feet. We moved outside and out of sight of the entryway. Neil looked sick. "He says if I give him what he wants, he'll let Mrs. Burner go."

"What is it?"

"That's just it. I don't know. He said it's something Carina gave to me."

"Did she give you anything that last day, or the day before?"

He made a gentle snort. "The day before she was so mad she wouldn't have given me a glass of water if my hair was on fire. And after the thing with Carson, I don't remember her giving me anything."

"But she wasn't angry with you after you helped her calm her brother down."

"No." He ran a hand over his chin, probably unused to being clean-shaven. "She was having a bad time with whatever was wrong between them."

"She'd learned something about Carson that upset her."

"Right. She was worried how Stan would react when he found out. At one point she said, 'Carson, just tell the truth. He'll forgive you.' It sounded like she left out the word *eventually.*"

"Do you think that's true? Would Wozniak have forgiven Carson anything, given time?"

Brown sighed. "For years, Carson screwed up and his dad bailed him out, but things changed about the time we got married. I think Carina was worried about Stan's reaction."

"You got no indication of what he'd done?"

He shrugged. "Something Stan would find hard to forgive."

"From what I hear of Wozniak, that meant taking something that was his."

Neil grimaced ruefully. "Yeah. I'm the guy who'd know."

I read the meaning in his tone. "You took his little girl."

"That's how he saw it."

I stared across the parking lot, trying not to think about what might be happening to my sister. We had to figure out what her captor wanted. "Could Wozniak be behind this?"

"What do you mean?"

"He hates being cheated out of what's his, right?"

"Yeah."

"Suppose he found out Carson had cheated him. Could he have killed him in a rage?"

"Maybe by accident, if things got really hot. But what about Carina?"

"What if she tried to stop him and he struck her without knowing what he was doing?"

Neil shook his head. "Much as I'd like to give you a good substitute for me as Suspect Number One, I can't see Stan losing control like that. Not with his kids."

My mind returned to Faye, in peril and probably terrified. "What do we do now?"

"I don't know."

"You're supposed to trade this item for my sister at the falls."

Brown nodded. "I said I'd meet him on the trail, past the first viewpoint."

"Do you think we could pass something off as the item and get her back?"

"I don't even know what the thing he's after looks like." He raised his hands, palms up. "I tried to get him to give me a hint, but he was sure I knew what he wanted."

"And you have no idea."

"None." He tried a weak joke. "I should have asked if it was bigger than a breadbox."

I gave him a "not funny" glance then watched the traffic on the highway for a few seconds. "We'll have to fake it. How much time do we have?"

"Till two." I looked at my watch: a little more than four hours.

"Should we call the police?"

Neil shifted his feet. "I vote no. First, the only thing keeping Mrs. Burner alive is this guy's belief we're under his control. If the police show up, he might kill her and run."

"But police know how to deal with kidnappers."

He gestured at our distinctly rural surroundings. "Up here in the middle of nowhere? I doubt it. The locals are likely to be so excited about getting to arrest me that anything else we try to tell them will get lost."

I had to agree. Brown was supposedly a double murderer, and no police officer I'd met thus far had found reason to doubt his guilt. I was someone they didn't know, a middle-aged woman claiming to be a private investigator. Would the police put off arresting one of Michigan's most sought-after fugitives on my word alone? I'd always thought of the police as friends, but I had to rethink that in this instance.

"If we don't call for help, what do you suggest?"

"Not sure." He scratched his head. "If I knew what he wants, he could have it."

That seemed to be the place to start unraveling the problem. "Okay. Think carefully about that last day. Did Carina give you anything at all?" As he opened his mouth to repeat his earlier negative, I put up a cautioning hand. "Think. Not something she said was important. Maybe not anything that seemed related to what was going on. Just something."

Seeing my purpose, Brown closed his eyes, letting himself go over the events of that day. Several moments passed before he spoke. "Ultrasound pictures of our baby."

"Pictures?"

"Not actual pictures. They were on a flash drive. As I was leaving, she stuck it in my jacket pocket, said something about the latest baby pictures. I almost gave it back, since I didn't have a computer at my rental. I figured she'd get mad if I mentioned it, so I said okay and left."

"Did you look at the pictures?"

"Never got the chance."

"Do you have the flash drive?"

He thought about it. "I kept it in my pocket for a long time. It reminded me of her and the baby we would have had—." His voice softened as he remembered the baby had actually come into the world. He tried her name on his tongue. "Brooke."

"Where is the drive now?"

He twitched his shoulders, shaking off the past. "When I moved into Haike's lodge, I set it on a rafter that runs over the doorway. You wouldn't notice it, but it's there."

"Neil, that might be what this guy is looking for."

"Why?"

"It has something on it Carina wanted you to hold for her."

The light dawned. "Whatever she had on her brother."

"It might have been her insurance that he'd do as he promised."

His face lit as he figured it out. "If I had the evidence, he couldn't change his mind."

"It has to be what the kidnapper wants." I considered the possibilities for a few seconds. "Take my vehicle, go back to the cabin, get the flash, and bring it to the park. I'll rent a car and go there so I can scout the territory a little. We need to avoid surprises."

Brown looked at me doubtfully. "I didn't mean for you to get involved in this. I can go alone. I'll get Mrs. Burner back somehow, but both of you shouldn't be in danger."

Gesturing at a rack of gift items just inside the motel door I said, "I'll buy some tacky clothes and carry a camera, like a tourist. You need someone to watch your back, and if I get out there, I can make sure there's just the one guy." He still looked unwilling, but I gave him what I hoped was a confident smile. "Just get that drive and return as fast as you can."

"Okay." He grinned, and I saw a hint of the brother Meri Brown was so fond of. "I don't have a current license to drive, but it hasn't been an issue in the last six years."

As I handed over the car keys, I struggled with doubts. Once the kidnapper got the drive, he might try to kill all of us. Did I have the right to put Neil in danger in order to get my sister back? Should I call the local police and report a possible crime at Tahquamenon Falls?

In the end I decided Neil was right. The police were likely to scare the guy away, with deadly results for Faye. There'd be rangers on duty at Tahquamenon, and while they weren't trained cops, they'd come running if our bad guy started shooting.

"Mr. Brown?" I said as he turned to go. "Bring a gun back with you, a pistol, if you've got one. I don't have much experience with deer rifles."

CHAPTER TWENTY-FIVE

Retta

I called Dale the morning after my visit to WOZ Industries. My sisters were still away, but I got him to admit they were in the U.P. He insisted he didn't know their exact location, and I thought he was mostly telling the truth. I tried calling them, but Barbara Ann seldom answers her cell if she knows it's me, and Faye always shuts hers down to save on the battery, no matter how many times I tell her it's silly to have a phone that doesn't connect.

When I thanked Dale and hung up, I was feeling like a little kid again. I wrote down everything I'd learned so far in an email and sent it to Faye, hoping she'd see I was contributing. Even then, it didn't feel like I'd done enough to really impress them.

What else was there? I'd spoken with Stanley and visited his employees. I didn't dare go back to Susie with more questions, though she knew more than she admitted. Who else might know something about the old case?

When I can't decide what to do, it helps to get out of my empty house and go mobile. I changed my clothes, put on a little makeup, and went into town, planning nothing in particular. When it seemed my only option was a touch-up to my nails, I saw our new police chief exit the city building. A double possibility! Not only might he have information on the Wozniak case, he was really cute. I parked—almost abandoned—my car and hurried over to his.

"Chief Neuencamp?"

"Yes." His back was to me, and his tone was merely polite until he turned. I can't help it. I love that change that occurs somewhere behind the eyes when a man appreciates me as a woman. Subtle things happen: pot bellies recede a little, shoulders straighten, and eyes drop. The time it takes for his gaze to return to her face lets a woman know what kind of man she's facing.

This one got back to business quickly. "What can I do for you, Mrs., uh, ma'am?"

Now, I might have overlooked his forgetting my name after just one meeting, but *ma'am* is not my favorite term of address. The first time a clerk used it on me, I almost left the store. When did I stop being *Miss*? Though Barbara disagrees, I prefer *Honey* or *Sweetie* to *Ma'am*, which sounds *old!* With my best forgiving smile, I prompted, "I'm Margaretta Stilson."

"Oh, yeah. After our, um, meeting, I got to thinking. Are you related to—"

I stepped in to speed things up. "My late husband."

"That was a terrible thing, his getting shot." I lowered my lashes, but his keys jingled in his hand. He was trying to be polite, but he wanted me to state my business.

"If you're on your way to lunch, may I join you? There are things I'd like to discuss."

Was it a woman asking a strange man to have lunch with her that surprised him, or the fact that I had an agenda? After the slightest pause he said, "If you don't mind driving your own car. I'm due at the County Commission meeting at one. Is Barney's all right with you?"

Barney's was on the lowbrow end of Allport's dining choices, but there was nothing wrong with the food. I guessed its utilitarian aspect would minimize gossip about the new chief dining with an attractive widow. At least as much as gossip in a small town is ever minimized.

When I arrived a few minutes behind him, the chief rose gallantly and held my chair. It's a charming custom, but my theory is it's designed to give a man a good, long look at a woman's backside. Not that Neuencamp seemed that type, but you never know.

Once he sat down again, a waitress brought us menus. I asked for iced tea; he ordered a Coke. She recommended the special, and I listened, because whatever Barney says is special on a given day usually is. Today it was a panini, however. Too messy for a first-time meal with a man. I chose a salad, and the chief ordered the French dip. With fries. He must have a great metabolism to stay trim at his age with all that fat and calories.

"What's on your mind, Ms. Stilson?" he asked when the waitress had retreated, menus under one arm and gum cracking at full power.

So he wasn't much for small talk. "I mentioned my sisters, Chief. May I call you Rory?"

"Of course."

"I'm Retta. As I told you, they run a detective agency here in town." Pressing my lips together as a little rebellious streak rose I said, "I sometimes help with their cases."

He took the straw out of his drink, set it aside, and took a long swallow. "I met Barb."

"Really?" Ms. Hermit already knew the new man in town?

"A couple of times now." I couldn't tell what he thought of her, but it was probably negative. Barbara Ann comes off as cold, at least that's what I've heard. I hoped she hadn't alienated the new chief already. Making no excuses for her, I forged ahead.

"We're looking into a cold case. I arranged help from the state police detective who was lead on it, and Faye spoke with Tom Stevens, but I wonder if there might be something in the old chief's files that could help. I mean, Kowaleski probably kept his own notes, right?"

"Most of us do." Neither of us mentioned the sad fact that the old chief's stuff was probably still in the office. There'd been no one to give it to when he died.

The waitress set down a little tub of coleslaw for Rory and a breadstick for me. The one thing that separates Barney's from other diners is the breadstick. Although I'm sure they go directly to my hips, I cannot resist them. I tore the warm, buttery thing in half and took a bite.

"If I stop by after your meeting, do you think I could get a look at those notes?"

His eyes crinkled briefly. "Tell you what. I'll review them tonight. Tomorrow I'll share what I think can be shared." His hands spread in a gesture that said it was the best he would do.

I know men, know when there's one I can't charm into bending his principles—at least not so early in a relationship. "That's very kind of you." Taking up the rest of my breadstick, I asked, "How did you come to northern Michigan from Chicago?"

The rest of the lunch was pleasant. Rory was certainly attractive, and he revealed polite interest in me without stooping to condescension, flattery, or drooling. He was the type a woman of mature age doesn't often meet in a small town, and I left feeling good about the future.

I was slightly disappointed that I had to wait until morning to learn what was in Kowaleski's notes. The upside to the matter, of course, would be visiting Rory again to find out.

There was lots of day left, so I searched my brain for a person with an inside view of the Wozniak family dynamic at the time of the murders. The police hadn't uncovered a suspect other than Neil Brown, but honestly, they hadn't looked very hard. Someone had to know what Carina really thought of her husband. I just had to figure out who that someone was.

CHAPTER TWENTY-SIX

Barb

As soon as Brown left, I asked at the motel desk about car rental. As the clerk began the process of finding me a vehicle, I tried on a hat from the souvenir rack that said I LOVE DA U.P. Pairing that with a sweatshirt picturing the falls, I added one of those disposable cameras as a prop.

When the rental car was delivered to the hotel, I headed to Tahquamenon, looking like Clark Griswold's mother. The area was waking up to spring. I passed beautiful chalets and rustic lodges where visitors to the falls could stay, play, and, of course, gamble. The U.P. has plenty of casinos. Apparently, love of nature and lucky numbers go hand-in-hand.

Though the roadside was dotted with clumps of green, pine and cedar, the maple, beech and oak trees were just sprouting leaves. Without nature's cover, I also saw the faded hopes and dreams of a multitude of property owners: failed motels, aging cabins, and boarded businesses. FOR SALE signs hung from mailbox posts, fences, and trees. Michigan's tough economy had turned second homes and summer businesses into luxuries many could no longer afford.

At the entrance to Tahquamenon State Park, I paid the entry fee and proceeded, noting the unexpected presence of a microbrewery on park property. *Unusual in a state park*, I thought as I turned left and parked. My vehicle had the lot all to itself, and the sound of my door slamming echoed in the silence. A pickup truck sat next to the restroom building, and lights shone inside. At least I wasn't totally alone.

Following the signs, I made my way to the main trail, which led to a cross-trail where more signs informed me that the Upper Falls were to the right, the Lower Falls to the left. We hadn't thought of that. How preposterous would it be if we missed getting my sister back because we went in the opposite direction the kidnapper did!

After a short trek to the left I came to a wooden staircase that descended to the rushing water. Turning, I went back and followed the trail to the Lower Falls. The rushing water made a constant roar, and I glimpsed its swirling movement between the trees. A sturdy wood fence kept visitors on the trail and away from the abrupt drop-off.

Not far along the path I came to a second set of steps that led to a different viewing area. It was ninety-four steps down, according to the sign. A boast or a warning?

Leaning over the banister, I surveyed the view below. A boxed overhang at the waterline provided a perfect photo op for tourists, the falls at one side and the forest across the river a charming backdrop. I was briefly mesmerized by the sheer power of the rushing, churning water. It was hard to tear my gaze away, but I wasn't here to appreciate nature's power.

What I wanted was a place to hide so I could cover Brown while he exchanged the flash drive for my sister. After exploring the trail from all directions, I chose a likely spot where I could follow, whichever way they went. If Neil brought me a gun, I'd be close enough to shoot the kidnapper if necessary. Could I actually do it? Yes, if it meant my sister's life.

Hoping I had an advantage now that I knew the terrain, I started back to the parking lot. There was a lot to worry about, and I'm good at it. Was Faye all right, or had the man killed her and thrown her body into the deep Michigan woods? Would Neil return, having a vehicle and a head start? And even if those two questions were answered my way, did I have time to get the gun from Neil and get to my chosen hiding spot before the kidnapper arrived?

As I left the trees, I saw that it was too late. Next to my car sat a dirty white Ford. My heart sank. I didn't have the gun; I didn't have Neil's help; I didn't have the flash drive. I had no way to bargain for my sister's life.

As I came closer, however, the lone figure leaning against the car became clearer, and my shoulders relaxed. It was Faye, smoking a cigarette and looking very grumpy.

"Faye!" I hurried forward as she stubbed the butt against the sole of her shoe.

"Hi."

I am not a frequent hugger, but I embraced her, biting my lip to control the tears of relief that threatened. "How did you get away?"

She pulled away and faced me, one eyebrow raised in comic disgust. "It was only one guy, Barb, and not a very smart one at that." I pulled out a tissue and wiped my nose, running from relief this time, not from allergies. "Come on," she said. "I'll introduce you."

She took keys from her pocket, checked the area for onlookers, and, seeing none, opened the trunk. A head popped up. At a nod from Faye, the occupant clambered out, an embarrassed grin on his face. I stared in disbelief as he brushed dust from his jeans, settled his clothes into place, and pushed back straight blond hair that fell back over his eyes as soon as it was released.

"Barb, meet Gabe."

"Are you the one who shot at us?"

"No." His tone was definite. "You gotta understand. I had *no* idea he'd start shooting."

Faye regarded him as if he were a carpet stain. "Apparently Gabe has a partner."

The little man made an objection-like noise, but she glared him down. "Gabe *had* an *associate* who fired at us. He thinks the guy has since returned to Allport."

"He left me!" Gabe's tone was outraged, as if he thought we'd commiserate.

"Left you?"

"Yeah, the chicken-sh—"

"Tell her what you're doing up here." Faye's tone revealed irritation. Gabe nodded obediently.

"We was hired to follow you ladies and see if you found that Brown guy. We was supposed to get a certain piece of property back that he stole from our employer. I thought it was cool when you found him, but then, Z—my associate—pulls out a gun and starts blastin' away."

He paused to let me absorb that much, clicking his tongue in disgust. "I almost sh—I mean, I was real scared when you guys fired back. I'm non-violent, y'know?" He actually raised two fingers in a sign of peace not often seen since the '60s. "It was s'pose to be a simple job. Find Brown; take our employer's property back; get paid."

"So what went wrong?"

Gabe looked to Faye, didn't like what he saw, and turned back to me. For once, I was the more sympathetic listener, perhaps because I wasn't the one who'd been kidnapped. Actually, Gabe reminded me of a succession of low-level, low-wattage but not necessarily evil criminals I'd dealt with over the years. They don't mean to be mean, and they spill their guts within minutes of being caught.

"We was supposed to wait until you two left then go after Brown and get the thing-y."

Faye took a drag on her cigarette. "Apparently the mysterious Z is not so non-violent as Gabe here. Must have thought putting a few rounds through the cabin would send us running."

"He got nervous," Gabe defended his associate's action. "You ladies stayed in there a long time. He had to do something."

"Associate Z did not expect return fire," Faye rubbed her chin lightly, perhaps to banish a smile. "Apparently, he panicked and ran—*drove* away, rather, leaving Gabe behind."

"He shoulda stayed. I mean, we weren't gonna get paid if we didn't come back with the thing-y." Gabe stuck out a hand, turning it palm up in a gesture that implied his next move was obvious. "I figure Z's out of the picture, so the money's all mine if I get what we came for."

"So you kidnapped my sister."

Gabe looked at the pavement. "I wouldna hurt her. I needed something to trade, is all."

"And the object of all this? The thing-y you were supposed to get?"

"It's a flash drive." Gabe didn't seem sure what that was. "Our guy wants it back."

"And who is this guy?"

He shrugged. "Well, when I say I know him, I don't mean I really *know* him. He's somebody Z knows."

"Did you get a name?"

"Uh, no."

"Can you describe him?"

Gabe looked nervous. "I only talked to him on the phone, but Zack said he was cool."

"So some guy feeds you this story and you believe it? You follow two innocent women to the U.P., shoot up a cabin, and kidnap one of them, all on the word of a voice on the phone?"

"The guy killed his wife, didn't he? Besides, the dude gave us each five hundred up front and promised five hundred more when we brought back the thing-y."

"I see. A thousand bucks buys a lot of credulity."

"Huh?"

"Does your employer know you decided to try kidnapping?"

Gabe chewed at a fingernail. "Uh, yeah. He wasn't thrilled to hear it."

"But if you get the flash drive, it will be okay?"

"Yeah." He pointed at Faye, almost accusingly. "She walked right into it. I mean, she comes outside to smoke. There's nobody around. I had to take a chance or lose the money."

"He threw my phone into a ditch after he called you." Faye glared at Gabe as she added, "I *hate* getting used to a new phone."

"I'm *sorry*." He sounded sincere, as if telephonic interruption topped kidnapping.

I got back to business. "Your employer expects you to return to Allport with this drive."

"I would have, too, except she attacked me." Faye clicked her tongue and rolled her eyes skyward. "She hit me with her purse."

He sounded like a kid tattling on a playmate, but he was right. Faye's purse should be registered as a lethal weapon.

"You set the pathetic jackknife you waved at me on the seat," Faye said coolly. "In that situation I'm supposed to be afraid of a guy who weighs a third less than I do?"

I hid a smile, picturing her turning on the pipsqueak. Though I'd never seen her tough side, I'd guessed there was one. Women who raise teenage boys develop a certain fearlessness.

Faye rolled her neck side to side. "Genius here has the impression there's something valuable on this flash drive, industrial secrets, maybe. I think he's told us all he knows."

"Yeah. He wants it back real bad. Your guy stole it, so I was justicated in using force."

"*Justified*, and no, you weren't. You shot at us."

"I told you, it wasn't me." He shivered at the memory. "I couldn't believe he did that."

"So what did you do after your associate ran away like the coward he is?"

"Besides calling him every bad name I could think of?" He looked from Faye to me, but neither of us reacted to his attempt at humor. "I stayed down and quiet. When you all piled into the Chevy and left, I searched the cabin." He shrugged. "Didn't find it."

"You thought we'd run and not take this valuable flash drive with us?" I asked.

Gabe shrugged again. Apparently he was good at it. "I guess so."

Faye raised her brows. "Gabe operates on the premise that everyone in the world thinks exactly as he does."

After wiping his nose on a knuckle, he said, "There was this old car with the keys in it, and I figured I'd see if I could find you. I mean what's north except Paradise? I had to drive around town for a long time, but then I saw your car at the motel."

"Should have hidden it," I muttered, and Gabe nodded, acknowledging my mistake.

"How many '57 Chevys does a guy see in a day? I hung around, thinking I could make things right with the boss." Jabbing a finger at Faye, he said, "She comes outside, and I decide to be a entrepreneur." He was proud of the four-syllable word, though he said "ahn ter PEN yur." Resentment returned as he added, "Who knew I had a couple over-the-hill Charlie's Angels?"

"What do we do with him?" I asked Faye.

She appeared to want to smack him but said instead, "We take him back to Allport."

I pulled her aside, whispering, "Faye, that's kidnapping."

"He kidnapped me first!"

"That doesn't justify us doing the same thing."

"You mean 'justicate' it?" She sighed. "You're probably right."

I eyed Gabe, who gave no sign of thinking about an escape. If we had him arrested here, we'd lose track of him, and the local police would take Neil into custody as well.

"Tell you what. I'll do my lawyer bit on him. If he doesn't agree to come back with us and tell his story, we'll risk the kidnapping charge."

CHAPTER TWENTY-SEVEN

Retta

Yet another call to Dale revealed that Barbara and Faye had run into something and had to stay in the U.P. a while longer. He sounded a little fuzzy on the details, but that might have been because she'd told him not to give me any.

The clock at the bank read one-fifteen when I ended the call. I ran through a mental list of people who might have known Carina Wozniak Brown well enough to provide hints to her personality. One good prospect came to mind: the beauty salon. When you spend hours with a person on a regular basis, grateful for their ministrations and lulled by the pampering you receive, it's easy to let secrets slip out. I didn't know who Carina's stylist had been, but my own stylist would. It was time to touch up my nails after all.

The Hair Place had expanded its offerings a few years back. Patsy, the owner, took out one of the chairs, reduced her staff by one, and hired a Vietnamese woman who performs magic on fingers and toes. I had to wait, having no appointment, but that was all to the good, because as I chatted with Patsy, apparently aimlessly, I found out what I wanted to know.

"She didn't get her hair done here," she told me, raising brows as thin as copper wire. "Drove all the way to Dorville, to some foreigner." Patsy glanced at Mei, the manicurist, who made no sign she'd heard. It always appeared Mei's English wasn't good, though there were times when I suspected she understood everything. It was probably better to pretend ignorance around Patsy, to whom the only real American is one who shares her religion, her skin tone, her views on NASCAR, and her fanatical devotion to Toby Keith.

I don't agree with her views, of course, but it's never a good idea to upset a competent stylist once you've found one.

It was just after two when I left the salon. An hour to Dorville. I could easily find the shop before closing. I hoped the unknown French woman took walk-ins.

CHAPTER TWENTY-EIGHT

Barb

The battle of wits with Gabe wasn't much of a challenge. Within three minutes he'd agreed to go back to Allport with us and tell his story. Though I made it clear he'd face charges, I offered to leave out the kidnapping part. He was almost pathetically grateful.

Brown arrived, having found the flash drive and hurried back to rescue Faye. He was as surprised as I'd been to find her unharmed, in fact, triumphant. Once all was explained again, we discussed how to proceed. Duty demanded we take Brown to Allport, but I didn't know how to tell him that, or Faye either, for that matter. He was a step ahead of me.

"I've got to go back," he said. "Maybe this thing has something on it that will clear me."

"You should take a look before we go," Faye said, and I agreed. We had to know.

We had no device with us capable of reading a flash drive, so we went in search of the nearest library. While Faye chaperoned Gabe, Brown and I entered and asked to use a computer. After listening to the library rules for use, showing I.D., and signing a form promising not to visit porn sites or engage in internet gambling, we were shown to an aged PC.

I inserted the flash into the machine and listened as it engaged with a soft whirr. There were several files on the drive, some .exe and others .doc. Ignoring the former, I hovered over the names of the four .doc files. Each had last been accessed the day before Carson and Carina Wozniak were murdered.

Starting with the topmost one, *Fishing,* I clicked to open the file. It contained links to various sites, and I looked to Neil for an explanation. "Stan's only hobby." Pointing at one link, he said, "I think that's the place he was planning to try that year at Christmas time." Indicating another link he said, "And that's where he went the year before."

"So these are probably Wozniak's files. Any idea why your wife had them on her flash?"

He frowned at the drive sticking out of the USB port, the WOZ Industries logo imprinted on its casing. "Carina had a drive like this, but hers just had pictures on it."

I thought about Carina's house guest. "Did Carson have one?"

"Stan might have given him one. He bought them by the gross."

"And they all looked exactly alike?"

He nodded. "You get a discount that way."

Closing that file, I went to the next, *Pierce.* It contained information about the lake where Stan's house was located: depths, dimensions, and other specifics. Looking again to Neil, I got a shrug. We saw nothing interesting, though it added to my belief these were Wozniak's files.

The next one was labeled *Water Bills, 2002.* I clicked on it and got a list consisting of four lines. Each began with initials: AM, MT, CI, *and* NYCT, followed by dollar amounts and notations, *UsageQ1, UsageQ2,* and so on. I guessed that *Q* stood for quarter.

"Does this mean anything to you?"

"Nope."

The last file was named *Cinfo*. When I opened it, I saw a list titled *Carson's Investments*. There were eight listings, each describing a project Carson had proposed, the amount he'd been given, and the results in dollars. All of the final amounts were negative. I pictured Stan printing the list off and waving it in front of his son's face while he promised there'd be no more money.

After I closed the file, Neil and I stared at the screen for a while, contemplating the titles of the files we'd just examined. None of them gave me a clue as to what had happened. None of them contained information worth stealing or killing for, as far as I could tell. Pocketing the drive, I said, "It would have been nice to find something simple. I guess we'd better go."

He seemed reluctant to leave, probably disappointed the flash contained nothing that proved his innocence. Even if he was eventually cleared of murder charges, he had a lot to face between now and then. And if he wasn't cleared, he was on his way to prison, probably for life. I gave him what I hoped was an encouraging smile. "If you're innocent, Mr. Brown, we'll prove it. Faye wants Brooke to get her daddy back." He smiled grimly, compliant but not convinced.

We left the library and rejoined Faye and her captive, who was wheedling unsuccessfully for a soda and some Cheetos.

Taking Faye aside, I told her what we'd seen on the flash drive. "What would Wozniak's reaction have been if he learned someone stole some files from his home computer?"

"If it was Neil, he'd have had him arrested."

"What if Carina or Carson did it?"

"Why would they?"

I wasn't sure, but I was convinced one of Stan's children had put those files on the flash. Either had plenty of opportunity and would have known Stan's habits. "I don't know about the son, but Carina had given her husband an ultimatum, and he moved out rather than bow to Stan's wishes. Maybe she thought if they had money, she could have Neil and the life she wanted."

"Then why the murders?"

"Maybe one of them found out what the other was doing. That could have led to the fight Neil interrupted. And maybe after he left, it started up again."

"That would explain one death, but not two," Faye argued.

"You're right." I sighed. "At least the long drive will give us time to think it through."

We decided Brown, Faye, and Gabe would take Brown's car back to Allport while I drove my own. Gabe had a cell phone, as did I, so we could communicate if we got separated. Faye would drive and Brown would, ironically, guard the prisoner lest he decide to bolt. Hitting the "Go home" button on my GPS, I followed its flat-voiced commands, checking the mirror often to assure that Faye was safe in the driver's seat of the other car.

CHAPTER TWENTY-NINE

Retta

The shop was called *Entrez*, and the French theme was carried out everywhere: white, lacy furniture, draped pastel curtains, and prints of Paris landmarks on the wall. The stylist's name was Simone. Her French accent was real, though Michigan-isms had crept into her vocabulary over the twenty years she'd been here.

Claiming I had to attend a funeral, I asked for a trim. Eyeing me critically over the wet head of her current customer, Simone said, "Return in twenty minutes. I will fit you in."

After browsing a couple of over-priced clothing stores, I returned. The customer was putting on her glasses as Simone swept up clumps of gray hair littering the floor. Soon I was in the chair, and she stood behind me as we both faced the mirror. "A trim, you say?"

"Not more than half an inch." I didn't want Patsy to suspect I'd gone to another stylist. "This funeral is unexpected, but I want to look my best."

Simone raised her brows briefly, which I interpreted as irritation. She probably wanted to try something creative with my hair, which stylists often tell me is perfect to work with: full-bodied, thick, and with just enough curl to make it easy to style.

Choosing her tools, she wet a section with a squirt bottle and began clipping the hair into manageable blocks. I waited for a question, and it wasn't long in coming. "Where do you live?"

I had my story ready. "Detroit, but I'm staying at a cabin near Allport, on Pierce Lake."

"Ah, yes. I once had a customer who lived on that lake." Her eyes met mine in the mirror. "I thought her family owned it."

"Someone owns most of it," I responded. "There's a huge house on the opposite side that looks like something from *Architectural Digest*."

She chuckled. "That sounds right. Her father is quite concerned with money, I think."

"And is she as concerned with it as her father?"

Simone pressed her lips together for a second. "She died."

"Oh. I'm sorry to hear it."

Hairdressers are great listeners, but to whom do they ever get to talk? I was the perfect candidate: a stranger to tell an old story to. "She was murdered by her husband."

"How awful!"

"Yes." For a few seconds there was only the grind of scissor blades meeting. Bits of hair fell onto the plastic cape over my shoulders. I tried not to shudder. "I was surprised, you know?" Her sentences ended with the Gallic rise, and *you know?* might well have been *n'est pas?* "I thought he was crazy for her. But maybe that was it, you know? Maybe a little too crazy."

"You met him?"

"He came in on her first visit. After that, he would wait in the car. She said he was silly about her pregnancy, but I think she liked that he worried about her."

"So you were surprised when he killed her?"

"Who knows which of us is capable of such a thing?" Simone said philosophically. "But he seemed...gentle, even in dirty jeans and work boots."

"She married a working man? I thought you said her dad was rich."

Simone chuckled. "This girl, she was like a matador, and her father was the bull."

"She goaded him."

"That is the word. Her father wanted her to marry someone in his business. Instead she chose this construction worker, very handsome, but not a man for the suit and tie, you know?"

"You think she chose—" I caught myself and didn't use Brown's name. "—this guy because her father disapproved?"

She thought about it. "I think she loved him as much as a spoiled girl can love anybody."

"That's good."

She snipped for a while then said thoughtfully, "The last time she came here, she said they would move to Detroit soon. He didn't want to, but she said he would do as she wanted."

"And that's why he killed her?"

A shrug. "The TV said they fought. Her brother was there, and he was killed, too."

I was thinking back to something she'd said earlier. "Her father wanted her to marry someone else? Someone who worked for him?"

"His 'right-hand toad,' she called him."

Carina might have said *toady*, but there wasn't much difference. Eric DuBois was Stan's right-hand man. Had she rejected DuBois because she didn't like him, or because Stanley did?

After tipping Simone generously for not butchering my hair, I drove back to Allport, my mind digesting and dissecting what I'd learned. Stanley Wozniak had hoped for a connection between his daughter and Eric, but Carina chose Neil, married Neil, and became pregnant with Neil's baby. It seemed highly unlikely DuBois would have waited a year then killed Carina to frame Neil. What would it have accomplished? No girl, no fortune, no in with the boss. Unless he was a lunatic, DuBois gained nothing. I knew Faye wouldn't like it, but Neil Brown was still the most likely candidate for life in prison

CHAPTER THIRTY

Barb

We took the eastern leg of 123 southward to I-75, just north of St. Ignace. Soon we saw the Mackinac Bridge towering gracefully over the straits. I wondered how Faye would do driving across, since she usually shuts her eyes on the section where grid-work makes a car sway and rumble. She handled it well, probably unwilling to show weakness in Gabe's presence.

We planned to go directly to the police department, where Neil would surrender himself. Faye and I would introduce Gabe and tell the part of the story we could attest to. Nobody expected Neil would be set free immediately, but we had to begin somewhere.

It was almost five o'clock when we arrived at the Allport P.D. Tom Stevens was surprisingly calm at the appearance of his longest-sought suspect, but word spread quickly. Soon people began passing his office door, moving in slow motion as they tried to get a look at us. Several city employees invented reasons to collect in the hallway. Tom frowned at them intermittently as he listened and tried to look as if he had an open mind.

"You understand I'm taking you into custody," he told Neil when we finished.

"Yes, sir."

Tom fell into his old lecturing way. "You gave the legal system a lot of headaches, son."

"It was a mistake to run," Neil agreed. "Because I wasn't here, nobody looked for the person who really killed my wife. If I'd told my side of it, maybe he'd have been caught."

"Or you'd have gone to prison," Faye put in. I hoped she wouldn't start telling Tom his job, though I had to admit, his obvious assumption Neil was guilty made me nervous.

Brown seemed resigned as he was taken for processing, an officer on either side. Once he left, Stevens turned to us. "Not wise, going up there on your own."

"We weren't sure it was actually him."

"Well, you were lucky. He coulda hit you both over the head like he did his wife."

"You don't know he did that."

Stevens folded his hands on the desk. "Faye, you've seen the evidence against him."

Her voice rose a notch, and I sensed trouble ahead. "Why did someone send Gabe here to follow us up there and steal a flash drive from Neil?"

Her question reminded Tom of the other player present. "Oh, yeah." Without moving, Gabe seemed to shrink into his chair. "Mr. Wills is acquainted with the Allport P.D., ain't you?"

Gabe didn't answer. He seemed to find the floor tiles really interesting.

"That doesn't make his story less credible," Faye insisted. "He had no reason to follow us except that someone hired him to see if we found Neil."

Stevens rubbed both cheeks with a beefy, spread hand. "*If* some guy hired Mr. Sleazy here, it only proves somebody was interested in finding Brown. If old Gabe went off the deep end and started shooting, he's in big trouble."

Gabe found his voice. "I told you, my associate did the shooting."

"A person you refuse to name and who probably doesn't exist."

He seemed insulted at the slur on his honesty. "He does too!"

Faye interrupted before Gabe could go into his story again. "And the flash drive?"

"Maybe somebody thinks it has evidence against Brown on it."

"By somebody you mean Stan Wozniak." Faye's tone was as sharp.

"I didn't say that."

"You didn't have to."

There it was. Stevens believed Stan Wozniak had hired Gabe Wills to follow us. Any deeper purpose would not be considered. With a warning glance to Faye, I rose from my chair. Her neck was splotched with red, which meant she was furious, but she followed my lead.

"Thank you, Officer Stevens." I was almost as frustrated as my sister. Somewhere along the line, I'd become convinced Neil was innocent, but Stevens pooh-poohed the whole idea. Could he not see there was something going on that needed investigation?

No. He'd gladly take the credit for apprehending a suspect who'd eluded the law for years, and he was unwilling to complicate the accepted story with possible alternatives.

As we left, Faye blew out a breath of frustration. "You know he'll charge Gabe with stalking or something and ignore the rest of it."

"We're going to appeal to a higher power."

"What?"

"The new chief is a former Chicago police officer. He won't have preconceived ideas of this case, and he's got more investigative experience than the rest of the department put together." I paused. "And there's one other thing that might make him want to help us."

"What's that?"

"When we had dinner the other evening, he mentioned that he finds me attractive." I left my sister wide-eyed and gasping as I turned toward the car, hiding a grin I couldn't suppress.

CHAPTER THIRTY-ONE

Retta

I arrived at the chief's office at eight-fifteen the next morning, time enough to let Rory settle in but hoping to catch him before anyone else got in the way.

"Mrs. Stilson," he said as I entered. Since a couple of deputies were present, it seemed we were going to keep things businesslike.

"Chief." I nodded to the others. "Did you have a chance to look into that matter?"

"I did." His glance took in my outfit, chosen carefully to be attractive without seeming overly planned. "Please, come on back."

The room he led me to wasn't inviting, even if the inhabitant was. The dingy-yellow walls were scraped and scratched by years of wear. There was almost no furniture, just a battered desk, an office chair with cracks in its leather back, and two straight chairs for guests. "They're going to paint," he said apologetically. "I decided not to move my stuff in until they finish."

"If you'd like a female perspective, I could help with color and fabric choices," I offered. "Just a few little things can really brighten things, but I know men are no good at that."

"It's nice of you to offer." He had his back to me, and I couldn't see his face, but his voice seemed a shade cooler. "Coffee?"

Surprisingly good coffee came from a complicated-looking machine behind his desk. After I'd complimented the blend, he dropped a bombshell. "I suppose you know we have Neil Brown in custody, since it was your sisters who brought him in."

Adjusting my jacket to give myself a moment, I wondered if I should admit they hadn't told me. He'd wonder why I wasn't in on such big news. "I haven't spoken to them since they left for the U.P. You know how many dead spots there are up there."

"I see." It couldn't tell from his tone how much he did see, but he left it alone. "Do you still want to know what was in Kowaleski's notes?" He stumbled over the Polish pronunciation.

"It's Kuh-vuh-LES-ski, but we called him K. And, yes. It might help us wrap things up."

Consulting a notebook lying open before him, he said, "I found it interesting that Kow—uh, K, thought one witness was lying. He said something didn't ring true in her statements."

"Sue Mason." When he looked up, surprised at my deductive powers, I added, "A woman can tell when another woman has a thing for a man. If Brown was in trouble, she'd try to help."

"K thought she probably saw Brown before he took off."

"The truck at the dispatch office."

Rory nodded. "K figured she didn't know anything specific, so he dropped it."

I picked at a sliver of wood sticking out from the desk corner. Rory frowned, so I put my hands in my lap. "Sue's a good person. At worst, she told Brown the police were after him, maybe urged him to run. It's what someone with a soft spot for an old flame might do."

He looked down at the notebook again. "He wasn't willing to ruin her reputation because she showed bad judgment that made no difference in the end."

A soft knock interrupted, and a young officer stuck his head in. "Sorry, Chief, but you told me to let you know. They're here."

"Thanks, Gates." Rory rose, signaling he had other things to do.

I meant to thank him and slip out, promising we'd get together again soon, but I stopped dead when I saw who'd come to speak with the new chief.

CHAPTER THIRTY-TWO

Faye

Arranging to meet Barb outside the chief's office at 8:30, I went in early to visit Neil Brown. He'd been put in the tiny cell the city uses to hold prisoners until arrangements are made for whatever comes next. After reading the email Retta had sent summarizing what she learned in our absence, I wanted to clarify some things with Neil.

Despite the fact that the cell was completely open and eight feet from the doorway, the guy on duty made a big deal of asking formally if Neil wanted to talk to me. He almost smiled as he gave assent. At first we talked about food and rest and what he might need me to bring him. The deputy soon lost interest, and I turned to what I really wanted to know.

"Where did you leave your truck when you went to see Carina that day?"

"On the street," Neil answered. "There was a spot right in front. Why?"

"That's a point for us," I said. "The man Wozniak saw left on foot. My sister checked it out, and she says he couldn't have seen you clearly from where he was."

"He couldn't have seen me at all," Neil said. "I was long gone by the time he got there."

"But don't you get it? It proves he's mistaken."

He gave me a reproachful look. "Do you think he'd ever admit that?"

"No." We fell silent, and the sounds of the room broke into my focus. The phone rang. Feet shuffled. The deputy spoke to someone about a missing bicycle. Everyday stuff, but nothing was everyday for Neil, locked in, suspected of murder, and unable to do anything about it.

No doubt he regretted coming back to Allport. Overnight he'd gone pale under his tan and his eyes looked sunken. I promised myself we'd try harder to clear him. But how?

"I've been thinking about the files on that drive," he said. "Something on it isn't what it appears to be. Otherwise, why were those guys so anxious to get it?"

"Kidnapping is a pretty drastic step."

"Gabe wanted the money, but the person who sent him for it is afraid."

"Of what?"

He shrugged. "That it'll prove I'm innocent, maybe?"

"Because if you are, the police will start looking for someone else."

He nodded. "Three of the files make sense to me. Stan might keep track of fishing spots and information on Pierce Lake. The one listing Carson's failures is like him, too. Keeping track of what the kid cost him."

"And the fourth?"

"That's the odd one."

"Because it lists old water bills?"

"Because Stan doesn't get water bills. He's got a well."

I hadn't thought of that. "We plan to show the drive to Chief Neuencamp this morning. We'll see what we can come up with together."

Neil made a doubtful grimace. "I hope the chief's more willing to listen than Stevens was." His eyelids drooped. "Meri visited last night. I told her not to come back."

Recalling what Neil didn't yet know, that his sister was facing life-threatening surgery, I faked a confident smile, assured him we were on the case, and left him in that awful place.

I was still thinking about my talk with Neil when we got to the chief's office. Barb seemed to get stuck in the doorway. Peering around her, I saw Retta, her chair pulled up close to the desk. She rose from her chair, giving the impression that a noose hung from the ceiling had been pulled tight. "I think we're done with plans for the grant, aren't we, Chief?"

"Yes," he replied blandly. "That's under control, but you might want to stay."

"Stay?" Retta and Barb spoke at once.

"It will save repeating things later." He looked at them in turn. "Is that okay?"

Barb nodded stiffly, her face blank. Retta's smile was thin as water. "If I can help."

For a while the chief seemed to be the only person in the room who could function. He herded Barb and me in and went across the hall to get another chair. Though I was curious about Retta's presence, the image of Neil in that cell kept resurfacing in my mind. We'd brought him back to what might be life in prison. Even though Barb and Retta sat there with tension crackling between them like gathering lightening, I had to convince the chief Neil was innocent.

Once we were seated, the chief said, "You must be Ms. Burner. Rory Neuencamp."

"Faye. It's nice to meet you, chief." Barb stayed silent, so I gave him a synopsis. Of course he'd heard it from Tom, but he'd probably slanted things to make Neil seem guilty.

"Mr. Brown turned himself in voluntarily," I finished. "He wants to set things straight."

"A few years behind schedule," Neuencamp said mildly.

"He didn't think anyone would listen to his side of it," I argued. "That's why he ran away." Assuming an air of confidence I added, "We plan to prove he didn't kill his wife."

"I see." Neuencamp's gaze sought my sister's. Barb shifted in her chair but said nothing.

"Gabe, the man we, um, convinced to return with us, will tell you he was hired by someone to retrieve this flash drive." Digging into the zipper pocket of my purse, I took out the drive. I'd refused to give it to Tom, arguing it was too important to entrust to anyone but the chief. "What's on this could be what got Carina and Carson killed."

I looked to Barb. "Neil says look at the water file. Stan doesn't get water bills."

Retta made a sound like a hiccup, and we all turned to look at her. "The computer tech at WOZ told Stanley to hide his financial files under an innocent-looking title, like an electric bill."

"An old one that no one would take any interest in." Barb had returned from whatever planet she'd been visiting. She leaned toward Neuencamp. "Chief, you need to look at the file."

He seemed doubtful. "Do we know who this drive belongs to?"

"It was given to Brown by his wife, who's deceased. I think the law would call it his."

"But the drive might contain sensitive information."

She regarded him coolly. "You won't know unless you look, will you?"

With a shrug the chief plugged the drive into his computer. As he waited for it to load he asked, "The water bill is the important one?"

Barb shrugged. "Brown's right. Stan would have a well out there."

Neuencamp clicked on the file. "What are the letters at the beginning of each line?"

"They didn't ring any bells." Barb clearly wished she could go around the desk and look over his shoulder, but she stayed where she was.

"Read them off, please, Rory." I looked at Retta, who'd taken out a pen and a scrap of paper. Quickly I did the same, writing down each entry as he read it off. I leaned so Barb could see my list, and we all fell silent, trying to fit words to the initials. "AM, MT, CI, and NYSB."

Retta got the first item. "Allport Merchant. They use AM as their logo."

After a moment's thought, I said, "MT could be Michigan Trust. They're based in Detroit, where Wozniak lived for years."

"If they're banks, that would make NYSB New York State Bank," Barb said.

The chief nodded. "What's CI?"

There was another silence as we thought about possible bank names. Connecticut International? Cincinnati Investments? Commercial & Industrial?

"The only things that come to my mind aren't banks," I said. "Counter Intelligence. Confidential Informant. Certifiably Insane." I was getting desperate.

Barb looked up at the chief. "Not a bank. Think offshore accounts."

Neuencamp smiled. "Cayman Islands."

"They're all places where Stanley has money!" Retta beamed at us, though her wattage dimmed a little when she met Barb's gaze and didn't get an answering beam.

The chief was studying the screen. "If this was my code, the numbers after each one wouldn't be amounts. They'd be the account numbers."

"And Usage_Q1 and so on are the passwords." Retta said. "He's got capitals, a number, and special characters in each one, just like the computer guy advised."

"You need to ask Wozniak about this," Barb said, and I cringed a little at her bossy tone.

The chief didn't seem to mind. "He might be a little touchy about us looking at his files."

"Which is why we have to tell him. If he hasn't changed his passwords in the last six years he's an idiot, but he certainly needs to change them now."

"Since there was no love lost between Stanley and Neil," Retta said, "maybe the son and the son-in-law joined forces to steal Stanley's money."

"If that were the case, why were Carina and Carson murdered?"

"Something went wrong. Brown killed them, but then he couldn't access the money because he was afraid they'd track him down."

For once I found Retta as irritating as Barb did. How could she believe Neil was a killer? I reminded myself she'd never met him. She was just staying neutral, like a good investigator.

Touching a notebook on his desk, Neuencamp spoke to Barb. "I'm been reading up on the case. Can you tell me why you think Brown might be innocent?"

She ticked off the points on her fingers. "He's had the drive all these years and never used it, which indicates he didn't know what was on it. Someone followed us to the U.P. and demanded he hand it over, and I'm almost sure Neil had no idea what they were talking about." Noticing that Barb's "Mr. Brown" and "Brown" references had become "Neil," I smiled to myself. She believed in him too.

For the first time, Retta spoke directly to Barb. "If Carina gave that flash drive to her husband, she'd probably figured out her brother planned to steal their dad's money."

"Why Carson?"

"He stayed at Stanley's house for the first few days of his visit, even though things hadn't been good between them. I think he wanted a chance to get at his dad's computer." She explained to Barb and the chief what she'd learned at WOZ, ending with Art Chalmers' impression Carson had been concerned for the safety of Stan's financial information.

Barb presented a theory. "Carson stays at Stan's and copies any files he thinks might be the right one to his own flash drive."

Entering the spirit of things, Neuencamp leaned back in the chair. "His sister found out about it somehow, which is why she was upset that morning."

"Everybody's flash drive looked the same," I reminded them. "She probably picked up Carson's thinking she had her own and saw what was on it."

"So she confronts Carson, asking him what he's doing with Stan's files."

"Which started the argument Neil interrupted," Barb said. "His DNA and blood got on Carson's clothing when he defended his wife."

Neuencamp seemed to return to cop mode. "Just how strongly did he defend her?"

"Neil says they were both alive when he left," Barb said.

"So who killed them?"

She hesitated, probably unwilling to accuse anyone. "It's possible Wozniak didn't react well when he learned what his son intended."

I doubted the chief knew Wozniak well, being new to Allport. Could he accept the idea that a prominent businessman had caught his son stealing from him and killed him in anger?

"Carina was there," Barb said. "She saw what happened, and that's why she was killed."

"It's possible," Neuencamp said, "but there are a couple of things to keep in mind." Flipping through the notebook, he consulted a couple of pages. "First, Carson was hit as he bent over her, indicating the wife was struck first. Second, the police processed Wozniak's clothing. He didn't have the kind of blood spatter a person would get from bashing two people's heads in. He had blood on his hands and shirt front, consistent with him holding his children to his chest."

I got an image of a frantic father cradling his dead son and almost felt sorry for Wozniak. Still, other than Neil he was the best suspect. "He'd have regretted it as soon as it was over."

Neuencamp rearranged the things on his desk, a classic signal that a meeting is about to end. "Let me look into this. I haven't talked to Brown yet, haven't had much chance to talk to Tom, either." To Barb he said, "I'll be objective. That's all I can offer right now."

"That's all we ask, Chief." She rose and we left, leaving Retta and the chief together.

When we got outside, however, Barb stopped on the sidewalk, allowing me time for a smoke. I lit up, feeling far from cheerful about Neil's future. Chief Neuencamp had listened politely, but that didn't mean he believed us. And it was hard to walk away, knowing Brooke's daddy would soon be transferred to the county lock-up.

"What do you think she was doing in there?"

I exhaled before answering. "Butting in, I suppose. Or batting her false eyelashes at the new chief to see if he's susceptible to her charms." I glanced at my reflection in the window of the building. My face looked its age, maybe more. "I wonder what it's like to get any man you want just by being you. I don't think I ever had that power, and I sure don't have it now."

"I never begrudged Retta her ability to charm men," Barb said vaguely. I noticed, though, that she spoke in past tense.

CHAPTER THIRTY-THREE

Retta

I was surprised to find Barbara Ann and Faye waiting for me when I left the police station. I'd stopped at the ladies' room, mostly to be sure they were gone before I left. Seeing them waiting I flinched a little, but Barbara didn't accuse me of sticking my nose in their business. Instead she asked in her usual blunt way, "Stan Wozniak likes you, right?"

"He does." I waited, guessing she wanted a favor. "What?" I finally prompted.

"I need to meet him somewhere outside his office, somewhere he'll have to be social." After a moment she added, "Where he can't order me off the property."

My mind had been running ahead, and I was ready. "How about dinner with him this evening at a table full of local VIPs? He'll have to be civil."

I'd been trying for months to get my sister involved with AllBoosters, an organization I practically founded. Its purpose is civic good works, but Barbara Ann has no patience for organized philanthropy. "The most effective kindness is one-to-one," she always says. While that's nice, people united accomplish bigger things than one can do alone. Being recognized as a good person doesn't hurt your popularity, either. Barbara's lone wolf attitude has always been her problem. One of them.

Stan Wozniak understands the importance not only of giving to charity but being seen to do so. He'd be at the AllBoosters' Spring

Festival tonight. I'd asked Barbara to come months ago. She'd bought a ticket, but it was clear she'd had no intention of going. Until now.

"All right," she said with a sigh of resignation. "What does one wear to this gala event?"

"It's formal. I'll come over and help you choose something."

Faye made a little choking sound. "No, you won't," Barbara said. "I can dress myself."

My tongue got the better of me. "You'll arrive looking like a misplaced librarian."

Faye dropped her cigarette butt on the ground, stepped on it, then bent to pick it up and dispose of it in a nearby can. I suspected she was also getting out of the line of fire.

"I'll try not to disappoint you, Retta," Barbara said, ignoring the too-innocent look on Faye's face. "But I will *not* show up sparkling, flowing, or over-exposed."

It was a slap at me, but Barbara Ann is too inhibited to enjoy clothes the way a woman should. It didn't bother me a bit that the dress I'd chosen for the evening sparkled, flowed and, if it didn't *over*-expose me, at least offered enticing possibilities.

"Why do you need to talk to Stanley?"

"He could be a murderer. I want to see him operate."

That was just ridiculous. "Stanley would never hurt his children, though I'm sure he used his money as punishment."

"Threatening to let them '...hang, beg, starve, die in the streets?'"

"What?" Faye and I spoke at once.

Barbara waved a hand. "I was quoting Juliet's father."

"Juliet?"

"Capulet." She made a never-mind gesture. "Wozniak is the Lord Capulet type. Money is his god, so he uses it to make others toe the line—his line."

Not much for Shakespeare, I merely hummed agreeably. "You'll see. Stanley's no killer."

Faye looked unhappy. "We've got to give the new chief reason to investigate this case and not just go along with what everyone said six years ago."

"He promised he'd be objective," Barbara said. "Maybe he'll find something the others missed." Her mouth turned down a little. "I just hope he isn't easily swayed. Wozniak is bound to press him to charge Neil with murder."

"Maybe I can help there, too," I told them. "I think our new chief likes me, so I might be able to balance out Stanley's hard sell with a little soft soap."

***

You could have heard my gasp in Lansing when I picked Barbara up that evening. She looked really good. Her hair, cut too short for my taste, was styled in soft curls. The dress, a long, slender thing in navy that draped nicely, softened her rather thin figure. As I could have predicted, she'd minimalized the accessories, tiny gold hoop earrings with a necklace of larger hoops. I must admit, the understatement worked. She'd even taken time for mascara.

"You look very pretty," Barbara told me. "I suppose the outfit is new?"

"It's a small town. Once you've worn a dress everyone's seen it, so you need a new one."

"Do you."

I hated it when she used that tone, like I was six and she was sixteen and the ultimate expert in cool. It wasn't like that anymore. Barbara had stopped trying, and I hadn't. I was pleased to see she'd tried a little tonight. A dowdy dinner companion is a terrible bore.

"I hope you'll avoid topics like global warming and fracking," I told her. "Nobody comes to these things for a lecture."

Barbara turned to regard me with that one raised eyebrow. "I once danced with the Vice President and managed not to blurt out that I'd voted for the other guy. I won't step on any toes."

When we entered the hall together, we caused a bit of a stir. I had chosen a deep red dress, perfect for my colors, and had Patsy brighten my highlights a little. It was fun to see the men react to our entrance and the women react to their reaction.

I'd arranged for us to be seated with Stanley Wozniak. He rose as we approached, smiling and stepping away from the table to hug me. "Retta. Good to see you again." His eyes turned a darker color when he realized who was with me.

"Stanley, this is my sister, Barbara Evans."

As we'd hoped, he chose to be polite in a social setting. "Good evening, Barbara."

"Barb."

I guess she thinks it's more professional, but her name sounds like a weapon when she shortens it like that.

"This is my attorney, Calvin Combs." Stan indicated the only other person at the table, a well-dressed gentleman with white hair and over-tanned skin. "He rode up with me from Detroit today for a few days' R & R." He smiled. "My date, since you didn't answer my call, Retta."

I gave him my Mona Lisa smile in response. The cash bar was open, and Stanley offered to get us each something. While he was gone, others assigned to our table arrived, the Catholic priest and the Comptons, an oversized couple known for supporting local arts. Greetings and introductions were exchanged. Stanley returned with wine for Barbara and me, cocktails for himself and his guest, and promptly went off with orders for the new arrivals.

"Such a nice man," Mrs. Compton crooned, listing over the table like a sinking freighter. I thought her name was Betty, and she wasn't known for good judgment, in art or men.

We settled in for the polite conversation required at these affairs: where a person went in Florida last winter, or Arizona, or Texas. That's good for at least twenty minutes. Which is better? Which is more economical? Which has the best golf courses?

After that comes gardening, much-discussed in Michigan in spring, because it takes skill and judgment to succeed at it. Plant too early and frost will kill your tender new shoots. Plant too late and they won't have time to bear fruit. Everyone talks about it, though most of the people at our table hired someone else to do the heavy work.

Barbara said little, but what she did say was pleasant and interesting. I noticed she was adept at deflecting questions about her former life, turning the conversation back to the questioner. "Yes," I heard her tell Father Fred, "I practiced law for a long time in Tacoma. What do you think of the church's position on amnesty for illegal aliens?"

Shortly before the meal was served, the last seat at our table filled. Rory Neuencamp entered the hall, looking ill at ease but oh, so handsome. He'd opted for black slacks with a black turtleneck under a gray jacket. I'd seen the look in *GQ* last fall, but I suspected

Rory's choices were his own, no matter the trend. Still, it worked for him.

I saw the hostess take his ticket and point him to our table, and I flashed him a smile of welcome. Next to me, Barbara tensed as she saw him approaching, probably uncomfortable in the company of someone who knew a lot more than she did about crime and catching criminals.

"Chief Neuencamp," I said as he reached us. "So nice to see you."

I made introductions, and Rory took a seat. Mrs. Compton launched into a gushing speech of welcome that prevented real communication for a while. When the emcee stepped up to the microphone, conversation halted.

Tables were chosen for order of service in the buffet line. Our group was called to go third. (I'm lucky that way!) As we stood to head to the food tables, I maneuvered Barbara into place next to Stanley. The line was all the way across the dance floor, which meant she'd have plenty of time to speak with him in comparative privacy. Mrs. Compton was still monopolizing Rory. I chatted with Mr. Combs and eavesdropped on Barbara at the same time.

Typically, Barbara Ann didn't even try to warm Stanley up before getting to the point. "Mr. Wozniak, I want you to know our agency means no disrespect to you or your family."

"Then leave it alone," he ordered. "You found Brown, now let the law deal with him."

"But there is some doubt as to his guilt. It's our business to—"

"A detective agency? His tone made it sound like she'd opened a house of prostitution.

"If he's guilty, we'll accept that. But we've discovered some things—"

"He's wrapped a couple of gullible women around his finger." His voice remained low, but the intensity was like an ocean wave splashing over her. "Don't you think I know that? Brown convinced my daughter he was a good man, but after she married him, she saw his true nature. When she decided to divorce him, he murdered her." Stanley's eyes narrowed as he finished. "Brown took my children from me, and I intend to see that he pays. Don't get in my way, Mrs. Evans."

As Barbara frowned in that way that made her look at least five years older, I felt someone brush past me. Rory stepped between the two of them, putting a hand on her arm. "Ms. Evans, sorry to interrupt, but could we talk about those vandals you reported? If you don't mind losing a few places in line, we could catch up on the case before we settle down to dinner."

For a moment Barbara looked down at his hand on her arm, her expression an odd one I couldn't decipher. Then she said, "Of course, Chief Neuencamp."

Rory's hand went to Barbara's elbow in the classic gesture of a gentleman, and the two of them stepped back to his place in line. That left me next to a still-smoldering Stanley Wozniak, who struggled to regain control. After a long, tense silence he turned to me, asking, "Where's your house in Florida, Retta? I don't have much sense of the geography down there."

Taking the cue, I described my second home as my mind went on its own track. As far as I knew, there'd been no vandalism. Turning sideways to glance at them from under my lashes, I watched as Rory and Barbara chatted comfortably. Our new chief had stepped in to rescue my sister from Stanley's anger. What a nice guy he was—but I'd already figured that out!

The rest of the evening was uneventful but a little surreal. Barbara and Stanley were amicable to the group as a whole, though neither spoke directly to the other again. When we returned with our plates, she traded places so I sat next to Stanley. The meal was unexceptional, the usual baked chicken, Swedish meatballs, and corn and mashed potatoes on the side. As we ate, the chief divided his time among the diners equally, as a municipal employee must. Afterward there was dancing, and he danced with me twice. He asked Barbara once, but she looked so stiff in his arms that it couldn't have been much fun for either of them.

The door prize giveaway dragged on too long, but the gifts were worth the wait. Barbara won a booklet of coupons for car washes, which pleased her since she's a little obsessive about her car. I won the fifty-fifty drawing and turned my half over to AllBoosters. I got a big round of applause.

On the way home, she said, "I suppose you heard Wozniak's threat."

"I wouldn't call it a threat, Barbara."

She clucked impatiently. "Do you consider 'Do not get in my way' a polite request?"

"I don't think he meant he'd hurt you. He just meant he's determined."

"Then who sent two guys to follow us to the U.P. and get that flash drive from Neil?"

"But he's a respected businessman, known all over the state."

"And respected businessmen are caught in criminal activities every day."

While I'm not as interested in the front two sections of the *Detroit Free Press* as Barbara Ann is, I'm not totally ignorant. I couldn't argue with her on that point.

CHAPTER THIRTY-FOUR

Barb

Faye and I spent the next morning in the office. I knew she was tied in knots because we'd been instrumental in Neil's arrest. I was trying to look at the whole thing objectively, since I saw that she couldn't. Embarrassing as last night had been, it was clear Wozniak truly believed Brown had killed his children. Overnight I'd come to the conclusion he hadn't done it, since I didn't think that sort of hatred could be faked.

It could have been Brown who stole Wozniak's financial information. If Carson and Carina found out and called him to the apartment to confront him, he might have killed them and run away. He might have been afraid to use the information he'd stolen lest he be caught. We had only Brown's word for some things, and he might be a clever liar.

On the other hand, there were arguments for his honesty. He could easily have done away with us when we walked into his lodge full of deer rifles. He'd been willing to hand the drive over to save Faye, which argued he hadn't known what was on it. And while I didn't know a lot about off-shore accounts, I thought that if a man had account numbers, passwords, and six years, he'd have been able to figure out how to withdraw the funds.

Another factor argued for Brown's innocence. Someone had sent Gabe and the elusive "Z" to retrieve the flash drive. If Stan didn't hire them, who was after the information? It had to be that another person was in on the scheme to drain Stan's accounts. If so, he or she was probably responsible for Carson and Carina's deaths.

I'd wanted to ask Wozniak about who that might have been, but he'd made it clear he wasn't going to talk to me.

I was wondering if Faye might convince Stan to talk with her mom-like approach when, like manna from heaven, my opportunity came. The phone rang, and ALLPORT P.D. came up on the screen. At my hello, Rory asked, "Want to go with me to visit Stan Wozniak?"

"You saw the way he treated me last night," I told him. "I'm not in his good graces."

"I think I can convince him you need to be there. Can we meet at WOZ in half an hour?"

Promising Faye I'd fill her in as soon as possible, I headed north, forcing myself to maintain a prudent speed and obey all traffic lights. I might have passed through a few that were more orange than yellow. On the trip, I thought about what I wanted to ask Stan.

When my question list got to three, I stopped myself. Rory would do the talking. I had no right to be there. Which made me ask what had led him to invite me.

Anger. I'd seen the look on his face when Stan rejected my conciliatory overture. I'd known other men like Wozniak whose gentility was a veneer that barely covered the nastiness beneath. I had no power and I was female, so Wozniak saw no need to treat me politely. Recalling Rory's intervention and subsequent kindness, I guessed he'd felt sorry for me. *Retta's old maid sister*, he probably thought. *Poor thing doesn't have a chance against a guy like Stan.*

This was the chief's way of letting me get a little of my own back with the owner of WOZ Industries. If it really had Wozniak's account information on it, the fact that I'd seen it would no doubt be enough to convince Stan to change his passwords immediately.

Once I understood my role, I tried to let go and enjoy the ride. It was one of those soft spring days that lets you know the worst really is over. The leaves were turning from that tentative, early green to a more robust color. The road was lined with weed-flowers that would stand only until the county got time to send a mower around to flatten them.

Rory and I met in the parking lot and went inside together. He offered no explanation for me to Stan's secretary, a doe-eyed brunette who looked more like Miss October than Ms. Efficiency. Rory's uniform got her all fluttery. "Certainly, Chief. I'll let him know you're here."

Word had spread that Neil Brown was back, and people probably assumed the new chief had come to inform the victims' father personally. It's what a lot of them would have done to score points with the wealthiest man in the county.

Wozniak wasn't happy to see me at Rory's side. His eyes hardened and his lips tightened, but he didn't object when Rory said, "Mr. Wozniak, we met last night, but I didn't think it was appropriate to discuss this matter at a social event. I'm sure you remember Ms. Evans. We're here because the arrest made in the deaths of your children has raised some questions."

"Please sit." The request might have been directed at both of us, but I doubted it. Rory twisted a chair into place for me and I sat. The doe-girl hovered nearby. "Can Bambi get you something? Coffee?"

"No, thank you." I detected a glint of enjoyment in Rory's eyes. "You've probably heard that Neil Brown turned himself in to us. Ms. Evans spent some time with him and convinced him it was the right thing to do."

Wozniak shifted in his chair. "I'm sure she meant well."

"Things we heard from Mr. Brown give us cause to re-examine what happened that day."

Wozniak's prominent Adam's apple bobbed once before he answered. "Really."

Rory turned to me. "Barb, would you like to explain?"

Taken aback, I had to gather my wits. Wozniak turned to me, his cold stare indicating he was one hundred percent certain we didn't need to re-examine the case.

"Mr. Wozniak, while my sister and I were at Mr. Brown's residence, someone shot at us. Later, she was kidnapped by a man who demanded that Neil give up a flash drive your daughter gave him the day she died."

Rory took a photograph of the drive from a manila folder he'd brought along and set it on the desk. "Do you recognize that?"

"Everyone here has at least one," Wozniak replied with an impatient wave of his hand.

"This one contains a file with what looks like access information to financial accounts, one of which is in the Cayman Islands."

That surprised him, at least that's what I thought I saw before his face went blank again.

Rory asked quietly, "Might those passwords be yours?"

Wozniak tapped the photograph. "As I said, there are hundreds of those drives around here. I couldn't say whose files would be on it."

Rory took a sheet of paper from the folder and laid it beside the photo. "This is a printout of one of the files on the drive. Now can you identify it?"

His face went pale, and he set his hands on the edge of the desk, as if holding himself in his chair. "You say Carina gave Brown this?"

Rory gave me a tiny nod, and I explained. "Carina and Carson were fighting when Neil arrived at the apartment that day. Neil intervened and Carson gave up, promising he'd do what Carina wanted him to. Your daughter told Neil the matter was between you and them, but as he was leaving, she gave him the drive. He says they were both alive when he left them."

Wozniak summoned his anger once more, shaking his head as if to keep my words from getting in. "He killed my children!" Picking the paper up, he shook it at Rory and me. "Carina must have found out he planned to rob me and told her brother. When Brown found out, he killed them." His eyes turned red. "I'd give him the money right now if it brought my children back!"

Rory asked softly, "Does that file contain information about your personal finances?"

Stan nodded, still emotional. "My son would not steal from me. He—he wouldn't."

Rory picked up the papers and put them back into the folder. "We'll find out the truth, no matter who's guilty. I suggest you change the passwords on your accounts, even if those aren't current. Someone stole that information, and we don't know who it was."

I was pretty sure I knew. Carson had been at Stan's house. Neil hadn't. Carina had been angry with Carson over something he'd done that would upset his father. Carson had cultivated a friendship with the tech. Carson had wanted to be a big shot in California, but his father had cut off the funding. Carson had stolen the files, but he'd probably needed help with the rest of it, someone to help him transfer money from Stan's files to somewhere else.

Stan wasn't about to admit any of that. "If my son were foolish enough to share my private information with anyone, it would have been with the only person he knew in Allport, his brother-in-law. Carson was young and perhaps a little unwise in the area of finance."

"You're saying he might have planned something with Brown and then wanted to back out at the last minute?" It sounded all too plausible when Rory said it.

"Carson might have been briefly misled, but he would never have followed through." Stan's anger rose again, and he returned to what his type does best, threats. "No matter what the reasons were, we all know who killed my children. Ms. Evans might not want to face the facts, but I expect, Chief Neuencamp, that Neil Brown will be held in custody until his trial. He's an obvious flight risk, and I've waited six years. Now, do your job and see justice done."

Rory rose, nodded in a manner that was barely polite, and said to me, "I think we should let Mr. Wozniak get back to business, Barb." There were no further pleasantries as we left, but I sensed Stan's stare aimed at the center of my back like a steel-tipped dart.

As we stepped out of the elevator we met two men waiting to go up. One I recognized, Eric DuBois. The other had such a grumpy expression that he looked like a cartoon character, complete with everything but the black cloud over his head.

"Mrs. Evans, nice to see you again," Eric said. Turning to Rory he put out a hand. "You must be Chief Neuencamp. Eric DuBois."

Rory shook hands with Eric then turned to the other man, whose bottom lip pressed upward, making an upside down smile. He took Rory's hand in what seemed to me a reluctant gesture. "Miles Bonworth," he said, barely moving his lips. The accountant Retta had mentioned.

Eric seemed embarrassed at the man's unfriendly attitude. "Miles, this is Barbara Evans of the Smart Detective Agency."

Bonworth looked me over appraisingly. "I thought you'd already caught your *perp*."

"There are always loose ends to tie up in a case such as this," Rory answered smoothly. "Mrs. Evans came with me today to help with that."

Once again I was pleased at the skill with which he made my presence seem natural and necessary. The curve of Bonworth's lips went even deeper.

"As a matter of fact, I have questions you might answer." Rory turned to Eric. "Could I ask you to entertain Ms. Evans for a few minutes while I speak briefly with Mr. Bonworth?"

The tiniest glance from Rory gave me a clue to what he had in mind. These men had the know-how to have helped Carson in his scheme. One of them might be a killer. My job was to assess the likelihood that Eric DuBois was the one while Rory tackled Mr. Grump.

Eric agreed with a hint of gallantry, Bonworth with much less good grace, mumbling about having work to do, but we got back into the elevator and rode up to the second floor again. I saw Eric glance at the door to Stan's office and wondered if he was recalling how angry his boss had been at my first visit. Nevertheless, he ushered me into his office, set a chair for me, and asked the assistant to get us cold drinks.

"So what has the chief of police got on his mind?" he asked with a knowing smile.

I wasn't sure how much to tell, since a lot of what I thought I knew wasn't proven. "The murder case has gotten a little more complicated," I told him. "It seems someone intended to raid Mr. Wozniak's personal accounts, though it never happened."

He was silent for a few seconds, but his expression made me think he wasn't surprised. "You think Carson was angry because Stan cut him off."

"That's one possibility. Someone copied Stan's access information, which means that person was in the house and opened Stan's personal computer. The question is could Carson have pulled something like that off by himself?"

DuBois thought about it. "I think so. I mean, just about anyone can copy a file."

"But would he have known how to move funds from an off-shore account?"

"I'm not sure." He gave me a direct look. "He might have had help in the family."

I heard the warning in his voice. "You're thinking Neil."

His smile was grim. "Actually I was thinking both Neil and Carina."

"Why?"

He bit his lip briefly then made a "why-not?" gesture. "I like Stan. I really do. He's tough to work for, but we get along okay. That said, he had some issues as a father. He used money to reward and punish his kids, and they resented it."

"I heard he cut Carson off the year before."

"Yeah. Carson was a screw-up, but Stan didn't help. The kid was always trying to plan some big thing that would make his dad proud of him. It was easy for unscrupulous types to suck him in and take his money. When Stan said no more, Carson was just a twenty-something, no-skills schmuck, and there are plenty of those in

California. Last I knew he was working in a mom-and-pop pizza place and living in an apartment above it."

"Quite a come-down from movie producer."

"Exactly. Carson was desperate."

"And Carina?"

"Her dad had put her in a really rough spot. She had to choose between Neil and Stan."

"The job in Detroit."

"Right. She'd almost convinced Neil to take it, but she knew it was a bad thing."

"If Neil gave in to Stan's demands once, he'd be forced to do it again and again."

"Exactly."

"So you're saying the three of them conspired to rob Stan?"

Eric held up a hand. "I don't *know* anything. You're wondering who might have helped Carson out, and that's what came to mind." He gave a huff of dry humor. "Stan might not have even reported it. He wouldn't want anyone to know his own children stole from him."

My mind was picking at the edges of Eric's theory. "I'm pretty sure Neil Brown doesn't know much about off-shore accounts."

"No, but Carina did. She looked like her brain was fluff with her green fingernails and her baby-doll dresses, but she was very aware of Stan's wealth. She came here all the time, and I'd see her picking up information. Once she sweet-talked Miles Bonworth into taking her to lunch, and Art Chalmers in technical support practically ate out of her hand."

Rory appeared in the doorway, and I rose from my chair. "Well, I'll let you get back to work, Eric. Thanks for the hospitality—and the information."

Eric rose like the gentleman he was, but I thought he was relieved. He no doubt hoped Stan never found out he'd spoken to me, and he probably did have lots to do, so it had been good of him to be gracious about the interruption.

Once we were outside, Rory asked, "Did you find out anything?"

I told him Eric's theory, ending with, "It's plausible, except I can't see Neil going along. He just isn't the type to do something underhanded like that."

"People can be deceptive," Rory said, and I had to admit he was right. Neil had had six years to practice his innocent act, if in fact that's what he was doing.

"What'd you learn from the money man, Bonworth?"

"The world is a mess. People are idiots. Our only salvation is mathematics." Rory smiled before continuing. "He doesn't think the son was smart enough to plan the scheme on his own. He hinted that Eric DuBois, is our culprit, probably because Bonworth hoped to be in the position DuBois now holds." He raised one eyebrow. "Mr. Bonworth claims DuBois 'cuddled up' to the boss after his kids were murdered and 'slithered' into place next to the throne."

"This all stems from jealousy?"

Rory shrugged. "It could have been DuBois, I suppose. He'd have the know-how."

"As would Bonworth."

"True. I just can't see the guy allying with anyone long enough to hatch a plot. He's a real loner. Besides, it seems like he doesn't need to *have* money. He just needs to *control* it."

"It's kind of a psychological game, isn't it—trying to figure out a person's motives."

"That's how the interesting cases are."

"Speaking of motives, why did you invite me to come out here with you? Were you mad at Stan for being a jerk to me last night?"

Rory's tone was teasing. "Maybe I guessed your appearance at a charity ball was motivated by the chance to get to meet him."

Retta might have told him that little tidbit, but I didn't want to think where or when that had happened. While they were dancing last night, looking as smooth as if they'd been partners for years? Afterward, maybe, once she'd dropped me off at home?

"So why did you help me?" I asked to banish the images that were forming in my head.

"Well, I think you're right. Wozniak doesn't want to admit it, but Carson planned to steal from him. That Cayman Island account had over a million dollars in it, if our code-breaking skills are correct."

I shook my head. "But according to Neil's story, Carson had agreed to give up the plan and confess. It would have been over."

"But his partner hadn't agreed. Carson must have called to warn him it had all come apart. The kid didn't realize that to protect himself from prosecution, the guy had to stop him."

"By killing him. But he had to kill Carina, too, because she knew who he was."

"When he threw suspicion onto Brown, he must have thought he'd cleaned up the mess nicely." Rory opened the car door for me, and I got in and rolled the window down as he finished, "He didn't get the money, but he managed to stay out of prison."

"But when Faye and I went looking for Neil, we stirred it all up again."

"He must have taken the flash drive he thought had the files on it. Later he found out he had the wrong one. Since Carson's drive never showed up, he guessed Brown had it." Rory sighed. "If your friend Neil had looked at that thing, he might have cleared himself years ago."

I was stuck on the *who* rather than the *what if*. "We keep talking about this partner, but we have no idea who he is," I said, glancing back at the WOZ building. "Carson wasn't from Allport, so he didn't know many people. Who would he have hatched this plot with?"

"According to your sister, he made it a point to meet the computer tech, but she thought he was a little too wimpy to be a murderer."

Again I quelled a pang of jealousy at the thought of Retta and Rory with their heads together, discussing my case. "I bet you've seen all kinds of murderers in your career," I said, "even wimpy ones."

Rory nodded. "My grand-dad used to say, 'Stuck in a corner, any dog'll bite.'"

I rolled my eyes. "Homespun wisdom?"

He leaned down, resting his elbows on the window frame. "I did have another reason for the invitation. I wanted to see you again."

Caught off guard, I tried for a careless grin. "La, Chief Neuencamp, you'll turn a girl's head with such talk!" Wishing him good day, I drove off, wondering if our new cop thought a little too much of himself. He was obviously romancing my sister. Was he looking to make it a family affair?

CHAPTER THIRTY-FIVE

Retta

When Barbara Ann called, there was traffic noise in the background. I hoped she was using hands free, but she didn't give me time to ask. "Retta, I know you've been picking Faye's brain about the Brown case, and I know you've done some sn—some work on your own. We need to put together everything we can, so I'd like—" I felt her reluctance drip through the airwaves. "I'd like you to come to the office and compare notes."

I stirred my soup, homemade, not store-bought, savoring the smell of perfectly caramelized onion. "I thought the police were handling things now."

"We both know Stan Wozniak will do everything he can to hurt Neil's case." She sighed deeply. "Pooling our information will maximize effectiveness for our client."

My heart did a little flippity-flop at the words *we* and *our*. "You're right. Could we meet at Joe's instead of your office? They have a Mexican buffet on Thursdays."

"Don't do that." Her tone was sharp.

"Do what?"

"Change things. You always do it."

"I don't--"

"Yes, you do. I ask you to come here; you suggest we go to Joe's. I ask for a cantaloupe from the store; you bring a casaba, which is somehow better. Faye suggests a two-day shopping trip to

Saginaw; you shift it to four days in Grand Rapids. Stop changing things. Do as I ask."

It wasn't fair, especially the part about the trip to Grand Rapids. I'd extended it so we could all see *Jesus Christ Superstar*, my favorite show, which I knew neither of them had seen. Faye said afterward she liked it a lot. Barbara Ann was a little grumpy about it, but how can you not love the music in that show, even if you aren't a church-goer?

When Barbara gets on her high horse, I just back off. "All right. I'll come to the office." I'd get Faye to go to Joe's with me afterward. "Faye seems pretty sure Mr. Brown is innocent."

"Yes." Barbara sounded unsure, which isn't like her at all. "We haven't got much the police will call evidence, though."

"You don't think Rory will be fair?"

Her tone of voice changed. "How exactly did you meet the new police chief?"

"By accident, really."

"While you were working for the Smart Detective Agency, right?"

Despite my desire to be pleasant, I gave a little huff of exasperation. "Barbara Ann, I'm not trying to take over your business. I don't stick my nose in where I'm not wanted." I heard a snort but went right on. "I know people in Allport, and you don't. And the ones Faye knows—well, they aren't going to get you the answers you need."

When she replied she sounded like the old Barbara, patient with Baby Sister but not convinced. "Okay. Stop in as soon as you can." I heard her draw a big breath and waited for the rest of it. "We'll pay you for your time, and this in no way means you're part of this agency. I understand you have contacts, but you'll just be a consultant, paid for your time."

I bit back a snippy response. "You don't have to pay me."

"We'll accept your help on an hourly basis at our regular rate for subcontracted work."

"I'll be there in half an hour." I almost thanked her but caught myself in time. If we were going to be all business, I was offering expertise, so I didn't need to grovel.

For Barbara Ann's benefit I gushed over the office décor when I arrived as if I'd never seen it before. Faye seemed uncomfortable, and Barbara just looked at me like she does.

"I spoke with the mayor this morning," I told them. "She's all a-flutter because CNN is sending a team in, and she asked me what she should wear." I chuckled. "No doubt she's hoping to look slim and thirty-something--like that's going to happen!" Faye smiled politely, but neither of them was interested in our mayor's fashion faux pas.

Barbara led the way into her office and offered me a seat. Faye followed, taking what I assumed was her accustomed place on the right side of an oversized mahogany desk. I glanced around, since I hadn't been allowed in here yet. Lovely, but cold, like the inhabitant. I made a mental note to buy some bright throw pillows for the pale green divan and maybe some silk flowers to soften the severe black stoneware pieces set around the room. As if she read my mind, Barbara frowned. She'd see how much they helped once they were there.

Barbara took me through everything: what I'd learned from Stanley, his employees, and K's notes on the case. She stopped me several times to get details, and I have to admit she made me recall things I hadn't paid much attention to at the time. Faye took notes.

Once she made me repeat a segment. "The tech told Carson about his dad's passwords?"

I scooted my chair closer to the desk. "Art Chalmers. He said Carson was concerned."

"Would he have told Retta that if he'd been in on the theft?" Faye asked Barbara.

"Probably not."

"But Art would know everyone's log-on information." I caught myself frowning, which I try not to do. It makes lines. "He didn't seem like the type, but who knows?"

Faye leaned forward. "Whoever the partner was, he'd have been desperate to keep them from telling Stan."

"But Carson didn't know that many people in Allport."

"What about Stan's main man—? What's his name?" Faye consulted her notes.

"Eric DuBois," I supplied. "He's had a position of trust for years. If he'd wanted to steal from Stan, he could easily have done it by now."

She nodded reluctantly. "Who else is there?"

"The accountant, I suppose, Bonworth. He's an ornery cuss who feels unappreciated."

Barbara huffed in frustration. "Now we're guessing by personality type. We need more to go on than the fact that you find him unpleasant."

"Honestly," I said flatly, "the most likely person is Mr. Brown. Carson was his brother-in-law. He was there. They fought." I turned an onyx clock on Barbara's desk a little so it didn't line up with the edge like a soldier on watch. She reached out and put it back.

"We accept that possibility. We're looking at alternate scenarios."

That put me in my place. I wasn't supposed to suggest Neil Brown was anything but lily white. It wasn't productive, but I didn't want to argue now that we were working as a team.

This is how it should be, I told myself. *We all have strengths. We need each other. And Barbara Ann needs a plant or two to make this office less sterile-looking.*

When Barbara finally rose, pushing back her chair, she seemed a little warmer, more like the big sister I remembered. "Thanks for the help, Retta. You've clarified several things for us."

Things had gone so well that I ventured a suggestion. "You know, I could help you design your stationery. Something feminine but businesslike, you know?"

Faye's face froze, and Barbara Ann's flushed. "We have stationery."

"But you're going to want—"

"No, we're not."

I dropped it. I could always come back to it later.

CHAPTER THIRTY-SIX

Faye

Once our consultant was gone, Barb said, "You keep telling her things."

"You have to admit that Retta's been helpful."

She took three tissues from a box on her desk, put one in each pocket of her sweater, and wiped her nose with the third. "We agreed she wouldn't be part of this agency."

"Retta understands that. She just wants to help."

Barb rolled her eyes." She doesn't know how to help. She only knows how to micromanage."

"Barb, I can't look her in the eye and tell her we don't want her around."

She huffed a breath of air toward her scalp, where a faint sheen signaled a hot flash. "Promise me you won't let her worm her way into our business."

"But she's got contacts, and she's smart as a whip."

I got a stern look. "She does some things well, but she'll drive us crazy."

"I just want us to succeed with this, for you, me, Meredith, and Neil." I added honestly, "She asks me stuff, and I tell her before I realize what I'm doing."

"That's your sister's forte," Barb responded with a grimace. "Swooping in at our weakest moments and using them to her advantage."

***

That afternoon I got a call from the EMT who'd cared for Carina. Annamarie wasn't nearly as hard to talk to as her mother had been, but she claimed she couldn't tell me anything new. "Mrs. Brown was never conscious," she told me. "No last words naming her killer or like that."

"Can you picture the scene for me and tell me everything you saw and heard?"

She hummed a negative. "Chaos is the only word for it. My partner was working on the guy, swearing because he was beyond help. The radio dispatcher was squawking, asking what was going on. Wozniak was stomping around behind us, shouting and swearing he'd get Brown for killing his kids. I was trying to stabilize her so we could get her to the hospital."

"A lot to handle."

"It always is. I didn't have time to notice what the room looked like, except it was messed up like there'd been a fight."

"I see. Well--"

Apparently unaware that I'd spoken, Annamarie added one thing. "I did wonder afterward, though, about her jewelry."

"Carina's jewelry?"

"Yeah. I remember telling Harry it was funny she still wore her wedding ring, since Wozniak went on and on about her abusive husband. She had on a necklace, too, a string of those metal beads with letters on them. It said CARINA AND NEIL, with a little heart bead at either end. It was kinda weird. Why was she wearing those things if her marriage was so awful?"

CHAPTER THIRTY-SEVEN

Barb

Local News Team
WDDD TV
543 Eaton Rd.
Gratiot, Michigan

Dear Marti, Jason, and Phil:

I applaud your efforts to present local news in an interesting way. Your enthusiasm is evident and most of the time, the features are worthwhile.

I feel compelled to write, however, to acquaint you with two facts of the English language. First, things that freeze in winter are thawed, *not* unthawed. *There is no such word, and it is contrary to logic to say it.*

Second, police do not bust down *doors. They might* burst in. *They might* break down *a door. While it's acceptable to use the word* bust *to describe a certain type of arrest, that has nothing to do with the door itself.*

You all look very nice. Please try to speak well, too.

A Viewer

Following established practice, I prepared the letter and envelope, put it in the zipper bag, and headed out for my morning walk, the bag in my pants pocket. I planned to go all the way to the post office, skipping nearby mailboxes to further protect my anonymity.

The air was just cool enough to encourage a healthy pace. My nose felt chilled at first, but once I'd gone a few blocks, I warmed enough to unzip my jacket halfway.

After launching my latest Correction Event, I circled the block and headed for home. The streets were empty, and I relished the quiet. It was something I'd had to seek out in the city, hence the habit of walking early in the morning. I was never a runner, too much strain on the feet and knees, but a brisk walk with slow-downs and speed-ups works for me. I can eat pretty much anything and maintain a reasonable weight for my age and body style.

That hasn't done much good. Fearing I'd said it aloud, I looked around to see if anyone was nearby. There was no point in dwelling on the fact that Retta had staked out the new police chief for herself. I really didn't want a relationship anyway, having had my share over the years and finding each one unsatisfactory in the end. It didn't matter if Rory succumbed to Retta's considerable charms. At least that's what I told myself.

At one of Allport's major streets, Biscayne, I quickened my pace and crossed, though traffic was not a concern. Five blocks from home. I continued down Mallett, passing a closed print shop and a run-down café. It wasn't a bad part of town, but there weren't as many good parts since the recession. Lots of businesses had closed in financial distress, and many that were left had no money to spend on cosmetic repairs.

A rumbly sound caught my attention. Turning, I saw an old, noisy pickup truck behind me. I was well out of the driver's way, but he slowed, craning his neck as if I were about to jump out in front of him. I turned down the side street that would take me home.

Soon I heard the truck behind me again. When it didn't pass, I got an odd feeling at the back of my neck. The feeling persisted until the truck turned into an alley behind me. Rolling my shoulders, I relaxed my tense neck. Probably the owner of one of the stores had come in early to get a head start on work.

Failure to trust my instincts cost me. As I passed the alley, someone grabbed me from behind. It was a man, not much taller than I but strong, with an arm as hard as the pump handle in Neil's faraway cabin. After the first moment of shock, I tried to remember my training. *Use his weight against him. Stomp his instep. Kick his groin. Gouge his eyes.* None of it seemed likely to happen. I was too busy trying to breathe.

The arm pressed against my windpipe was unrelenting. I clawed at it, but thick fabric protected the attacker's skin. I kicked backward, but my running shoes had no hard edges. It might have hurt him, but not nearly as much as he was hurting me. As I fought for air, bits of thought floated by. *Why?* was foremost, but there were others. *Who wants me dead? How can I stop this?* and *What made me think I could be a detective?*

Despite the futility of it, a primal, defensive spirit rose from my subconscious. I could not let my life end in an alley, at least not without a fight. Drawing on reserves I didn't know I had, I forced myself to think. *Pull at the arm. Get a tiny breath. Gather strength. Pull again. Breathe again. Think. Think!* It isn't easy when you're fighting to stay conscious.

Every enemy has a weakness. I had to find his. With one hand I pulled desperately on the arm that pressed against my throat, trying to suck in a breath of air. With the other I followed the fabric of the canvas jacket to where it ended. A glove covered the hand, but there was a gap between. I stabbed all five nails into it, pressing my thumb into the soft underside of his wrist, between the chords. He yelped and loosened his grip just a hair, allowing me a breath of air that was almost enough. The blackness that had begun to close across my vision like stage curtains receded momentarily. Too soon, the arm tightened again. In the fraction of a second before my thoughts clouded again, I went for his eyes. *Upward and behind*, I told myself. *Jab hard!*

I missed one eye completely, but the other I hit spot on. Air rushed into my lungs as my attacker screamed in pain and released me. I staggered a step forward then spun around, foolishly turning to look at him instead of running away. He wore a ragged Carhartt coverall and had a ski mask over his face. He'd put both hands over his left eye, and the right was closed in sympathy. I moved in to do the groin kick that would put him on the ground and render him helpless.

He wasn't as defenseless as I thought, because he turned sideways, and my foot connected with his leg instead. Still covering the injured eye with one hand, he caught my left foot with the other and pushed hard on my outstretched leg. I had to fight to keep the other one under me. Luckily, or maybe not so much, the building at my back kept me upright, but my head slammed into it hard enough to stun me for a few seconds.

When I recovered, my attacker was limping away, body bent forward as he nursed the damaged eye. He reached his vehicle, threw himself inside, and started the engine. I suppose I should have given chase, but I slumped against the cool bricks, head spinning. At the last second, I recovered enough to think about getting the license plate number. Pushing myself forward, I staggered toward the truck as the driver jammed it into gear and pulled away. The plate was illegible, covered in smeared-on mud.

Faye was making coffee when I got home. One look and she knew I was in trouble. Helping me to a chair, she put her hands on my upper arms, steadying me as post-traumatic shakes took over my body. I told her in gasping phrases what had happened, and her face went white. Once I finished, she knelt beside the chair, hugging me tightly until I gained control of my muscles again. When I stopped shaking she moved to the counter, poured a cup of coffee from the carafe, and set it in front of me. "Drink." Obediently, I gulped the fresh brew, not caring that it was too hot and lacking my usual two spoons of sugar.

"When they taught us the eye-gouging thing in self-defense class," I told her, "I recall thinking I could never do it. But when you're going to die, you can do anything."

Tears came then. Faye cried a little too. We faced something we'd acknowledged intellectually but not internalized emotionally. You don't poke around in crimes and people's lives without arousing anger. Someone wanted me dead.

"You have to go see your friend the chief," Faye said finally.

I felt my face go blank. "He isn't my friend."

"But you said—"

"We ate in the same restaurant one night and shared a table. He was polite, that's all."

Faye supplied us both with fresh tissues from a nearby box, and we mopped up. "Friend or not, you need to tell him what's happened."

"He'll probably say I deserved what I got for sticking my nose into police matters." She was right, though. I had to report this. I pushed fear away. Yes, I'd been terrified. But did I want to quit?

Hell, no. Anger began replacing fear. I'd get better. I'd be smarter, more careful. I'd win.

Half an hour later I was escorted into the chief's office, which had changed drastically since yesterday. Unopened paint cans were stacked in one corner, there was blue tape around the windows and doors, and plastic tarps covered the floor. The plan, my guide informed me, was to paint over the weekend. "We waited till he got here so he could pick the color he wanted."

When Rory arrived, apologetic for being elsewhere in the building when I showed up, he escorted me down the hall to a meeting room with a long, scarred table and ten chairs. He pulled out a chair for me at one end and took the one next to it, so that our shoulders were almost touching. To my great joy, he didn't even hint I'd got what I deserved. Instead, listening carefully to my story, he wrote points down on a legal pad he'd grabbed from his desk. Seeing my glance, he grinned briefly. "I can't think without a pen in my hand, so I take lots of notes."

"I'm the same way." That sounded too personal somehow, like I was trying to make us seem *simpatico*. I returned to the facts of my experience. "Anyway, the guy took off in a beat-up black pickup. The license plate was muddy, which I think was intentional rather than natural."

"Any idea of the make or model?"

"Dodge, I think. Had to be from the '90s. Rust around the fenders, a piece of trim missing on the side. Dent in the tailgate, like someone dropped a tree on it."

"That's good." Rory's eyes slid to the open door and back to me. "You all right, Barb?"

"I'm fine. I was shaken, of course, and my throat is bruised. But overall, I was lucky."

"Smart," he corrected. "You didn't panic. You took your shot and stayed alive."

I had to work to conceal the pride I felt at his words. I'd expected censure, blame, and maybe even orders to cease and desist. I'd gotten praise. From a cop, and not just a small-town guardian of the peace, but a professional with experience in dealing with the real thing.

"I appreciate your saying so."

He tapped his chin with a finger. "Any idea why you were attacked?"

"We only have one case right now. Neil Brown."

"Tom Stevens thinks we've got our man."

I gave him a look. "And Tom doesn't think girls should worry their pretty little heads with things like murder." Hearing the disdain in my own voice, I added, "The attack might have been random. I mean, how could anyone have known I'd be out there this morning?"

Rory didn't look like he believed it. "Seems planned, with the plate obscured and all."

"Wozniak might be afraid we'll get Neil released."

"I shouldn't have taken you out there," he said regretfully. "It focused his anger on you."

"My attacker wasn't Stan—too stocky. Would he hire someone to keep me from helping Neil?"

"Someone paid those guys to follow you to the U.P." Rory clicked his pen point away and stood. "Whatever the reason, the danger is real. I'll have officers check your home several times a day. And when you go to work—"

"I work from home." I took out a business card and laid it on the table. Rory took it up, read it, as it is polite to do, and nodded, passing a thumb over the embossed logo.

"We'll find this guy, Barb."

Again I had to hide my emotions when he said "we."

"Hello!" The voice from the hallway was all too familiar. "Rory, are you back here? Your office is a—" Retta stuck her head into the doorway, her eyes widening as she recognized me. "I didn't know you were busy. It's just that the grant is due in--"

She took one look at me and knew, as sisters must, I suppose. "Barbara, what's wrong?"

I stood, bending to pick up my jacket. "Nothing," I said, shooting Rory a look. "Just checking in." He looked at me, then at Retta, then back at me. "I appreciate your time, Chief."

"I'll call when I've done some preliminary work, Ms. Evans."

"You have my card."

"Yes. Well, um, take care."

"I will."

At home, I told Faye most of it. I said I was impressed by the chief's manner, I said I trusted him to do what he could to help, and I said Retta had come along. I didn't say that she and the chief would probably lunch together at noon. I didn't want to say it out loud.

CHAPTER THIRTY-EIGHT

Retta

Rory seemed distracted, and I guessed he was busy with the Brown case. He answered my grant questions so tersely I decided not to ask him to lunch again, as I'd planned. Instead I thanked him and left. Once the case was settled and Barbara and Faye weren't breathing down his neck, Rory and I could get to know each other better.

My phone rang as I left the police station, and I hurried to my car and closed the door against the traffic noise before answering. The screen said it was Faye. "What's up, girlfriend?"

"Retta?" I knew from her voice something was wrong. In a tumble of words, the story came out: Barbara had been attacked, and though she'd escaped any real hurt, Faye was terrified.

"The chief says he'll provide protection, but he can't guard her day and night." I was thinking about the look Barbara Ann had tossed at him. I realized it meant, *Don't tell Retta.* I returned my attention to Faye, whose voice teetered toward tears. "I shouldn't have pushed her into this stupid detective thing. How could I live with myself if—"

"Easy, Faye. In the first place, Barbara Ann never in her life did anything she didn't want to do, so you didn't push her into anything. In the second place, it sounds like she handled herself pretty well. Third, it could be a simple mugging, unpleasant but not likely to happen twice. And finally, if Rory says he'll protect her, you can trust him to do it."

All the while I was reassuring Faye, however, I knew she was right. This felt like it was about Neil Brown, and the city didn't have the manpower to provide full-time security for one citizen. "We need to solve this ourselves," I said. "Tell me every single thing you can."

Faye's fear *of* Barbara was almost as great as her fear *for* Barbara. "I don't think—"

"You don't have to tell her I know. Now what did she say about the guy?"

Once I had all the information Faye could provide, I considered my options. A black pickup truck and a man with a possible eye injury. I assumed Rory would check the emergency room to see if anyone had gone for treatment, so I concentrated on the vehicle. If its condition was as bad as Barbara said, it would need parts. Guys who drive junkers get their parts at junkyards, and there are only two in Allport. It might be worthwhile to visit them.

Inventing a story about a man who'd helped me when my car broke down, I told the overall-clad guy at the first one I'd been in a hurry and hadn't had any cash with me. "I'd like to give him a few bucks, you know? Men like that aren't common nowadays."

He knew exactly who I meant. "That's Zack Dymond," he said. "He musta been in a good mood, though. Usually he wouldna helped unless you paid him up front."

"Does he live in town?"

He slid a hand under his bibs and scratched. "On Deer Point Road. I think in a trailer."

There was no phone listing for a Zack Dymond, but there was a listing for G. Dymond, 2123 Deer Point Road. I guessed G. Dymond might be a relative, and I was right. When I called, she sounded interested in hearing more about the prize her son had won from the Allport Chamber of Commerce. "He ain't got a phone," she told me, "but I'll tell 'im. He's got a trailer on the property, and he usually comes over for supper." *Failure to Launch*, Michigan style.

When supper-time came, I was sitting along the road between Mrs. Dymond's run-down farmhouse and her son's even worse-looking trailer. I'd backed my Escalade into the trees on an old logging road, hoping I'd be able to get it out again. In spring the shoulders of tertiary roads can be pretty soft, as couples who stop for some "private time" often learn to their chagrin.

Not knowing how long the wait would be, I'd brought along a diet soda, some wheat crackers, and the latest *Celebrity Tracker* magazine. At first I felt like Kinsey Milhone, but I soon realized stake-outs are boring. You can't do anything that might distract you from what you're watching, so mostly you sit and wish there was a bathroom nearby.

At five-twenty, the trailer's storm door flew open and slammed against the exterior siding with a metallic thud. Apparently the closing mechanism had succumbed to wind or hard treatment. Onto the minimal, unvarnished porch stepped Zack, rubbing his belly as if he'd just finished a nap. Grabbing my binoculars, I took a look. Even from that distance, it was easy to tell the guy had a spectacular shiner. I followed him as he made his way to Momma's and dinner. There was no sign of the truck, but a barn behind the house was closed up tight. The ancient structure listed dangerously to one side, but I've known some that stood for years like that. A great hiding place for a vehicle the police might be looking for.

As soon as Zack disappeared into the house, I started my car and put it into gear. It pulled smoothly back onto the road, and I was back in town before six. On the chance an unmarried, new-to-the-job police chief might stay past normal hours, I stopped at Rory's office. He was working, shirt-sleeves folded back, and I noted nicely muscled arms. Weight-lifter, maybe?

Rory was putting papers into file drawers almost at random, and I guessed he was clearing the room for the painters. When I told him what I'd discovered and how, his expression went from curiosity to disbelief and finally to admiration. "That's good work, Mrs.—Retta."

I shrugged. "You're married to a cop for fifteen years, you start thinking like one."

"Wouldn't it have been smarter to tell me your idea and let us follow it up?"

There it was. Nobody ever appreciates what you do for them. They always think you're being nosy or pushy. "I have no intention of taking over your job, Rory. But my sister was attacked, and you were busy with all that's happened. I simply did some initial digging before giving you something else to do." I raised my hands. "He never saw me."

"That's good." After a moment he added, "And I can appreciate your reasoning." I saw in his gaze a new respect, a realization he'd misjudged me. We were actually getting somewhere.

***

The next morning, Rory called. "I thought you'd want to know your investigation led to the detention of one Zackary Dymond, known to some as "Z". The truck was in the mother's barn, as you guessed, and we got tire impressions from the alley that I think are going to match."

"That's great, Rory."

"Zack's one of the two who followed your sisters to the U.P., and according to Gabe, he fired the shots at them." I suppressed a gasp of surprise. I'd make sure Faye spilled those details!

Unaware of my ignorance, Rory went on. "The downside is that Zack isn't the pushover Gabe Wells is. He isn't talking."

"What do you think is going on?"

His tone changed as the professional law officer persona took over. "It's too early to say, but I thank you for your help. Now I'll let you get back to your schedule."

And you'll get back to yours. That was okay, though. I wasn't just an attractive woman to Rory now. He realized I had a brain as well.

CHAPTER THIRTY-NINE

Faye

The chief and I met for the second time when he stopped to tell Barb he'd apprehended her attacker. It was Saturday, and he looked friendlier in jeans and a dark green pullover.

Barb looked a little flustered when I told her he was downstairs. She didn't appear until Neuencamp was seated in the office and I'd brought him a glass of iced tea. Though she was dressed casually, she wasn't wearing the same shirt she'd had on earlier.

He filled us in on Zack's arrest. "We bluffed our way to a confession, told him the skin under your fingernails matched his." He grinned disarmingly. "With all the cop shows nowadays, people think we get stuff like that at the touch of a button."

In response to a question from Barb, Neuencamp said we couldn't visit Dymond unless he asked for us. That was disappointing. On TV P.I.'s always seem able to talk their way into an interrogation or a jail cell. In real life, the attackee doesn't get to face her attacker and sweat out of him the reason for his crimes.

The chief shared what he could, but in the end it wasn't much help. Dymond admitted to accosting Barb but said his intention had been robbery. He hadn't meant to hurt her, but when she fought back, he'd grabbed her in self-defense.

"He's a liar."

Neuencamp gave a tight nod. "I'm not sure if he was supposed to kill you, hurt you, or just scare you, but Zack is no purse-snatcher."

"Especially since I wasn't carrying a purse."

He shifted uncomfortably. "You should know he'll probably be released."

I heard the outrage in my voice. "Released! He attacked Barb!"

"He's hired a lawyer. Monday first thing, I'll bet he's out on bail."

"He *hired* a lawyer? Not a P.D.?" Barb asked.

"Nope. His mother hired..." Pulling a notebook from his hip pocket, he checked. "...Jamison Warren, who's apparently the local hotshot."

"He's pretty good," I volunteered.

"Pompous," Barb sneered. "The kind of lawyer that gives us all a bad name."

"Well, Jamison will argue it was all a huge misunderstanding."

"And the judge will buy that?"

He raised his hands in resignation. "No witnesses. If it hadn't been for your sister, he might have gotten away with it."

"My sister?"

I heard the horror in Barb's tone, but the chief said, "Retta didn't tell you? She hunted down his vehicle and steered us to him."

Barb's gaze slid over to me. "I wonder how she heard about it."

Sensing trouble, the chief set his glass on the desk, rose, and moved to the door in a strategic retreat. "I'll ask the court to issue an order forbidding Zach to come anywhere near you. It's the best we can do." With that he was gone. While Rory Neuencamp might have been a brave man, he was wise enough not to mix in the family dynamics of three sleuthing sisters.

***

I knocked at the door of the farmhouse, shifting my purse so the strap stayed on my shoulder. It was Sunday morning, and I'd come to see what I could learn from Glenda Dymond before her son was released on Monday. Before they put their heads together and concocted a story.

The woman who came to the door was, in a word, substantial. Her frame wasn't overly padded with flesh, but there was enough to suggest a Teutonic opera diva. Her hair, wrapped around her head in a tight braid, added to the effect. She stood erect, hands at her sides. "Ya?"

"I saw on your sign you sell fresh eggs?"

"Ya." It was more foreign than slang, a musical slide that revealed Nordic heritage.

"Could I have a dozen, please?"

"Sure. Wait here."

"Do you mind if I come along? I'd love to see your chickens."

She looked down at my shoes. "Watch where you walk. They don't care where they squirt." Taking a basket from a nail she went off, not waiting to see if I'd changed my mind.

I followed her to the back of the house, where a chicken coop almost as crooked as the barn rested against a shed next to it. At least thirty chickens scattered as we passed, but they didn't go far. In seconds they were back to pecking for wormy treats.

Mrs. Dymond had to stoop double to get into the dark hen-house, but she wasn't inside long. That was good, because an unfriendly-looking rooster had begun eyeing me. White feathers shone along his sides, and he carried his scaly red head upright, his beady eyes letting me know what he thought of interlopers. The hens ignored both of us, but I sensed in the rooster's posture a readiness to charge on the slightest provocation.

"Get, you!" Mrs. Dymond shooed the bird with a hand. "Thinks he owns the place."

"A nice specimen," I observed, feeling better now that the rooster had retreated.

"He keeps 'em laying. When he can't do that, he's Sunday supper." She waved again at the bird, who trailed after us. "He'll be tough by then, sure as hell." I followed her to the porch, where she separated a container from a stack in the corner and began putting eggs into it.

"You live here all alone?" I asked.

"Ya. My son lives close, though."

"Oh, that's good. He can help with chores and things."

She glanced at me with dark amusement. "Ya."

I searched for a way to get her talking. "These days a woman alone has to be careful. Someone was attacked the other day, right in town."

There was a pause. "What'd you hear?"

"Well, she was running, you know, for exercise." A faint sniff conveyed Mrs. Dymond's attitude toward those whose daily activities didn't provide adequate physical conditioning. "A man stepped out of an alley and grabbed her. She got free, but he might have killed her."

"He prob'ly just wanted her money. He wouldna hurt her."

I widened my eyes. "Who knows what a man like that had in mind?"

She stopped for a moment, one hand kneading the muscles at the back of her waist. "That's right, who knows? You weren't there. I wasn't there. We don't know what he wanted. Maybe she's one of them snooty types that deserve to get scared a little, running all alone in her expensive shoes. You weren't there. I wasn't there. We don't know."

And that, I thought, *is how a mother justifies her son's crimes.*

Digging in my wallet for two dollar bills, I tried again. "Did you hear they caught the guy who killed his wife a few years back? That rich girl, Carrie something."

"Carina."

"Right. My friend said she was kind of snooty, too."

Her jaw jutted. "Better not say that where her father can hear you."

I took a step back as if surprised. "You know Mr. Wozniak?"

"My son works for him sometime at his place out on Pierce Lake."

"Oh," I let admiration vibrate in my voice. "They say it's really something."

She folded work-roughened hands against her middle. "Mr. Wozniak knows it was Brown that murdered his kids."

I couldn't resist turning her own words against her. "But he wasn't there. You weren't there. Like you said, we don't know."

She eyed me coldly. "Well, I betcha one thing. Old Stan's gonna see that Brown pays for what he did."

***

"Why would killing me help Stan Wozniak?" Barb countered when I presented my argument. It was Monday morning, and Dale, Barb, and I had breakfasted together. Barb insists I don't have to feed her, but I worry about her eating take-out and packaged dinners. Besides, cooking for two almost isn't worth the effort. I always make too much, so why not share?

After Dale went to the garage to putter, I'd recounted my visit to Mrs. Dymond and the conclusions I'd reached. "Two possibilities," I told her. "First, Stan killed his own children and blamed it on Neil. Now he doesn't want anyone proving Neil didn't do it."

"But he didn't have time. Seconds after he entered the building he was calling 9-1-1."

"Maybe he went earlier, killed them, then sneaked back later to 'discover' the bodies."

"He was with other people all morning. Besides, this wasn't a heat of anger thing, remember? Carina and Carson were both struck from behind."

I cleared the plates, setting them in the sink and running warm water over them. Yes, I have a dishwasher, but I don't much care for it. Soapy water is relaxing.

"Okay, second possibility. Stan didn't kill the kids, but he's got something else to hide."

"That's a little more believable, but then we have two separate problems."

"Right. Stan's secret and the identity of whoever really killed his kids."

"Maybe it's time I contacted Eric DuBois again. He might know something."

We were interrupted by Barb's phone. "It's Rory." She stared at the device as if it might bite, but I poked her elbow and she answered. "Barb Evans."

As she listened, her face tightened. "Where is that?" ... "No, but my sister will. Thanks."

She closed the phone with a snap and stood, setting her chair neatly against the kitchen table. "Come on, Faye. We're about to visit our first murder scene."

"Who?" I croaked.

"Zack Dymond. He was released from jail this morning, and he's already dead."

CHAPTER FORTY

Barb

Visiting a crime scene was not what I had imagined. There was no drama to it, and no pathos, really, since the body had been taken away by the time we arrived. Rory stood talking quietly to a woman in a sheriff's department uniform. When he noticed us, he said something to her and touched her shoulder in a way that seemed both reassuring and congratulatory. I guessed she'd been first on scene and had little experience with violent death.

He approached where we'd stopped at the edge of the area, aware we shouldn't trample the scene. All business, he began where he'd left off on the phone. "Dymond left the county jail at five. Apparently they let prisoners out as early as possible on release day so they don't have to feed them." He seemed faintly amused by the miserly but efficient practice. "Zack griped about having to walk home, said his mother was busy. I guess she makes morning deliveries."

"Eggs," Faye supplied.

"Anyway, that's the last anyone saw of him. One of the workers was outside having a last cigarette before starting her shift. She didn't see which way he went, but she was a little surprised at how soon he disappeared. From that we theorize someone picked him up."

"And brought him out here." At Faye's direction, I'd driven to a spot called Bayner's Roost. Not far from Zack's trailer, it was down a side road used mostly by kids looking for a place to party.

After leaving the car we'd walked a short distance to an open, grassy space with the remains of a fire pit in the center, ringed by rocks and dug down to sand level.

"Someone drove him out here, got him out of the car somehow, and ran him down?"

"Judging from fresh beer cans we found over there, I picture it happening this way," Rory said. "Someone Zack knows picks him up near the jail. They come out here to talk things over. The friend has brought along a twelve-pack to celebrate Zack's release."

"Could be a source of prints," Faye said, and I twitched a little at her assumption he wouldn't have considered that.

Apparently used to advice from the laity, Rory nodded. "We're checking. Anyway, at some point Zack gets out of the vehicle, maybe to answer nature's call. The driver says he'll turn the car around then pick him up. We found where he did that about fifty feet farther along."

"But instead of picking Zack up, the other guy ran him down."

"Right."

"He might have been out here a long time before someone found him," I said, looking around. Even the view from the two-track was screened by a scraggly stand of jack pines.

"Luck," Rory agreed. "A local guy was out looking for his black lab. He found the dog, and the dog had found Zack, right where his supposed friend left him."

"You think they fought about something?"

His lips tightened as he shook his head. "I think Zack's death was the intention all along. The vehicle will be a dead end."

"Because it was stolen?"

"Because on Zack's belt buckle we found black paint with traces of rust. I think he was run down with his own truck, which is probably back in his mother's barn by now."

Rory was correct. When told what had happened, Mrs. Diamond said stoically, "He never killed nobody." Her son had been bad; she knew it. Now he was dead; he couldn't get any worse.

She willingly led Rory and the sheriff's deputy to the barn, opening a large door that slid along the outer wall to reveal Zack's beat-up Dodge. Its use as a murder weapon was apparent in the broken grill and the blood on the hood. When Mrs. Dymond gasped and turned away, Faye put an arm around her shoulders, leading her gently out of the barn. Rory and I approached the vehicle, circling in opposite directions. "Is this the truck you saw in the alley?"

The plate was still caked with dirt. "Yes." I pointed out the missing trim. "That's what I recall. And the rust."

"Okay." Pulling out his phone, he called the crime scene team still at the site of Zack's murder. As he talked, Faye returned, her expression revealing empathy for the man's mother.

"We'll go over it," he said when he finished, "but I'll bet it's clean. Whoever did this is staying a step ahead of us."

Faye's eyes widened as a thought hit her. "A guy called a while back trying to hire us to investigate a kidnapping. We thought it was a joke, but it might have been Zack trying to distract us from this case."

"Possible," I agreed. "It seems whoever hired him to stop us left the method up to him."

"The mastermind didn't choose very well. A high school student could have done better."

"Zack was no genius. The shots he fired at Neil's cabin made us *more* suspicious, and the attack in the alley failed to put me out of commission."

"And he trusted someone who brought him out here and killed him," Rory added.

Zack was a threat because he might have been convinced to tell who hired him. I made a mental note to investigate his background, but I doubted there was any possibility of his involvement in the deaths of Carson and Carina. He'd have been fourteen, maybe fifteen at the time. Still, I was learning that good detective work meant seeking out information, even when it was difficult to do or loathsome to contemplate. I was tired of surprises I should have foreseen.

***

It was raining the next morning when the three of us went to see Chief Neuencamp. Faye had called and asked Retta to meet us there. She readily agreed, which was no surprise to me. She got to act like a detective *and* bat her eyes at the chief.

Rory met us at the front and led us to his transformed office. The room was now a soft beige, and the furnishings were much different. The desk was highly-polished oak, the chairs were similar in tone with tapestry-covered seats. The sense of order and serenity pleased me. After a look around, Retta gave one of the smiles she summons when she's about to tell you how far short you've fallen of her standards. "Very nice, Chief, but you know what would really set it off? A copper mobile. I know a Native American artist I can put you in touch with. It'll be perfect, artistic and nicely in keeping with your heritage."

"I'm pretty happy with it as it is." His tone was emotionless but definite. No discussion.

She was quick; I have to give her that. "Oh, of course, Rory—Chief." She tittered sweetly. "I'm just happy your home away from home has been rejuvenated." She was babbling, probably because she wasn't used to a man looking directly at her and saying no.

Rory changed the subject to the matter at hand. He told us a little about the crime scene team's findings, which bore out the scenario he'd imagined. They had no suspects, since no one had seen the driver of the truck and both Gabe and Neil were locked up.

"I know how we could catch him," Retta said. "Barbara Ann tells everyone she's going out to Bayner's Roost to look at the scene again. The killer follows her out there and you and your people charge in and arrest him."

"Mrs. Stilson." I felt like smiling at the step back Rory took in his relationship with my sister. "This man murdered Zack Dymond."

"And he probably killed Carina Brown and Carson Wozniak." Faye never passed up the chance to plug Neil's innocence.

"I don't think Zach was supposed to kill Barb," Retta argued. "He sounds more like a mean-spirited screw-up to me. I bet he was sent to scare you and derail your investigation."

Faye made a rude noise. "What's going on here? Carson can't tell who his partner was. Wozniak thinks Neil's guilty, so he isn't looking in any other direction."

"Even the scheme to steal the money can be laid at Neil's feet," I put in. "The killer could have simply waited for the hoopla to die down."

"Something's out there that makes this person nervous," Rory said. "A hint to his identity he's afraid we're going to find." Looking at me, he added, "Since you were attacked, I'd guess it has something to do with you."

They all turned to me, but I shrugged helplessly. "No idea."

Rory stood, dismissing us. "Think about it. I'll do what I can from here."

"Can you let Neil go?" Faye asked. "Like you said, he couldn't have killed Zack."

He shook his head. "That doesn't change the evidence. But I'll talk to him, tell him we have a new operating theory. That should bolster his spirits a little."

Faye gave him her best smile. "Thank you, chief."

"Yes, thank you, Rory." Retta gave him a flirty smile. She couldn't help it.

Rory glanced at me, and I tried to keep a blank expression. "Chief."

"I'll be in touch." His eyes sought mine, but I dug in my purse for car keys.

"Thanks." I brushed past Retta, unwilling to look back at them standing so close.

CHAPTER FORTY-ONE

Faye

I backed out of the drug store, using my butt to open the door, since my arms were full.

"Hey, lady, can I help you with that?"

I turned to find Doris Larsen, a woman I knew slightly from church.

"I've got the load balanced, but if you'd unlock the car door, that would be great."

Taking the keys from my hand and moving ahead of me, Doris unlocked the passenger side and stood back so I could dump several prescriptions, a half-gallon of milk, and two value-packs of toilet paper onto the seat. "It was on sale," I told her with a grin.

"What's this I hear about you starting a detective agency?"

My grin turned to a grimace. "It's true."

She squeezed my arm. "You'll have to tell me all about it."

Closing the car door, I admitted, "Actually, it's scarier than I thought. My sister was attacked the other day because of a case we're working on." I'd suffered guilt pangs ever since, although Retta's reminder that Barb only did as she wanted had helped a little.

Doris' eyes grew wide. "Is she all right?"

"She's fine. And they know who did it, so she's safe now." I didn't add that the guy was dead. Something clicked in my head, and I asked, "Didn't you work at WOZ Industries once?"

"Half the town does or did," she replied cheerfully. "I left a few years back when Jim and I started our own business."

"Did you know Stan Wozniak's children?"

"Not really. I mean, we saw them sometimes, but I don't think I ever spoke to either of them." She gave a little chuckle. "Phyllis used to say they had a contest going to see who could say the least to the likes of us." She raised a pinky finger in a prim gesture. "So above us, you know." Looking ashamed, she added, "I'm sure they were nice when you got to know them."

I was thinking. "Who's Phyllis?"

"Phyllis Nesmith. Well, she's not Nesmith anymore. She was Stan's secretary once upon a time, but now she's Mrs. Eric DuBois."

CHAPTER FORTY-TWO

Barb

Eric DuBois' home had once belonged to one of Allport's lumber barons. It was made of fieldstone, with a massive entry already lit by wrought-iron lanterns, though it was only a little after five. The porch, though a spot so large probably merited a fancier name, was empty. There wasn't a swing or rattan settee or one of those lacy-metalwork table and chair sets yet, but it had been swept clean of winter's detritus. The windows were shiny clean. Everything was. I made a mental note to do better with my own porch, which had cobwebs in its corners.

Checking my watch, I rang the bell, hearing the muffled sound of chimes inside the house. It was too early for Eric to be home, which was what I'd intended. After a few minutes, the door opened, and I introduced myself. Mrs. DuBois, who appeared totally surprised to have a visitor, invited me in, but her expression said she expected me to refuse. When I thanked her and entered, she smiled like a child who's talked someone into attending her tea party.

"Call me Phyllis," She said as I followed her into a living room that was tastefully decorated but hardly warm. At her urging I sat, while she teetered on the edge of a chair. A stunning brunette, she reminded me of Stan's current secretary: same figure, same doe-like eyes, same better-than-average chest. I wondered if the job description included *droits de signeur*.

Phyllis DuBois' clothes were as tasteful as her furniture, but she didn't look comfortable in either. "Would you like something to drink?" she asked. "I just made iced tea."

"Thanks," I replied. "Shall we sit in the kitchen? I'm always more comfortable there."

She smiled genuinely for the first time. "Me too, but Eric says visitors deserve better." She led the way past an elegant dining room and indicated a small table in one corner of the kitchen, where she seemed to relax a little. There was something in the oven, pork, I guessed from the smell. This room, too, was squeaky clean, the appliances upscale and shiny, but touches of Phyllis' personality showed. Cute oven mitts hung on a plastic hook, pictures of a gap-toothed boy decorated the refrigerator, and a hand-embroidered set of covers hid the smaller appliances.

"Did you do these?" I asked.

Turning from pouring tea into tall glasses half-filled with ice, she blushed. "Yes."

I ran a finger over the image of a bright bouquet of flowers. "My grandmother used to embroider. I think it's beautiful, but I haven't the patience for it."

"It isn't hard if you practice. I'm trying to get real good at it."

There was a pause, and I knew she was wondering what I'd come for. "Your husband probably told you we're looking into the Brown murder case."

"No, he didn't." She shook her head. "It was awful, though. Really sad."

"I understand you were working for Mr. Wozniak at the time."

"Before I got married, I was quite the career girl." She laughed in a way that deprecated both her career and herself.

"I was hoping you might go over what happened that day. We came to the case late, so we have to rely on those who were there for information."

Phyllis looked doubtful. "It's all in the reports. I couldn't add anything."

"I'm sure you were helpful." I smiled as she handed me the glass of tea. "I'd just like to hear it from you, to get a clear idea."

She paused. "Sure. I guess."

"Great. Tell me everything you remember."

Her eyes rolled to the side as she thought. "It started out pretty normal." I felt my lips tense. What kind of secretary didn't know an adverb from an adjective? Forcing my mind away from grammar, I tried to listen to the message. "Eric and Mr. Wozniak were working on this contract that was giving them fits. They were at the lawyer's, and around eleven, Carina came by looking for her dad. When I told her he was out, she seemed real upset. She said I should have him call her as soon as possible."

"You knew Carina Brown pretty well?"

Another pause. "Not really. She came around a lot to see her dad."

"Your husband said she expected her father to drop everything when she called."

Phyllis seemed relieved that Eric had paved the way to the truth. "That's for sure. Carina could get her way like nobody else." Phyllis' gaze strayed to the window. "I used to wonder what it was like, having everybody jump when she said jump."

"You didn't like her?" I let it stay a question, though I thought I knew the answer.

She gave a timid shrug. "I guess I envied her."

"I suppose all that money has its allure."

Phyllis looked surprised. "It wasn't the money."

"Oh?"

She blushed, twisting her hands in her lap like a child. "I was crazy about Eric from the first time I saw him, but he only had eyes for her. He was always trying to impress her."

Not many women will admit they were their husband's second choice. Phyllis didn't seem to mind.

"When she married Neil I thought, 'Maybe Eric will notice me,' but he didn't." She smiled, but her eyes were sad. "I even used to try to look like Carina. When she came in that day, her fingernails were this really bright green. I said they looked cool and she said she'd never tried green before but she was hoping it would change her luck." She paused. "I guess her luck changed, but not in a good way."

"How did you and your husband finally start dating?" I asked.

"After Carina died, it was like Eric finally looked around and realized I was there."

"Was that soon after the murders?"

"Yeah. He asked me out, and in a few weeks, we was planning our wedding. I could hardly believe it."

I couldn't either. "Were Eric and Carson Wozniak friends?"

"Not really. At Carina's wedding Eric and him spent some time talking. That was the only time I know of they ever spoke to each other. Eric says they mostly talked about fishing."

"Did you see Carson during that last visit?"

"Yeah, a couple of times."

"Did he speak to anyone at the office, anyone in particular?"

"Not that I remember."

"We know he and his father argued sometimes. Were they angry with each other during that last visit?"

"No. In fact, Carson went out of his way to be nice to his dad. They had a real nice visit." Phyllis turned pensive. "I guess that's good, because Mr. Wozniak has those memories. But if Carson hadn't been at his sister's that day, he'd still be alive."

I wasn't so sure, but at that moment the back door opened and Eric entered. "Hey, Babe."

Phyllis sprang to her feet. "Eric!" She was smiling, but a note of distress sounded in her voice. I saw her glance around the spotless kitchen then seek her husband's eyes as if asking for something. Approval?

Whatever she wanted, she got a look I didn't like from him, very different from the affable manner I'd seen before. "I didn't know you were having company, Phyllis."

"I didn't either." She let out a brittle titter that cut off quickly.

Sensing trouble, I hastened to explain my presence. "When I learned your wife worked in Stan's office at the time of the murders, I thought she might contribute to the investigation."

"And did she?"

"I'm afraid not," Phyllis answered, though Eric had spoken to me and was looking at me. "You know how I am. I remember dumb stuff like Carina's nail polish, but if there was something important, I didn't notice." She turned to me. "That's why I stay home with our son now. I wasn't that great as a secretary."

Her dismissal of her own worth was setting my teeth on edge. "Thank you for your time, Mrs. DuBois. I won't keep you any longer." Something fluttered in my brain but didn't settle. I tried to catch hold of it. What had I just learned?

Eric turned gracious. "You mustn't leave on my account. Phyllis likes company, don't you, hon? I just came home to get some things I need, but I have to go back to work." He smiled at his wife. "Did you show Ms. Evans Buddy's room?"

"Uh, no."

"She might like to see the way we decorated it." Eric leaned toward me in fatherly pride. "Kid loves Thor."

I smiled politely, not sure exactly what that meant. "That's great."

"Show her, Phyllis."

She glanced at me. "I'm not sure—"

"It won't take long." Eric gave his wife a gentle push. "I'd do it, but I have to go."

"Supper will be ready in just a few—?"

"Go ahead and eat without me. I won't be back till late." He paused. "First, the room."

Obediently, Phyllis led me down the hall to her son's room. I was anxious to be on my way, but I didn't want to be rude. He seemed pretty proud of what they'd done.

The room was almost scary, with a huge figure of the comic book character looming over the bed, but the boy loved it. He showed me everything, the toys, the lamps, even the light switches, all tied to some movie franchise. I guessed nothing was too good for their only child.

When I finally left, the day was growing dim. Clouds had gathered overhead, and I guessed we were going to get rain overnight. Waving to nice-but-clueless Phyllis, I backed out of the DuBois' driveway and headed for town.

I hadn't gone a block when a voice sent a shockwave through me. "Mrs. Evans, there's a gun at your back. Turn left until you get back to 23. Then go south."

Eric DuBois was in my back seat. That flitting thought settled, too late to do me much good. Carina's green nail polish. She'd never worn green before, Phyllis said, but Eric had mentioned it. That meant he'd seen her that day. And where but at her apartment, where he murdered her and her brother?

I turned left. "You were Carson's partner in crime."

"Would have been. The crime never happened."

"Because you killed them."

"Because Carina found out." His voice turned wistful. "It was a dumb idea, but at the time, it seemed like so much money, you know?"

I turned left again at the end of the block. "So why do you want the flash drive now?"

"I didn't want it. I just wanted it destroyed."

"So you can go on being WOZ Industries' Number Two?"

"Ironic, isn't it? The murders made me indispensable to Stan. Turn here." I turned left again. "Neil can still take the blame if you don't tell anyone what you've figured out."

I stopped at the crossroad, heart pounding. His tone was off-hand, as if I'd guessed the ending. I had, but my mind protected me by blurring what was ahead.

"We talked that first day about my morning walks. You sent Zack to scare me."

"Zack was an idiot." He sat behind me, close enough that I didn't think I could jump out of the car before he caught hold of me. "Keep driving."

My hands obeyed as my mind searched frantically for other possibilities. Could I run the car into the ditch and make him drop the gun? I doubted it. I'd wait for a better chance.

Forcing my voice to remain steady, I said, "They'll know I was at your house."

"That means nothing." Something cold touched my neck. "Turn."

A right turn took us south, down 23 and through Allport. Despite furious brain activity, I had no helpful ideas. Anything I did to get attention would be useless, since I'd die as a result.

At the last major intersection on the south end of Allport there was a stoplight. On the corner sat a gas station, a Subway, and a laundromat. The light turned yellow as we approached and I slowed, grateful for any opportunity to think. As I sat waiting for the green, I noticed a city police car at the gas pump. Just putting the hose back was Rory. He turned, saw me, and waved. I didn't return the gesture but gave him a look I hoped spoke volumes. Too soon the light turned, and DuBois said, "Go!" Rory's gaze followed me, but all I could detect in his expression was confusion. He probably thought I'd snubbed him for choosing my sister over me.

A car dealership, a few blocks of houses, some converted to small businesses, and then we were out of Allport. Where were we heading? Eric had to be making this up as he went, and I began talking to keep him from thinking too far ahead.

"You framed Neil for the murders?"

"Not intentionally. I went there to get the flash drive and calm that idiot Carson down."

Something he'd said at our first meeting came back to me, and I cursed my own stupidity. "The ball bat was beside the door, you said. I missed it at the time, but how could you have known where it was unless you were the one who used it as a weapon?"

"I was leery of you from the start, Ms. Smart Detective. As long as Brown stayed in hiding, everyone assumed he was guilty. But you found him despite my attempts to stop you."

"Clumsy attempts."

"Maybe." He sounded as if that didn't matter now. "I guessed he had the flash drive but doubted he'd get what it meant. If Stan ever saw it, he'd know."

"So you sent Gabe and Zack to get it back."

His answer was a growl. "Idiots."

"You went to a lot of trouble."

"I had to cover my mistakes." His tone was almost pleading, but the old anger was still there. "I spent five years kissing Stan's ass, and he started talking about bringing Carson 'on board.' I think you can guess where that would have put me!"

"In third place at best," I replied. "You were lucky Neil got the blame, but think about it. In the last week you've made mistakes, some little, like mentioning the bat and Carina's nail polish; some big, like murdering Zack. It's coming apart, Eric."

"My 'mistakes' as you call them, are pretty much taken care of if you aren't around to point them out to anyone." His tone changed. "He's going to retire soon, did you know that? I'll be head of WOZ Enterprises."

Things had turned out better than DuBois could have hoped. He'd gotten away with his crimes, and while he hadn't been able to steal Stan's money, he'd gained his trust, and along with it, power, prestige, and a very comfortable lifestyle. I wondered how much he'd embezzled from WOZ over the last five years.

"You're going to turn left in about a mile."

"Am I giving you a ride to your office?" I asked in an attempt at sarcasm.

"Not exactly. We're going to the Pit."

Dim understanding turned to stark terror. "My sister will figure this—"

"She won't. You didn't get it until now, and you haven't had time to tell anyone else." The rain began then, a medium-heavy dose requiring wipers. I felt like crying, too.

"The chief of police knows someone is after that flash drive."

I felt his shoulder against my seat as he shrugged. "There'll be some mystery over all this. Some blame might go to Stan, but they'll say he's had enough grief and they'll let it go. Brown will get most of it."

"But they'll know he didn't kill Zack, since he's in jail."

He chuckled. "Maybe you killed him. He did try to strangle you, after all. Killing a guy could make a person depressed, and who knows what she might do then?"

I slowed to make the turn onto Pit Lane, passing a young couple who shared an umbrella as they walked along, love apparently making them oblivious to the rain.

About a half mile down, DuBois said, "There's a two-track on the left. Turn onto it."

I saw it ahead, its center green, its tracks dim with age. Not well traveled, like a hundred old roads around Allport. As soon as we were around the first curve, he ordered me to stop. "We'll wait here for a while," he told me. "The Pit shuts down at dark, and I want to think this through. Like you say, I don't want to make any more mistakes."

There had to be someone around. Reading my mind, DuBois said, "There's a night man, but he patrols twice a shift in an old golf cart that sounds like a tank. We'll avoid him easy."

"Easily."

"What?"

"Nothing."

In the rearview mirror, I saw him shrug again, unaware of my attempt to make him a better speaker of English.

"Get out."

I'd been plotting an escape into the woods, and I looked at him in confusion. "What?"

"I said we have to wait until dark. I'll sit up front." He flipped the passenger seat forward. "You'll wait in the trunk."

CHAPTER FORTY-THREE

Faye

I made scalloped potatoes for dinner, with asparagus and homemade cloverleaf rolls. When Barb wasn't there at six, I figured she was delayed. At six-thirty, I checked her calendar, thinking she'd made an appointment I was unaware of. A call to her cell went to voicemail.

After I'd told her about Phyllis DuBois being Stan's former secretary, she'd gone to interview her. As far as I knew, that was all she intended. At quarter to seven, I told Dale to go ahead and eat, and I called Mrs. DuBois.

"Yes, I met Ms. Evans this afternoon," she told me. "We had a nice talk."

"Might anything you said have led her somewhere else?"

"Hmm. I don't think so. I just repeated what I told the police back then."

"There was nothing she seemed to find especially interesting?"

"I can't think of a thing."

Thanking her, I hung up, telling myself that a week ago, I wouldn't have worried when she was an hour late. The attack and all the other crazy stuff associated with the Brown case had made me jumpy. Barb had her phone. She'd call if she needed me.

By seven-thirty I was pacing, and Dale retreated to another room where he didn't have to watch. "She's fine," he insisted. "Probably met a friend and forgot all about eating with us."

Loyal to my sister, I didn't point out Barb didn't have any friends, at least not the type she'd meet casually and decide to share an evening out together. Rory! She'd had dinner with him once. Maybe it had happened again.

But she'd have called. Barb is considerate that way.

Unable to quiet my unease, I called the police station and asked for Chief Neuencamp. "He isn't here," an officer told me. "You can speak to the deputy chief."

Tom Stevens was as unhelpful as usual. "She's probably shopping," he told me in that "Now, honey" tone of his. "Barb's a grown woman. You can't be tracking her all over town."

"She was attacked a few days ago."

"And the guy that did it is dead. He can't hurt her now."

Mentioning that someone had hired and probably killed Zack wouldn't get me anywhere with Tom. "Is there a way I could speak to the chief?"

Patiently Tom replied, "You could talk to him, but it wouldn't do no good. He's gone to Saginaw to pick up a local low-life that got himself arrested down there."

I ended the call and sat for a while, phone in hand. Where could Barb be? What had distracted her so much she didn't think to let me know she wasn't coming home?

Retta came to mind. They'd seemed on friendly terms that morning. I called.

"Oh, hi, Faye. What are you up to?" Retta's voice faded in and out, and I heard soft clunks and doors opening and closing.

"What are you doing?"

"Changing my clothes, I've got Miss Allport tryouts tonight."

"Have you heard from Barb this afternoon?"

"No. Why?"

Fears tumbled out, and by the time I'd finished, I was almost in tears. "Where can she be, Retta? She never forgets to call. Never."

"No, I don't suppose she does." I heard a closet door close. "Get a jacket, Faye. It's cool and kind of rainy. I'll pick you up in ten."

CHAPTER FORTY-FOUR

Barb

Two hours in a car trunk is longer than you can imagine. If you have to inhabit one, a vintage Chevy is probably a good choice, but that doesn't mean it's comfortable. I'd banged a knee getting in, and it throbbed the whole time. It was dark, of course, and the air was dusty and unwholesome. I lay next to my bag of Correction Event supplies, and I mentally went through its contents, hoping there was something in there that might help me escape. Paint: no. Brushes: no. Black clothing: no. I resolved that if I got out of this mess, I'd add a few things to my kit, like a knife, a pair of handcuffs, and a gun.

I'd been in the trunk for a while when sounds interrupted my panicked thoughts. I'd been trying to convince myself I could survive in this cramped, dark space. Of course, if I did, it would only be to die later. The car shifted, and I heard the musical tones of a phone number being punched onto a keypad. I heard the burr of the phone ringing. The voice that answered, however, was only an occasional squawk.

"Gabe?" ... "Do you know who this is?" ... "That's right." ... "I need you to do something for me." ... "Don't be stupid. Zack probably irritated somebody in town and paid the price." ... "There's a thousand dollars in it for you." ... "It's a lame charge, Gabe. They'll never make it stick." ... "All right. I'll make it two thousand, but I need you to come right away." ... "I can give you a thousand now and the rest tomorrow morning when the banks open." ...

"That's good. Do you know where the viewing point for the Pit is?" ... "Right. Meet me there in an hour."

The phone clicked shut and DuBois began humming, pleased with himself. What was he planning? Gabe wasn't the type I'd call to help with a murder, so why was he joining us?

"No one was supposed to get hurt." I pictured DuBois turning his face toward the back of the car as he spoke. Did he expect me to answer? To ask for further explanation? Not likely. I was fighting to stay sane.

After a while he started in again. "It was Carson's idea. When Stan said no more money, he got desperate. They were barely speaking when he went home after Carina's wedding."

Mention of Carina seemed to divert his thoughts. "She should have married me. Stan wanted it, and I was willing. Carina was kind of a pain, but she was hot, you know?"

No, I don't, but you'd never have turned her into a scared rabbit like you did Phyllis.

"Carina wanted Brown, though. I think that was mostly to irritate her old man."

It was silent for a while up front, and I tried to think what I'd do when he opened the trunk. If I could kick the gun out of his hand, I might have time to escape. I tried to visualize it in my mind, practicing successful images so they'd turn into action when my chance came.

He started talking again. "So Carson's extremely unhappy with his dad, and we start talking at the reception. We were a little drunk, but Carson says Stan's stingy, and I say, 'You ought to work for him.' Pretty soon Carson's telling me how Stan's got money in an offshore account, a couple million. He bragged he could get at it, and we joked about helping ourselves. That was it, just joking, you know?"

I pictured them, two young males impatient to get what they thought they deserved, outdoing each other in bold proposals for stealing the old lion's wealth.

"A few months later, Carson calls me at home. He's been thinking about our little joke, and he says we can get away with taking the money." DuBois laughed, a brittle, rueful sound. "I was young, you know? It sounded good to me."

My arm was going numb, and I wriggled onto my back. The spare tire interfered somewhat, but I managed to make myself a little less uncomfortable.

"Carson's part was to find the files and copy them for me. My job was to figure out Stan's system and transfer the money to our own offshore account the next time Stan went fishing in some remote spot." His tone turned whiny. "It should have worked."

Surely Stan would have become suspicious when Carson started throwing money around like the storied drunken sailor, but would he accuse his own son of theft? DuBois would probably have been safe as long as Stan thought Carson alone was responsible.

But Carson had carelessly left the flash drive where Carina had mistaken it for hers. I pictured her frown as she realized whose files were on the drive and her realization that Carson had taken them from their father's house.

"Carson phoned as soon as Carina left that morning," Eric said. "We were at the lawyer's office, but I stepped out to take the call." His tone turned outraged. "I could not believe it. The guy comes to me—*he* comes to *me*—then freaks out when that bitch gets suspicious! He was going to tell everything. Stan would forgive Carson, but no way in hell would he forgive me."

Even in my misery I was enthralled, imagining DuBois' dreams turning to nightmares.

"So Stan and I go back to the office, and Phyllis says Carina wants him to come to her place right away. I remind him he's got a lunch meeting, and he says he'll see her later. When he leaves I slip out the back and drive into town. I park my car a couple blocks away and head for Carina's apartment. I didn't intend to hurt either of them, I swear. I thought I could make it work." He groaned softly at the memory of how that plan had twisted into something terrible.

"Carina answered the door, and she lit into me right away. How dare I plot against Stan with all he'd done for me—that kind of thing. It was like she was nuts, screaming and swearing. She says, 'You'll be sorry you talked Carson into stealing from Dad!' Me! She thought *I* talked Carson into it! *He* called *me*! The bat was sitting by the door--"

A thump on the car seat indicated DuBois relived the memory of killing Carina.

When he began again, his voice was calmer but still taut with emotion. "I didn't even realize what I'd done until I was standing over her with the bat in my hand. Then Carson comes out of the bathroom shouting, 'What did you do?' He bent over her, and I knew he wouldn't understand." He let out a breath that was almost a sob. "It was all his fault, and he didn't get it!"

When he spoke again it was creepy, because he described the image that had risen in my mind. "I was a mess, blood all over me. I grabbed Neil's hoodie and put it over my clothes. I shoved the bat up the sleeve and pulled the hood over my head. I didn't know Stan saw me leaving until later." He chuckled softly. "He thought it was Neil."

"I was pretty stirred up, but I knew I had to get back to WOZ. My suit was black, and I keep a fresh shirt in my office for emergencies. I let myself in the back door, washed up in my bathroom, and put on the clean shirt. That night I took the hoodie, the bat, and my bloody clothes and buried them."

After a long silence that made me think he was finished, DuBois spoke again, his voice low. "There was one more problem. Stan's secretary, Phyllis, came looking for me while I was gone. I made up a story about leaving to pay a speeding ticket. Phyllis isn't very smart, as you probably noticed, but she had a thing for me. When I asked her to keep it quiet, she agreed."

Had Phyllis suspected she'd been scammed? Probably not.

DuBois sighed deeply. "From then on, I was extra nice to Phyllis, so she wouldn't *want* to tell anyone I was gone for a while that day. I didn't intend to marry her, but I couldn't let her think too much, you know? It would have been easy to find out there wasn't any ticket, but Phyllis isn't the type who'd check up on her boyfriend." His laugh this time was bitter. "She's a looker, and they say I'm lucky. Long as you don't want someone to talk to, she's a great wife."

After that there was silence that felt like it lasted for days. I almost missed DuBois' voice after a while. I had a few questions, but I could guess the answers. He'd probably met Zach through Stan Wozniak and recognized a fellow human being who wasn't particularly human.

More and more, my body objected to its awkward position. I was still afraid. I tried to remain determined to escape, but I felt myself becoming lethargic. Everything stopped mattering. In the end I just waited, passive and stoical.

I'd sunk to a semi-conscious state when the lid opened and a flashlight beam hit my eyes. "Get out."

To my undying shame, I could not. DuBois had to help me. Once I stood on solid ground, I shut my eyes, waiting for the world to stop spinning.

After a few moments I felt a little better. It was dark, and rain was still falling. There was a quarter moon, visible from time to time as clouds scuffed across the sky. When my head settled and my body once again obeyed my commands, I looked to Eric to see what was next.

"Get in. You're driving."

I obeyed. He went to the other side, climbed in, and sank down, his back against the door. If anyone happened to see us on the road, it would appear I was headed for the Pit alone.

CHAPTER FORTY-FIVE

Retta

Faye was waiting out front, and she climbed in so fast I hardly had to slow the car down.

"Where should we start?" she asked.

"Mrs. DuBois says she left a little after five, right?"

"Right."

I mentioned a couple of places she might have gone, but Faye dismissed both. "Do you think we should call the police?"

"I tried that." Faye explained Tom's attitude and Rory's absence. "I thought she might have gone to see the chief with what she learned from Phyllis DuBois, but I can't contact him."

I pulled the car over to the curb. "I can." Grabbing my bag from the backseat, I took out my phone and told it, "Call Rory." In seconds, he was on the line. "Neuencamp."

"Rory, it's Retta Stilson. I understand you're on the road, but Faye's worried about Barbara. She didn't come home, and we wondered if you talked to her this afternoon."

"I didn't talk to her," he answered, "but I saw her leaving town. I was at the gas station when she went past, going south on 23."

"Hmm. I wonder where she'd have been going."

"I don't know," he answered. "Come to think of it, she looked unhappy. I thought she was mad at me." The phone crackled as he made a movement I couldn't identify. "No message?"

"No."

There was a pause before he said, "I don't like that."

I opened my mouth to reassure him, but then I glanced at Faye's white face. She was scared. "We're going to see what we can find out. I'll keep you informed."

"Please do."

I closed the phone and turned to Faye. "Rory saw Barbara on 23, going south."

She frowned. "Let's drive out that way. Maybe she had a flat tire or something."

Instead of saying she'd have called in that case, I put the car in gear and did as she said.

CHAPTER FORTY-SIX

Barb

I turned into the viewing point's parking area, a small space of dirt carved out of a thick stand of alder and birch trees. At the center of the area, a short flight of stairs led to the plank platform that I knew from my earlier visit revealed a spectacular view of Lake Huron, the expanse of the Pit, and a sheer drop to the Pit's floor, a hundred feet below.

"Get out," DuBois ordered. When I obeyed, he exited the other side and came around. Glancing at my flat shoes, he said, "Good choice. We have to do some walking."

I searched my mind for a way to delay him, but what good would it do? No one knew I was here. No amount of dragging my feet would help me now.

"Hey." With my already high stress level, the voice almost set me screaming. I turned to see Gabe approaching. It was difficult to make out his features in the dark, but there was no mistaking his shambling gait and slouched posture.

When he got close, Gabe stopped. "What's she doing here?"

DuBois stepped forward, pointing the gun at Gabe's chest. "She's going to be murdered."

"What?" Gabe was stunned. "I never killed nobody."

"Shut up and do as you're told." With a tense gesture, DuBois indicated that Gabe and I should go left. We paralleled the platform, coming around its southern end, where a six-foot fence continued along the rim of the Pit. I remembered that the fence angled away from the edge, making a wedge of land the local teens called Party City. Someone had cut a hole in the fence, low to the ground and just big enough to crawl through. No doubt the kids tested their courage by hanging out on the wrong side of the protective fence. In the faint light I saw beer cans and a "pocket-rocket" liquor bottle, all empty.

"Through the rabbit hole, Ms. Evans," DuBois said cheerfully.

Gabe looked at the fence then at Eric. Though not the brightest bulb in the chandelier, he was getting a glimmer. "Look, Mister. I don't want the money. I promise I'll keep quiet—"

"I said shut up. Ms. Evans, do as I said. Gabe, follow her through. Both of you, stop on the other side. Remember, a bullet goes a lot faster than you can run."

I couldn't bend myself low enough to pass through the hole, though an image of laughing teens scooting lightly to the other side came to mind. Older, stiffer, and less willing, I crawled through on hands and knees. Radiating fear, Gabe came so close behind me that my shoe brushed his arm. I turned, ostensibly to hold the fencing back for him, and stuck a tissue from my pocket through the diamond-shaped pattern of the fence wire.

DuBois did a good job of getting through without taking the light off us. I considered trying to kick at the gun as he squirmed through, but he kept a firm hold on it, using his elbows to bear his weight. "Head down the path," he ordered, aiming the light at a break in the trees more suited to the passage of deer than humans. "I'll shine the light ahead so you can see your way." He sounded almost solicitous, like a good WOZ Industries employee protecting guests on the property from harm. A person might not believe only one of us was going to be coming back.

Surreptitiously draping another tissue on a branch, I started walking. It was all I could do.

CHAPTER FORTY-SEVEN

Retta

The road was shiny with rain, and headlights of approaching cars blurred in the mist. We passed several vehicles heading into town, but saw no one heading out.

"I don't know what she'd be doing out here." I was due at the school in an hour, and I wondered if we were being silly, hunting down a grown woman who could come home for supper or not, as she chose. Faye was having none of it.

"WOZ Industries is this way."

"Yeah, but everyone's gone home by now, and it's a little early for teenage lovers."

The Pit was known for what the kids called "watching the submarine races on Lake Huron." Apparently they raced late every night.

"There!" Faye's voice startled me. Walking along the road was a couple sharing an umbrella and three bags of groceries. "Stop! Maybe they've seen her."

I pulled over, and Faye rolled down the window. "Did a '57 Chevy go by here?"

"Sweet car," said the young man, who was damp around the edges of his U of M sweatshirt. "We saw it on our way into town, a couple of hours ago."

"It went down Pit Lane," the girl said. Her sweatshirt was drier, since she held the umbrella. The sleeves hung over her hands and the band reached her knees. His spare, no doubt.

We thanked them and went on. I turned onto Pit Lane, driving slowly so Faye could peer down the trails and side roads. We went all the way to the WOZ entrance, where the guard at the shack stepped out, pulling a slicker over his head as he came.

"Ladies? What can I do for you?"

"Have you seen a woman in an old Chevy?"

"Why, no. Everybody's gone for the day."

Faye looked disappointed as I turned the car around and started back. The guard retreated to his shelter, waving as he disappeared. "Now what?" I asked.

"I don't know. Drive slowly, and I'll keep an eye out."

CHAPTER FORTY-EIGHT

Barb

We entered the woods, moving away from the gaping hole on our right. The Pit was huge, running for at least half a mile, and the fence that lined it ran close to the road for the convenience of construction and maintenance crews. We were on a small promontory that ended somewhere ahead at what had been the original viewing point. We'd come there as kids in the days when such things were protected only by a wooden railing and a sign that advised caution. I shuddered, remembering that I'd once climbed the fence and leaned over to tease Faye, laughing as she begged me to come away from the sheer drop.

Behind me Gabe moved in an almost catatonic state. Faced with death, he wasn't thinking; he was merely doing as he was told. When the trail turned again, I dropped my third and final tissue.

DuBois held the ridiculously small flashlight I kept in my car, lighting the ground just in front of us. He stayed centered behind Gabe and me, one hand holding the gun and the other the light. I told myself I should run, but there was nowhere to go. The cyclone fence, somewhere to the left, was six feet high. I might run smack into it in the dark and knock myself senseless. Even if I didn't, I'd never be able to scale it before DuBois caught up with me. Anywhere else I went would lead to exactly what he wanted, a fall over the edge to my death.

CHAPTER FORTY-NINE

Faye

"There!" My voice sounded loud in Retta's car, which has that sealed-like-a-can-of-tuna quietness inside. "There's someone at the viewing point."

I'd seen only a flash of white, but when she backed the car up a little, my heart started pounding. "It's the Chevy."

She backed up some more and pulled into the parking area. Barb's car was at the far end, up against the trees. Going down Pit Lane, it had been invisible from the road, but on our return, the white on the back fender showed just enough for me to spot it.

"Look!" Retta pointed to the opposite end of the open area. Harder to see due to its color was a dark Ford Ranger pickup, parked sideways so that it nestled under the trees.

Retta shut off the engine. "What do you think's going on?"

I had no idea. Barbara had her late-night outings, and I had no idea what she did. I couldn't imagine, however, that she'd come to meet a secret lover at the Pit.

Getting out, we went to the Chevy, which was unlocked and unoccupied. We skirted it and found nothing. Rain, now steady and stronger than before, was rapidly obscuring the footprints around it, and it was even harder to see them in the light of Retta's key-chain flashlight. Disgusted, I said, "We should each keep an emergency kit in our cars."

"Oh!" Retta scurried away, and soon the dome lights of her SUV revealed her digging in the well at the back. Closing the door softly, she hurried back with a black knapsack in hand. "Don insisted I have one," she whispered. "I've never used it, and I forget it's in there."

The bag contained a decent flashlight and a pack of unopened C batteries. With a silent prayer they weren't too old to work, I loaded the flashlight and tried it. A strong, bright beam of light rewarded my effort. Along with that was an umbrella, a candle for heat, some matches, a lighter, a bundle of flares, a small blanket, some MREs (army-style Meals, Ready to Eat) and two bottles of water. I handed the bag to Retta. "I'll be right back."

At the viewing point the footprints were clearer, since the trees sheltered the ground a little from the rain. A large pair of shoes with no visible tread, a slightly smaller pair with heavy tread, and a small pair with light tread that I thought were Barb's. Following them about twenty feet, I found a hole in the fence just large enough for a person to crawl through.

I stood frowning into the darkness. In unguarded moments, my sons had mentioned parties at the Pit. They'd laughed at WOZ Industries' efforts to keep them away from the dangerous drop. "They put up a fence," Jimmy once said scornfully, "we cut a hole. They fix the hole, we make another one."

Obviously, this was the hole that led to what they called Party City. Was I mistaken? Had these footprints been made by a trio of teenagers out for a few thrills along the edge of the Pit? I almost turned to go, but something white stopped me. Caught in one of the diamond-shaped holes formed by the wire, a tissue fluttered. It was damp but not soaked, so it hadn't been there long. Someone had gone through the hole in the fence fairly recently, someone who always had pockets full of tissues.

"What do you see?"

I jumped as Retta spoke at my elbow. "Barb went through there."

She peered into the night. "Why?"

We both listened for a moment, but the sound of rain dripping off everything around us covered any noise from the woods ahead.

Barb was on the wrong side of the fence. Since I couldn't think of a reason that made sense, I guessed it had nothing to do with her unfailingly reasonable self. "I'm going after her."

"Faye, that's crazy. I'll go."

I turned the flashlight on her. "Retta, you're wearing heels, nylons, and a skirt." She might have said I don't move as fast as I used to, but she didn't. Instead she said, "I'll follow the fence along the road on this side. Maybe I'll see or hear her."

There was a moment when each of us wanted to reassure the other, but neither could think of a way to do it. As a family we're nothing if not realists, and we both sensed this was bad. Touching my arm briefly, Retta turned and hurried away, looking a little like Gene Kelly as she splashed unheeding through the rain with a forgotten, folded umbrella over her shoulder.

I was glad she didn't stay to see me crawl through that fence. It wasn't a pretty sight from any angle, but from the back it was undoubtedly ugly. The hole was made by teenagers for teenagers, not for women with figures beyond Rubenesque. The fencing caught at my clothes, gouged my back, and held on as if desperate to stop me, only to suddenly let go and rebound against the post with a clang, almost launching me face-first into the mud.

Once through, I flashed the light ahead. The inevitable beer bottles, mashed paper cups, and bits of broken glass lay on my left. Inky blackness on my right hid the pit and the lake beyond it, but I knew it was there. A familiar feeling hit low in my gut, the sense I was being pulled toward that yawning gulf by an irresistible force. I imagined myself stepping forward: solid ground, solid ground, and then nothing beneath my foot but air.

Stop it! I told myself. *There's no time for this!*

For reassurance I bent and picked up a branch. Like a blind person using a cane, I tested the ground in front of me. It felt solid. With the stick, the light, and my fear for Barb's safety, I would ignore the fact that I was so close to the edge of the Pit. I would ignore my pounding heart and shaking legs. Ahead of me a path disappeared into the trees. A tissue lay on the ground, damp but not sodden. Lowering my head, I started down the path.

CHAPTER FIFTY

Barb

Passage was difficult, since the path was simply the way deer and adolescent explorers traveled. How far was it to the old viewing point? Would I be given the option of jumping?

I had a really dumb but somehow important argument with myself about whether it was better to go over the edge myself or make DuBois push me. Maybe he'd order Gabe to push me off. I might be able to handle him. Faye had. I made myself stop thinking in that direction.

Distracted by my own thoughts, I tripped over an exposed root and went down, partially stopping the fall with my hands but letting out a grunt of pain anyway. DuBois helped me up with an almost courteous gesture, but his comment wasn't reassuring. "It's not far now."

CHAPTER FIFTY-ONE

Retta

For reasons I'm not sure of now, I brought the emergency bag as I hurried along the roadway. It had been years since I'd been to the Pit, but I knew about the trail along the edge. In warm weather we'd sometimes cut school and gone there to peer down at the trucks at work, so far away they looked like toys in a sandbox. I'd always felt sorry for the boys, who felt required to show off their manly courage by testing the edge. My girlfriends and I had hung back and squealed as they pretended it was nothing to lean out or sit with legs dangling over empty space.

The rise of the lawsuit mentality had led to the Pit being lined with a much stronger fence in the mid '70s, complete with a secure viewing point, and a lot of Do Not Enter signs. Not that it stopped the kids, teenage delusions of invincibility being what they are.

As I traced the fence-line, the rain stopped. It didn't help my progress much, since the shoulder was already softened. Peering into the woods for a glimpse of Faye or Barbara, my heels sinking in with each step, I vowed to add walking shoes to the kit for future occasions.

When a light flashed beside me, it almost didn't register. Resisting the urge to call out, I leaned against the fence, hoping to see it again.

There! Another faint gleam deep in the trees. Was it Faye? I didn't think so. This light was weak and thin, where the flash from my kit had a strong, broad beam. I listened, straining my ears to hear past the last drips of water falling from the trees. Was something moving through the woods? I thought so. Suddenly there was an exclamation, part surprise, part pain. And clearly, I heard a man's voice say, "It's not far now."

There were people in there, at least two of them. One of them might be my sister, and she might be in trouble. I was on the wrong side of the fence, and it was doubtful I could climb it in heels. Faye was somewhere behind them, at least I hoped she was. But what could she do if Barbara was under some unknown threat?

Suddenly I remembered that the bag slung over my shoulder had flares in it. Don had told me they were simple to operate. "Just aim at the sky and tap the bottom," he'd said. "You can't miss." Setting the bag down on the wet ground, I began to rummage through it, hoping as I searched that flares age well.

CHAPTER FIFTY-TWO

Faye

"It's not far now."

The voice ahead stopped me dead in my tracks. Shutting off my flash, I tried to quiet my raspy breath. I was close enough that he might have heard me if he hadn't been focused on someone else. I listened until I heard movement again. They were heading away from me.

I followed, too slowly for my liking. Hampered by the darkness and my aging body, I struggled every step of the way. *If we all get out of this,* I promised myself, *I'll quit smoking.* Being completely honest, I added after a few steps, *At least I'll cut way, way down.*

CHAPTER FIFTY-THREE

Barb

I stumbled on, feeling blood running down my calf from the knee that had been smacked twice in the same place tonight. It wouldn't matter if I didn't think of a way to escape. If I could distract DuBois, I might hide in the trees. It probably wouldn't work, but what difference if Eric shot me or threw me over the edge? No one would know except Gabe, who wouldn't live to tell about it.

Since I'd been looking down at the tiny patch of light at my feet, I almost didn't see the fence before me. When I realized the way was blocked, I lurched to one side and came to a stop.

"Here we are," DuBois said with that disgusting cheerfulness.

He raised the flash to the sign. DANGER! DO NOT PASS THIS POINT! Beyond it on the right, the dark seemed lighter. I was seeing sky, not trees.

"We don't quarry on this side now," Eric said, sounding oddly like a tour guide. "It will be a while before anyone finds your bodies."

I was regretting my earlier decision not to try to escape on the pathway. Now I was trapped here, the fence on one side, Eric behind, and the Pit everywhere else. Nowhere to go.

"Just step over it," DuBois ordered. The barrier was four heavy posts sunk deeply into the ground and connected with three cross-boards. I could easily climb over it if I wanted to. I didn't.

Gabe was looking at me, eyes wide with terror. I waited for one of them to say, "Ladies first," but that didn't happen.

What did happen was a flare that lit the sky over our heads. I heard the hiss as it ascended but had no idea what it was until the light burst above us with a pop. A few seconds later, another hiss sounded. By that time I was already on the move. "Run!" I shouted to Gabe, giving him a shove. Amazingly, he responded to my order as easily as he had to DuBois earlier. Taking off like a startled chipmunk, he pushed past DuBois and ran back the way we'd come.

I chose a different direction, heading to where I was pretty sure the fence was. If I could get over it before DuBois decided which of us to chase, I had a good chance. The flares were great in that their appearance startled him, freezing him for a few seconds. The downside was they made it easy for him to see both his targets.

He came after me. Hiding behind the bole of a pine, I peeked out to see him look up at the flares, survey the woods around him, and then look directly at me.

His choice wasn't surprising, but something else was. Behind DuBois, Gabe had come back. Arms pumping, he ran straight at our common enemy.

An unlikely savior, Gabe was not coming to my rescue. Behind him came someone he found every bit as scary as DuBois: my sister Faye.

Gabe hit the unsuspecting DuBois full on in the back, sending him stumbling forward, out of control and into a tree. Eric's head hit the trunk before the rest of him did, and he staggered back, eyes glazed. Gabe reeled backward for a moment from the impact but soon regained command of his body and began to run again. He passed me like a shot, crashing through the branches like a herd of panicked elk.

As the last of the flare's light faded, Faye came on full tilt, following Gabe. She couldn't know DuBois was there, dazed but still deadly. His plan had gone badly awry, but I doubted he could recognize that now. He'd shoot Faye unless I stopped him.

"Faye! Down!" She stopped then obeyed, dropping to the ground just before a shot rang out. Her flash went out a second later, and I heard a scrabbling in the trees as she crawled to relative safety.

The scene had faded into darkness except for the faint glow of the flashlight DuBois had dropped when Gabe barreled into him. It lay on the ground, lighting his feet as he stood crouched on the pathway, trying to decide what to do next.

A metallic vibration told me Gabe had found the fence and begun climbing. DuBois turned, and I ducked down. Keeping low, I started in a wide circle around him.

In only a few seconds, he picked up his light, did a quick arc in my direction, then turned it off. He was taking no chance that Faye might be armed. A second shot echoed through the darkness, making me jump. It wasn't aimed at me. At least I didn't think so. Had DuBois shot Faye? I wanted to call out to her but dared not.

Silence followed as we all thought about what to do next. DuBois was between Faye and me. I couldn't move toward her. She had disappeared into the woods on the opposite side of the path, which meant the Pit edge was close. She couldn't retreat any farther.

With agonizing slowness, I began moving toward the spot where I'd last seen DuBois. If I could sneak up behind him I might surprise, even disarm him. The problem was remaining noiseless in the inky blackness as I guessed where he might be.

When I thought I was close, I stopped, holding my breath and waiting for him to move. It was hard to ignore the feeling that he might have heard or even felt my approach and was waiting, ready for me. Ready to kill me.

Suddenly there was a pop, followed by the now-familiar hiss, and another flare lit the sky. DuBois was about six feet away from me, and he looked up in surprise. I was surprised, too, but I recovered faster than he did. Pushing off from a tree trunk, I hit him with all the force I had. We tumbled to the ground together, both of us letting out grunts on impact. I landed on top, which was good, but he held onto the gun, which was not as good. He brought the butt of it down on my back with a force that shuddered down my spine.

Another force shook me, but it was secondary. I heard DuBois' curse, heard a clunk, and felt a second jolt. He groaned in pain. In the light of the flare, I saw a size eleven Walmart walking shoe had descended on his wrist and pinned it to the ground.

He might not have given up even then. After all, he was up against two aging women. I felt his muscles tense as he gathered his resources to throw us aside. He could still run, and neither Faye nor I would be able to catch him.

"I've called the police, and they're on the way." The voice came from the road. Retta! DuBois moaned once and slumped back. I guess a third sister on the scene was more than he could imagine. And more than he could handle.

CHAPTER FIFTY-FOUR

Faye

The man Barb had tackled gave up when I kicked the gun from his hand, picked it up, and pointed it at him. As the third flare faded overhead, I turned on my light. "You okay, Barb?"

"Yes," she replied, though she grimaced as she stood. "Banged up, but nothing's broken."

"What's going on in there?" Retta demanded.

"We're okay," I told her. "How about you?"

"Good," she called. "A man came over the fence, and I've got my gun on him. Is he a good guy or a bad guy?"

I was pretty sure Retta had no gun, but with her you never know. I looked to Barb. "Would that be Gabe she's talking about?"

"Yes."

"I thought I recognized the little creep, but he was moving pretty fast." I raised my voice. "Keep him under guard, Retta. We're going to want to talk to him."

"Okay," she called. "We'll meet you at the cars."

Turning back I asked Barb, "And who is this?"

"Eric DuBois, soon to be former second banana at WOZ Industries." She gave him a nudge with her foot. "Let's go."

She didn't have to ask me twice. The stress was getting to me, even though most of the danger seemed to be over. I was still on the wrong side of a fence that kept me from plunging into the Pit, but somehow it was a little better with Barb beside me.

I gave her the gun, since she has more experience with them, and I kept the light on the path ahead. When we got to the hole in the fence, Barb went through first, awkwardly but still more gracefully than I would. When she was situated, gun ready, on the other side, we sent DuBois through. Finally I wedged the flashlight into the fence so she could keep watch on him while I exited. I didn't mind a bit that the beam was aimed at him and not at me as I fought that demon wire a second time.

We found Retta standing behind Gabe, who grinned weakly, hands raised to indicate submission. When I stepped past him, I saw that Retta's "gun" was her umbrella. She shrugged. "He was climbing the fence, so he had his back to me."

Sirens wailed in the distance. We waited in silence, exhausted and still shaky from the adrenalin pumped into our systems. There was a lot that needed to be explained, but no one seemed to be in a hurry for that. DuBois maintained a stony silence, and even Gabe sensed that this time, there was no explaining away what he'd done.

The first police car on scene surprised us. Rory Neuencamp did a sliding turn, hit the brakes, and was out almost before it stopped. "Barb, are you all right?"

"Fine," she replied, but the waver in her voice said differently. Now that it was over, she looked ready to collapse.

"Give me that." He took the gun from her and turned to me with a silent request. Setting the light on the hood of the Chevy, I put a supporting arm around her. Actually, I wasn't that much better off, so we kind of held each other up.

"I thought you were on the way to Saginaw," I said to the chief.

"After Retta's call, I turned around." His tone shaded toward humor. "Somehow I had the idea you needed help, but I guess the three of you together are a match for just about anything."

"No, really," I told him. "We're very glad you're here. How did you find us?"

"Well, I heard the 9-1-1 call on the scanner, and then flares started lighting up the sky."

"Retta did that," I told him. "Good thinking, Sis."

"He was going to push me over the edge." Barb glared at DuBois, who scowled back.

"He tried to shoot me," I said, "but Barb knocked him down."

"How did you two find me out here?" she asked.

Retta flashed her most innocent smile. "Good detective work, that's how."

"Well, you saved my life." Her voice softened. "Thanks, Retta."

For once Baby Sister was speechless.

A county police car pulled in and two officers got out, hands on their weapons. "It's under control," Rory told them. "You can cuff these two."

"Do we need an ambulance?"

Rory looked at us, and we all shook our heads. "Guess not. Mirandize the prisoners and transport them in separate cars so they don't get a chance to make up a story." He turned to us. "Will you come to the station? I need to hear from all of you, and it might as well be together."

I looked at Barb, who nodded to indicate she was willing. "We can follow you there."

Retta said the last thing I expected. "Barbara Ann, why don't you ride with the chief? Faye can bring your car along, and we'll meet you there."

CHAPTER FIFTY-FIVE

Retta

I love it when things work out, and the Brown case went very well. Eric DuBois' lawyer tried to plead the murders down to manslaughter, but Stan put pressure on the D.A.'s office, and no deals were made. They used every delaying tactic imaginable, so the trial hasn't started yet. It really doesn't make much difference. He was denied bail, and nobody doubts a guilty verdict.

Faye actually spoke for the other guy, Gabe. He got some time in the county jail, but she talked to the people at her church, who got him into a GED program. She actually went to visit him and promised she'd help him get work once he's released. I tried to talk to Barbara about it, figuring she has more sway than I do on Faye's activities, but she shut me down with, "It isn't a bad idea. We might be able to use him here from time to time."

Neil Brown was released, so he was able to be at his sister's side when she went into surgery. The doctors were optimistic about their success, but brain tumors require a wait-and-see period during which Meredith would be checked frequently. In the meantime, she recovered and went back to her second-graders.

It would be a lie to say I wasn't surprised that Barbara Ann and Rory were attracted to each other. I'm usually better at picking up signs, but it wasn't the end of the world. There are other men out there, and a girl might miss one, but another will come along.

As far as the agency goes, I made no progress on changing the name. I bought the items I thought the place needed and was told I could take them back. I dropped off some ideas for a nicer logo and got no response whatsoever.

But—and it's a big one—Barbara Ann said in front of Rory and Faye that I'd saved her life. Later she told the reporters who interviewed her about her ordeal how smart I was and how much help I'd been.

I'd never by pushy about it, but I'll be part of the Smart Detective Agency yet.

ABOUT THE AUTHOR

Maggie writes mysteries, loves fine chocolate, and has three cats--Bobbi, Harry, and Jo--and two dogs, a lab named Barker and a rescue dog named Pie.

Maggie and her husband might be found hiking, but they seldom prepare properly for it. It's more of a "Let's see what's over that hill!" type of lifestyle.

You can contact Maggie at

https://www.facebook.com/maggie.pill

or

http://maggiepill.maggiepillmysteries.com/

Other Sleuth Sisters books available in print, audio, and e-formats:

Book #2--*3 Sleuths, 2 Dogs, 1 Murder (sample below)*

Book #3--*Murder in the Boonies*

Book #4--*Sleuthing at Sweet Springs*

Book #5—*Eat, Drink, and Be Wary*

SAMPLE: *3 SLEUTHS, 2 DOGS, 1 MURDER*

CHAPTER ONE

Retta

It's hard to say which is worse: hearing that your gentleman friend has been arrested for murder, or learning that the victim was his wife.

I was browsing my favorite on-line shoe site when the news came. I'd just added an item to my cart, a darling pair of navy pumps with little pink bows at the heel, when a distinctive ring-tone sounded. Reaching over, I touched the screen, and said, "Hey, Faye."

"Hi, Retta. Are you at home?"

"Yup, shopping from my living room, since we live two hours north of just about everywhere."

"Good." My sister's tone hinted at bad news. "Are you seeing a guy named Winston Darrow?"

I considered asking what concern that was of hers. My sisters leave me out of almost everything they do, and sometimes it hurts my feelings. A year ago they started a business without me—without even *telling* me. This year, because of storm damage to my second home in Florida, I was stuck in Michigan on the tenth of

January. Any other winter, I'd have been drinking wine in the afternoons with my girlfriends in Deerfield Beach.

Since I had to stick around, I'd let my sisters know I was available to help the Smart Detective Agency (though I hate that name). I hadn't been invited to take part. In fact, Barbara Ann had told me in her usual brusque way that I'm hard to work with because I'm bossy.

So when Faye asked about Winston Darrow I thought, *Why should I share my private affairs with them?*

Still, it isn't Faye's fault. With her middle child issues, insecurities, and lack of self-confidence, she gets bullied by Barbara Ann. I've told Faye that Barbara is too stubborn to take good help when it's offered, but she just smiles.

Knowing Faye wouldn't ask about my social life if it wasn't important, I answered without being snippy. "Winston and I met at a thing and hit it off. We've gone out a few times."

Unlike my sisters, I have a social life, and I'd met Winston at a Republican fund-raising dinner a month earlier. While I'm not political, I do support candidates who support the police. My husband, a state police officer, was killed ten years ago in the line of duty. Since then, through efforts to get better body armor state-wide, I've run into most of the movers and shakers of Michigan's Lower Peninsula at one time or another.

As single attendees, Winston and I had ended up sitting together. He was good-looking and charming, though a little shallow. He'd said he was divorced, which is why the news Faye was about to dump on me was a double shock.

"Mr. Darrow called our office this morning. He's being questioned about his wife's murder, and he's afraid he'll be charged. He wants the agency to help."

I heard my voice go up a notch. "Winston is married? I mean, he was married?"

"I'm sorry, Retta. His wife died early Sunday morning. Barb didn't promise him we'd take the case or anything."

My mind went in a dozen directions. Winston was married. That was Shock #1. It was embarrassing to learn I'd been lied to. Barbara would snicker up her sleeve, Faye was obviously feeling sorry for me, and soon my friends would hear that I'd been taken in by a smooth-talker who was possibly a murderer. I thought of people who'd seen us together, imagining their reactions. My face began to burn. How dare he do this to me!

"I don't mean to pry," Faye said. "I just want a sense of what kind of person he is."

She didn't sound disapproving or judgmental. That's how Faye is, and I appreciated it. Barbara would no doubt have added, "What were you thinking?" or something like that.

Winston Darrow's handsome face came to mind. He was smart. He was funny. Apparently he was also a liar. But a murderer? I recalled him cringing once when I'd squashed a cricket with a rolled-up magazine. I couldn't see him killing anything, much less a living, breathing, still-attached wife. "Winston isn't the murdering type. I'd bet on that."

"Good to know." Faye's voice was low, and I guessed she was trying to keep Barbara from hearing. "I thought I should tell you, because you're bound to be dragged into it."

Another shock. "What do you mean?"

"According to Mr. Darrow, the police hinted he'd shot his wife in order to be free to marry you."

I shook my head vigorously, though she couldn't see it. "That's ridiculous. We never even mentioned marriage. And she was shot?

Faye, Winston hates guns. It's one of the reasons I enjoyed his company—no long, boring stories about what he saw from his deer blind or what kind of rifle he picked up at the gun show last weekend."

"Well, he owned a gun, or his wife did, and it's missing."

"Which proves nothing unless that's what killed her." I was arguing Winston's case, which was odd in light of what he'd done.

I could almost see Faye raising a hand to calm me down. "If the police have a good case for domestic violence, we won't waste our time."

"It's not a waste." I sighed, irritated at both Winston and myself. "Winston isn't who I thought, but he's no murderer."

"He says he was with you Sunday night."

"Well, not *all* night, if that's what you're asking. He left around midnight." A series of painful images came to mind, people whispering behind their hands, hiding smug smiles. *He crawled out of Retta's bed, went back to his wife—and then shot her!*

"That doesn't help," Faye was saying. "Cops estimate the time of death was between eleven and two."

"So if he left my place at twelve, he had time to get home and kill her." I heard a sad little moan and realized it was me. "What are we going to do about this?"

"*You* aren't going to do anything," Faye said sternly. "You know Barb gets mad when you start giving advice."

"I never give advice, especially to Barbara I'm-Fine-on-My-Own Evans." Ideas gathered in my head as I spoke. "Tell her to call Rory Neuencamp and see what he knows. It's out of his jurisdiction, but cops talk to cops." That reminded me of something, and I asked, "Have Barbara and Rory started anything yet, or are they still avoiding each other like teenagers at a church mixer?"

"Um, they haven't gone out that I know of."

There's no pushing Barbara, but I resolved to say something to Rory the next time we met. It doesn't take a genius to see they're attracted to each other, but Barbara Ann would die in the desert before she'd ask anyone for a glass of water. And flirt? She doesn't know how!

I returned to the current problem. "Start checking divorce records in New Mexico. Winston told me he and his wife split three years ago."

Faye's reply sounded flat. "We'll do that, Retta."

"And keep me informed. Please," I added. Ending the call, I closed my iPad, too distracted to complete my purchase. I wandered the house for a while, letting Faye's news sink in. My dog Styx, asleep on his couch, raised his head as if to ask if we were going outside. I patted him, feeling soothed a little by contact with my best friend. "Not right now, baby." His head sank back to the couch, and he was snoring in seconds.

I must have mentioned my sisters' business at some point, so Winston had called their agency when trouble hit. Naturally he thought they'd help him prove his innocence for my sake.

Was he innocent?

Though angry he'd lied to me, I was pretty sure Winston Darrow wasn't capable of killing anyone. A couple of times he'd even joked about being a lover, not a fighter.

As someone who knew Winston well, I couldn't just sit around now that he was in trouble. Therefore the next question was clear: What should I do to help?

CHAPTER TWO

Barb

"So what did she say?"

Faye jumped a mile, and I chuckled to myself. She deserved a little scare for the covert call to Retta, but I'd known it would happen. Though tough when she needs to be, Faye is a softie who sometimes forgets that our baby sister drives us both insane with her meddling. Besides, this time she was correct. Retta was going to be named as the Other Woman in a murder investigation, so she had a right to know what we knew.

"He told her he's been divorced for three years." Faye's lip curled, betraying anger. "I'm betting this guy is a jerk."

"That doesn't make him a murderer," I replied. "Here's the odd thing, though. I did an online search for information on the Darrows, and there's next to nothing."

There's a lot to be learned about a person if you know where to look on the Internet, and the Smart Detective Agency has developed an impressive array of sources, thanks to Faye's office skills and my background as a lawyer. Checking my notes I read aloud, "Winston Darrow, born 1950, self-described entrepreneur. His wife Stacy has no job history. They're comfortable financially, own a home on a small lake between here and Gaylord, and have two vehicles: a Lexus and a Tundra. He's a member of the local Kiwanis Club, the Rotary, the Republican Party, and the Friends of the Library, but he doesn't attend meetings. Instead he shows up at social events like dinners and receptions. Mrs. Darrow stays home a lot. She's a member of a dozen on-line groups, most focused on reading mysteries and collecting Carnival glass."

"Good reading choice." Cozy mysteries are Faye's favorites. "Did you finish the report on the missing money at the hardware store?"

"Yes," I replied. "They're going to handle the embezzlement quietly, but the owner says with what we gave him, he can demand repayment in exchange for a lesser sentence. He's happy with that."

"Good," Faye said. "That clears our schedule so we can spend some time with Retta's friend." She glanced at me then looked down at her keyboard. "Might Chief Neuencamp help?"

The suggestion had obviously come from Retta. While our local police chief could probably help, I was reluctant to ask. First, I didn't want Rory to think we expected him to do our work. In addition, I didn't want to appear to seek out his company. Our relationship was cordial, and though my sisters had insisted he'd take it a step farther, he hadn't. I told myself he was learning the rules of a new job in a new town, and he'd naturally keep professional distance between the Allport police and the city's only detective agency. What I didn't like to think was that Rory considered me only a business acquaintance.

"Let's do a little more on our own," I told Faye. "When I talk to the chief, I want to have my facts straight."

We spent the rest of the morning digging, and when we finished, we'd added a few bits. The Darrows had moved to Michigan as newlyweds two years earlier from Taos, New Mexico. According to their marriage license, her maiden name was Stacy Kern, and she was fifteen years Winston's junior. Her parents, Alice (Duggan) and Charles Kern, were both listed as natives of Rutland, Vermont.

Stacy's lack of presence on social media—no Facebook, no Twitter, no Instagram—had me picturing a shy, plain girl who'd perhaps married a father figure. Winston had a Facebook page, and his timeline contained photos of him with a succession of different women. In each picture he looked confident and debonair while his companions looked startled, as people often do after multiple face-lifts.

The most recent photo was captioned WIN & STACY GOT MARRIED. The happy couple stood before a sprawling, red-brick courthouse, and when I set the cursor over it, TAOS, NEW MEXICO, came up. Unfortunately, the photographer hadn't timed the shot well, and the new Mrs. Darrow was digging in her purse for something. Though her face wasn't visible, Stacy had a knockout figure, revealed by a short, tight mini-dress, and a mass of dark hair. So much for shy and plain.

Had Winston Darrow murdered his wife in order to marry my sister Margaretta? She's an attractive woman, but as far as I'm concerned, Retta's charm fades each and every time she starts trying to run my life.

CHAPTER THREE

Faye

When Barb asked me to do the initial interview with Winston Darrow, I took it as a sign she doesn't think of me as just the office manager. I'd gathered intake information before, of course, but this was only our second murder investigation. Though the stakes were high, she trusted me to handle it.

Usually, I let Barb take the lead, bowing to her experience with the legal system, but I try to do my part. Sometimes I take the initiative, like when I handled Retta's stubbornness in the matter of payment.

Retta wants to be part of the Smart Detective Agency, but Barb refuses to make her a partner, citing her manipulative ways. I'll admit, Retta likes things her way, and she's nosed in several times already by sheer force of will. She really can be helpful, (I swear she knows half the people in the state) which makes it hard to leave her out completely. Barb's solution had been to call Retta a consulting expert and pay her a fee.

After a while, though, I noticed that Retta never cashed our checks. She didn't send them back or anything. They simply remained outstanding. When I asked about it she got evasive, claiming she forgot, but I suspected she was getting back at Barb for leaving her out. It became my problem, since I do the bookkeeping.

In the end I called her bank, got the routing numbers, and deposited the money directly into her account. That might not be possible everywhere, but in a small town it's doable. Retta could no longer "forget" to cash the checks, and I saved myself headaches Barb never even knew about.

Winston Darrow lived in Bonner County, thirty miles west of Allport as the crow flies. Since Bonner is mostly comprised of small lakes nestled among large forests, however, a direct route is nonexistent. Narrow country roads meander through touristy little villages, tracing lakeshores and skirting hills, so it took me an hour to get to the sheriff's office situated in Lawton. It was easy to find the county building once I got there, since it was by far the largest structure in town.

A cold wind pushed the door closed behind me with a bang that made everyone present look up. I introduced myself, ignoring the raised eyebrows at a woman of my age being a private investigator, and asked if I could see Winston Darrow. He was due in court for arraignment soon, and there was some discussion about whether he could have a visitor before he saw the judge. When nobody could think of a reason why he couldn't, I was shown into a bland room containing a table and three chairs with metal legs and one-piece plastic seats. A few minutes later a deputy brought our prospective client in.

Two decades ago, Darrow would have qualified as eye candy. He still didn't look bad: thick black hair with a touch of gray at the temples; a trim build, not athletic but hardly gone to seed; and large green eyes set into a fine-boned face. The favorable impression he might have made disappeared almost immediately when he stepped close, tilted his head down and to one side, and gave me a look meant to make me feel feminine and attractive. Instead I felt like backing out of the room.

"Mrs. Evans," he said in a mellow, low-pitched voice, "it's good of you to come so quickly." Taking my hand, he raised it slightly and I swear, only the look of warning on my face kept him from raising it to his lips.

Darrow's kind of charm never works on me. Stepping out of his personal space and re-possessing my hand, I said, "I'm Faye Burner, Barb's partner."

He smiled warmly to cover his mistake. "Mrs. Burner, sorry. Please call me Win."

He gazed into my eyes for that extra half-second men like him use to let a woman know she interests them, or to try to create that impression. I tried to maintain objectivity, but he hadn't gained a single point so far. Winston "Call me Win" brought words to my mind like *greaseball, sleazeball, egotist, lothario, scuz-bucket.* The list could have gone on.

Still, he'd just become a widower and might soon be a client, so I sat down on the hard chair and took out my notepad. "I'm sorry for your loss, Mr. Darrow. Please tell me what you can about your wife's death and I'll see if we can help."

"Win, please," he repeated. Sitting down opposite me, he glanced around the room. "Are the police listening?"

I shrugged. "They could be. This isn't a privileged conversation." Meeting his gaze, I asked, "Were you intending to tell me something you didn't tell them?"

"Of course not." He waved both hands dismissively. "I told them the truth, same as I'm going to tell you."

He was smooth, but I noted fraying at the edges of his persona. His un-shaven beard was grayer than his hair, betraying his age. His clothes were rumpled, and his eyes were slightly glassy. Maybe he was grieving. With visible effort, he pulled himself together and began his story.

"I was with Retta Stilson—your sister—Saturday night until about twelve. After we had dinner at that new Mediterranean restaurant, she invited me back to her place. She'd made a pie, and she said she'd never eat it all by herself." He tried to look innocent. I tried to look like I didn't care what he and my sister did after eating pie.

"When I left Retta's it was storming, and the east-west roads had drifted badly. The trip took longer than usual, white-knuckles all the way."

"What time did you get home?" I almost added "to your wife."

"About one-thirty. Everything was white, and I couldn't see the driveway posts. When I turned in, one wheel went off into the ditch. I tried to back out, but I just made things worse. The car was off the road far enough that it wasn't a hazard, so I left it there, figuring I'd call someone with a tractor in the morning. The house was dark, and my hands and feet were freezing from trying to push the car." He looked down. "I didn't look in on Stacy, just went to my own room and took a hot shower."

"You had separate rooms?"

He licked his lips. "Stacy likes—liked her privacy, and we had plenty of space." Darrow's voice dropped a little. "She'd lost interest in pretty much anything that had to do with me."

"Was that because you went around telling other women you were divorced?"

He tried for anger, but his reply sounded defensive. "We might as well have been."

*****END OF SAMPLE*****

CPSIA information can be obtained
at www.ICGtesting.com
Printed in the USA
LVHW01s2251200918
590775LV00002B/123/P